The Transparent Girl
and Other Stories

After the Empire:
The Francophone World and
Postcolonial France

Series Editor
Valérie Orlando, Illinois Wesleyan University

Advisory Board
Robert Bernasconi, Memphis University; Alec Hargreaves, Florida State University; Chima Korieh, Rowan University; Françoise Lionnet, UCLA; Obioma Nnaemeka, Indiana University; Kamal Salhi, University of Leeds; Tracy D. Sharpley-Whiting, Vanderbilt University; Nwachukwu Frank Ukadike, Tulane University

See www.lexingtonbooks.com/series for the series description and a complete list of published titles.

Recent and Forthcoming Titles

The Transparent Girl and Other Stories

Corinna Bille, Selected and
Translated by Monika Giacoppe
and Christiane P. Makward

LEXINGTON BOOKS

A division of
ROWMAN & LITTLEFIELD PUBLISHERS, INC.
Lanham • Boulder • New York • Toronto • Oxford

LEXINGTON BOOKS

A division of Rowman & Littlefield Publishers, Inc.
A wholly owned subsidary of The Rowman & Littlefield Publishing Group, Inc.
4501 Forbes Boulevard, Suite 200
Lanham, MD 20706

PO Box 317
Oxford
OX2 9RU, UK

British Library Cataloguing in Publication Information Available

The translators gratefully acknowledge a grant-in-aid from **Pro Helvetia, Arts Council
of Switzerland**.

Library of Congress Cataloging-in-Publication Data

Bille, S. Corinna, 1912–1979.
  [Short stories. English. Selections]
  The transparent girl and other stories / Corinna Bille ; selected and translated by
Monika Giacoppe and Christiane P. Makward.
     p. cm. — (After the empire)
  Includes bibliographical references and index.
   ISBN 0-7391-1169-8 (cloth : alk. paper) — ISBN 0-7391-1295-3 (pbk. : alk. paper)
   ISBN 978-0-7391-1169-7   ISBN 978-0-7391-1295-3
   1. Bille, S. Corinna, 1912–1979—Translations into English. I. Giacoppe, Monika, 1965–
II. Makward, Christiane P., 1941–   III. Title. IV. Series.
PQ2603.I442A2 2006
843'.912—dc22   2005030272

Printed in the United States of America

Contents

Acknowledgments

*O*ur warmest thanks go to Maurice Chappaz who let us choose freely among the works and graciously allowed us to translate them. Editions Gallimard also enabled us to secure the rights for several key stories, and we gladly acknowledge their cooperation in making this reader possible.

Several colleagues and friends have been instrumental in achieving a project we undertook several years ago out of a common enthusiasm for Corinna Bille's writing. Besides our series editor, Valérie Orlando, we are indebted to two exquisitely demanding readers who read the final version of the book: Professor Kathryn Grossman and Professor Alan Knight, both of the Pennsylvania State University.

Thanks to the new age facilities in communication, we were able to submit previous versions of stories to a number of colleagues within the professional association "Women in French" and to other volunteer scholars. We thank all of them warm-heartedly for giving us their time and comments: Dawn Cornelio, Timothy Cox, Wendy Greenberg, Margot Miller, Lynn Palermo, Jo Podol, Michele Scatton-Tessier, Carol Smucker, and Toni Wulff.

On questions of regional culture and elusive lexicon we owe special thanks to M. Alain Cordonier, of the Mediathèque du Valais in Sion, Switzerland, who researched and resolved several daunting questions for us.

The translators gratefully acknowledge a grant-in-aid from Pro Helvetia, Arts Council of Switzerland.

Introduction

$\mathscr{F}$or a Western world readership, Corinna Bille's environment will seem distant but only as remote as rocky Colorado or forested Tennessee, with a touch of rural Pennsylvania. Natural wilderness usually provides the setting for intimate distress as well as major dramas. The author's given name was Stéphanie, but she elected "Corinna" in celebration of her mother's twin villages of Upper Corin and Lower Corin in the Upper Rhône valley of the Swiss Alps. The canton of Valais is largely Francophone and Catholic, features that set it apart from the other Francophone cantons of Switzerland. Valais (Wallis in German) connects France to northern Italy. It was invaded and used for passage by many armies from antiquity to the Napoleonic wars. Its history is therefore rich in traces, archeological and biological, of other cultures, but the region owes its fame in modern Europe to the splendor of its mountains, with Mount Cervin (Matterhorn in German) as the crown jewel.

S. Corinna Bille (1912–1979) was the eldest of three children born to a pretty and wise peasant girl and the noted artist Edmond Bille. The peasant girl had originally served as a maid for his earlier children. Edmond, stained-glass master and religious folk art collector, lost his wealthy first wife and married Catherine Tapparel, who gave him Stéphanie, René-Pierre, and André. Corinna Bille lovingly imagined and recounted her parents' courtship in a novella entitled "Virginia 1891" (*Deux passions*, 1979). In this, the companion text of "Emerentia 1713," included in the present volume, Bille uses family correspondence and oral tradition to give flesh and substance to her own prehistory. She enjoyed a very positive relationship with her mother, born in 1891, and helped her through troublesome senility before losing her in 1974. Catherine, also called "Mamita," was a rich source of information about peasant life and traditions for Corinna Bille. The writer did not mythify her mother to the same extent Colette did with Sido (Mme. Sidonie Colette), but she constructed a powerful portrait on the similar basis of genuine devotion and interest.

Her childhood and young adult life were spent in her father's baroque mansion overlooking Sierre. She did wander far away to Paris on one occasion, and she enjoyed traveling to distant places (Russia, Africa, Lebanon, Ireland, Siberia), but she was long considered a "regionalist" writer. She indeed shared with both her parents a quasi-religious devotion to their part of the world, fondly referred to as "The Noble Country," as several poems strikingly show. She helped her father in his business as well as posed for him for a variety of works, most notably for a controversial Virgin and Child, commissioned for a village chapel (Chamoson). From childhood on, of course, she had access to a fairly rich family library. Her mother was very fond of reading to the children. Her father directed the children in plays and monitored Corinna's first attempts at writing. She grew up surrounded by artifacts and works in progress; she also assisted in the collection, restoration, and conservation of works of art. Her "Don Juan of a father" (witness the tiny cruel tale we included as "Don Juan in Heaven") owned one of the very first automobiles in Valais, and she fondly referred to her childhood as an extremely happy time between a loving, pious, refined mother and a fanciful, sanguine patriarch. He traveled frequently, sometimes with his wife, but he also enjoyed entertaining at home. As a young girl, Corinna Bille studied for a year in a parochial school in Luzern but was treated harshly there, so her father brought her home. In Sierre, she took secretarial and business law classes, helped her father, and wrote, having vowed at age sixteen to become a writer. She also took language and literature courses in Zurich for a year but never attended college. Her father was very "physical," and the children were able to enjoy winter sports and mountain trekking, a national passion for the Swiss. Bille grew into a graceful, six-foot, Venetian blonde girl, occasionally meeting "celebrity" visitors such as Louis-Ferdinand Ramuz, Benjamin Fondane, and Rainer Maria Rilke.

At age twenty-one she fell head over heels in love with a young French actor on the occasion of the making of a film adapted from a novel by Ramuz. She married the young man and went to live in Paris at the height of "Années Folles" and the peak of surrealist activity. But the marriage proved a cruel failure since it remained unconsummated. She wrote a candid report on it, death wish included, that was only published posthumously in *Le vrai conte de ma vie* under the heading "The White Wedding." Traces of her anguish during those two years can be found in stories such as "The Wild Demoiselle," "The Halloween Fiancés," or "The Saint," all three included in this volume. Corinna Bille returned to Sierre in 1936 and slowly restored her spirits through writing and other creative occupations but first had to be nursed through a lengthy struggle with pneumonia and tuberculosis. Surrounded with books and art lovers, devoting ample time to her own writing, Bille eventually developed a satisfying relationship with another budding writer, Georges Borgeaud, but they were not formally engaged.

When she was introduced to Maurice Chappaz (b. 1914), early in 1942, her romantic fate was sealed. She became his companion, gave birth to a first son two years later, eventually secured a divorce from her French husband, and married the poet in 1947. These were happy, passionate though destitute "Bohemian" years. Before the war, Corinna Bille had already published several stories and poems. Chappaz unfailingly supported publication of her works as well as his own. She never stopped writing, keeping notebooks, jotting down dreams, anecdotes, and stories told by her peasant relatives or read in the local press. She observed village life in a variety of settings, moving with her two babies (a second son was born in 1948) according to the time of year and the goodwill of their relatives (her family in Sierre, his uncle and aunts in Chable and Fully). Various sites and dwellings are reflected in the writings included in this volume, from "The Cat" and "The Last Confession" to the very last one, "The Messenger."

It was not until 1958 that a house of their own was built in Veyras, above Sierre, providing stability for the couple and their three children along with a niece Corinna raised as a companion for her daughter. School vacations were spent in various chalets owned by the family (one in the forest of the Rhône near Sierre, another high in the mountains above Chable), and finally their favorite refuge for summers became a chalet built by Chappaz in Val Réchy on the left bank of the Rhône, above St-Luc. To this particular spiritual harbor, an entire novella was devoted, entitled *Forêts Obscures* (*Dark Forests*). After twenty years in "the pink house" of Veyras, the children were out of the nest, and they decided to move the primary household from Sierre to Chable in lower Valais. The Chappaz family house, the "Bishops' House," known as "l'Abbaye," had indeed been a summer residence for the bishops of Sion. The couple had barely settled in Chable, and they had just returned from a summer trip to Siberia, when Corinna was diagnosed with cancer. She died in October 1979.

Bille's bibliography comprises the equivalent of about forty volumes. Major features of this monument include her broad range of inspiration and her formal freedom as well as a discreet playfulness and irony. She drew from real life stories and anecdotes from her own experiences, she reminisced motifs from art culture, and she exploited dream materials and her own jubilant fancy. Crystal clear syntax (albeit an occasional, odd use of past tenses), restraint in pathos, sobriety in description but with passion for detail in describing her natural environment, and splendid mastery of the French language: all these account for the esteem her writing enjoyed early on. The single most distinctive dimension of her work, which matured, it must be underlined, away from trends, groups, and theories, involves feminine sexuality. It is not "eroticism" in the common, phallocentric sense of the word. To appreciate the daring—and to understand why religious and conservative critics vituperated her work until fame shielded the author—it must be remembered that her first marriage took place in the 1930s, and that she happily gave birth to an illegitimate child during the war, twenty years ahead of the inception of the sexual revolution. Also to be underscored is the fact that she lived mostly in small towns and even villages without the benefit of urban anonymity. The Chappaz were in some ways pioneers of modern mores and ecological responsibility: Maurice denounced military and tourism development in Valais in a scathing satire, and the rape of natural beauty is the key of a poem such as "Parabole," included here, the very last of *One Hundred Tiny Cruel Tales*, which reads:

> Mechanics tear out my hair, heavy with potatoes they have planted. They burn the reddish hairs between my thighs. They breathe their foul fuel into my mouth.
>   The architects of the universe used my legs for a compass and broke them while they were spread wide apart. They consecrated the host of the new world on my worn-out back.

When true reproductive choice and sexual freedom became widespread in Western Europe, Bille was beyond childbearing age. Even though Swiss law was more progressive than French law on contraception in the 1960s, it never was banal, especially not in Catholic Valais. Bille's affirmation of woman's sexuality is unique in the Swiss-French context and is far more daring than Colette's, not to mention Simone de Beauvoir's. With unparalleled elegance, concision and clarity, Corinna Bille has shared her liberating vision of the woman's desire, pleasure, and vulnerability. Violence, rape, sibling incestuous desire (including one fulfilled passion in "The Knot" and a cruel one in "My Forest, My River," both included here), abandonment, sexual rapture, seeking deflowering, and even masturbation, that resounding silence of feminine literature, appear in her stories. Passion and pride in love, enduring even through capital punishment, lie at the core message of her best novel, *Theoda*.

Clearly a free spirit early on, and a rebel in some ways, Bille kept her distance from institutional religion. She retained, however, and even regenerated her relation to spiritual life and some aspects of Catholicism through personal relations and the company of her husband, poet Maurice Chappaz. Her last extra-marital affection was a chaste one; it was inspired by an aging and psychologically unstable priest (the phrasing "Alzheimer" had not surfaced at the time). The man was a friend and had been a confessor of the Chappaz couple: she nicknamed him "little white mouse" and enjoyed exploring her affection for him in an unpublished diary entitled "L'aventure fantastique" ("The Fantastic Adventure").

Corinna Bille gave numerous interviews in spite of her natural reserve with strangers and intellectuals. She confessed being fascinated by odd, even abnormal types: criminals, cretins, murderers, madmen, and even alcoholics—the "wino" (or "saoûlon" in Valais French) is traditionally looked upon with empathy because Valais has a very strong wine-making culture. Thus "weird" characters, mostly drawn from real life, and including an old-fashioned Russian healer and a clown, people Bille's texts. We retained "Crazies" among the selected Eight Tiny Cruel Tales to illustrate this vein. Bille's ironical gaze on religious institutions and mysticism is particularly well illustrated by "The Last Confession" in the present volume. Her most passionate indictment of the puritanical Christian tradition is voiced in the novella *Emerentia 1713*, which may be considered her masterpiece. Of this text—written in the mid-seventies under the shock of discovering the historical reality behind the story—Bille confided that her witch-child portrait owed something to Hawthorne's character Pearl in *The Scarlet Letter*.

Indeed, authors from the United States and Scandinavia were richly represented among her literary passions. Her reading of Dos Passos at age fifteen triggered her decision to become a writer, but she did not sustain the self-discipline, nor did she enjoy sufficient quiet and the material well-being necessary to undertake vast novelistic constructions over prolonged periods. Her genius is rooted in the excitement and joy of storytelling rather than in the analysis of social woes. She actually disowned psychology as a writer's tool. Bille excelled in the shorter genres. Her novels are extended novellas or French-style "récits": some are auto-fictional travelogues (e.g., *Les invités de Moscou* [*Guests in Moscow*]) and love-stories (*Oeil-de-mer* [*Eye-of-the-Sea*]). The early *Sabot de Vénus* (*Lady-Slipper*) gave her considerable trouble to achieve, embroidering as it does a simple village drama of adulterous passion and punishment.

NON-NARRATIVE WORKS

Corinna Bille's poetry deserves far more attention than it has received so far, this lack partly due to the fact that it was not easily accessible; it was only recently collected in three volumes through her husband's care. Apollinaire was one of her favorite French poets. She likely owes surrealist writers and artists some of her own delight with free verse and poetic prose writing, as well as her fascination with dreams. As with her handling of narrative forms, poetic writing in Bille's work is not clearly separate from prose poetry. This is particularly evident in the short-short story format, represented in our selection by sixteen "tiny tales." Some are clearly poems with allusive imagery and open signification, some are pure narratives whose very conciseness—as with master French poets such as Eluard or Jacob—legitimizes their status as poems (e.g., "The Horse"), and some are known to be dream material ("Lovesick") or surrealistic erotic fancy ("The Bird-Woman"). Others still echo pure emotional, universal experience ("The Mother") or conjure up familiar art motifs (Van Gogh's sunflowers and starry night in "Anguish"), hereby giving us the pleasure of recognizing and sharing.

This writer's predilection for shorter forms reflects her joy of creating over the tediousness of editing, which she compared to "housecleaning." We must imagine what tediousness it was indeed to type using real paper, carbon sheets for multiple copies, a real clanking typewriter with a fabric ribbon, not to mention the responsibility of typing her husband's texts as well as her own. Not surprisingly, she did leave an abundance of unpublished materials, especially works for the theatre and autobiographical texts. She told an interviewer,

> Theatre has always fascinated me. As a child I acted in plays adapted from Perrault and directed by my father. I was "Little Red Riding Hood" and the princess in "Puss in Boots." Then I organized shows with my schoolmates, and I invented half the stuff. At age twenty, I married an actor from l'Atelier Theatre. . . . That is how I became acquainted with the Cartel group, and occasionally watched rehearsals with Dullin. Back in Valais, I started writing poetry, short stories, and novels but I only dared tackle the theatre in 1961, when I was invited by the Geneva Radio to submit a short play. I wrote it [the text is "L'Etrangère," "The Outside Woman"] in one session as I've written all my plays. Indeed, when the idea comes, it's so sudden and overwhelming that I start seeing, hearing my characters. It won't let go of me until the final period. (quoted in *L'Oeuvre dramatique complète II*, p. 12)

One volume of dramatic texts published in 1963 contains six plays to be performed in two groups of three. They include rural farces and legends as well as love stories such as the eponymous "The Unknown Woman of the Upper-Rhône." This play dramatizes a recurring scenario I have determined to be her personal myth (in psycho-critical terms after Charles Mauron's method), namely "death on the installment plan." Indeed, in many short stories, in poems, and in several dramatic works, the first death is reversible: one comes back from death or is rescued, only to jump into death a second time. The first death is often a suicide. This storyline befits the surrealistic mode. It suggests that the death wish is not radical: the heroine (the vast majority of Bille's protagonists are women) commits suicide out of despair rather than a philosophical decision. Sometimes she is saved, sometimes it is a mock-death, as in Emerentia's story included here. In the present volume this pattern is best illustrated in "The Wild Demoiselle," eponymous of a 1974 collection that earned Bille the Goncourt award for the short story. The plot is clearly a new exploration and rewriting of the play "The Unknown Woman of the Upper-Rhône." Only one dramatic text by Bille has been translated into English (see "The Scent of Sulfur" in Makward and Miller, *Women's Drama from the French*).

CRITICISM AND FILM RESOURCES

No formal biography of Corinna Bille exists though a wealth of information is available in French on this short story writer, poet, playwright, and novelist whose stature is arguably second only to Germaine de Stael's, and who is definitely a major female presence in French-Swiss literary history. Bille is regularly anthologized and included in Swiss literature dictionaries and manuals, and a Swiss/Europa postage stamp even bears her portrait. She received the most prestigious French honor for short fiction, the Goncourt award for the short story in 1975. Several academic works have been devoted to Bille's work, with the bulk of her archives conserved since 1983 at the Swiss National Library in Bern, along with those of her husband, poet Maurice Chappaz.

Interested readers can find rich photographic documentation in Gilberte Favre's book, *Corinna Bille: le vrai conte de sa vie* (*Corinna Bille: The True Tale of Her Life*, 1981). A timeline of her life is included in *Le vrai conte de ma vie* (*The True Tale of My Life*, 1992), a massive, annotated montage of autobiographical and auto-fictional texts collected and edited by Christiane P. Makward from packets of notes and boxes prepared by the author herself: she was packing to move from Sierre to the village of Chable, near Martigny, only a few months before she died. Several bibliographies exist, but they are not up to date. A scientific one, with pre-editions and re-editions, appeared in the 1989 doctoral dissertation by Maryke de Courten, *L'Imaginaire dans l'oeuvre de Corinna Bille*. A slightly more complete but more compact bibliography (first edition only) is available in the *Dictionnaire littéraire des femmes de langue française*, by Christiane P. Makward and Madeleine Cottenet-Hage (1996). Readers will find below an updated version of the latter.

Quite a number of newly collected and edited texts by Bille have appeared in the past ten years, including the complete poetic works in three volumes, edited by Chappaz, and the complete dramatic works, in two volumes, edited by Christiane P. Makward. Likewise, the Geneva publishing house La Joie de Lire has collected and published her tales and stories for children in three volumes. Indeed, Maurice Chappaz (b. 1914) has devoted considerable energy in the twenty-five years since Bille's death, ensuring that her works remain in print and that her unpublished manuscripts are brought out with all due care. To a large extent, the process is completed though not closed.

Like many great authors, Corinna Bille was an obsessive writer. Raised entirely in the pre-electronic, pre-audiovisual era, she left an abundant correspondence: for example, a selection of her letters to her parents yielded a huge volume edited by Gabrielle Moix in 1995. Along with many albums of images and photographs that she composed for her pleasure, Bille left over twenty richly illustrated "Dream Notebooks" from which she tapped freely for two volumes of short-short stories (we selected eight from each book). As a painter's daughter, and sometimes a model, Bille adored images. She painted and drew, constructed collages and conserved magazine images, and her greatest treat was to take in a movie or two on occasional trips to Lausanne, the closest big city on Lake Geneva. None of the eighteen houses she once listed as a possible framework for her autobiography had a television set: to this day, Maurice Chappaz has not allowed a television set in "l'Abbaye," his house in Chable. In her maturity, a hearing impediment prevented Corinna Bille from enjoying much music on the radio, but it conversely enabled her to insulate herself easily from surrounding activities and noise.

It is fascinating to speculate how this "technologically free" person would have received movie versions of her work. Léa Pool of Quebec directed a "free" adaptation of "The Wild Demoiselle." The 1990 film is titled "The Savage Woman" for the English subtitled version. Three persons worked on the scenario to "translate" into a contemporary love story what Bille had conceived as a timeless, un-technological, pristine drama with medieval overtones. On its own terms, the adaptation is a good one. The site of the male protagonist's work, a modern, spectacular dam in Switzerland, is particularly well used in the film, though absent from Bille's text. In the most powerful scene, the "demoiselle" (actress Patricia Tulasne) is shown with her back to a formidable dam wall that dwarfs her while she utters a resounding peal of laughter: she has just understood the inevitability for her to re-disappear by committing suicide again. Such a scene is a remarkable "spin" on Bille's story.

Another film serves Bille's writing well, although it is curiously devoid of reference or credit to Bille's masterpiece included here, "Emerentia 1713." The 1982 Franco-Swiss television long feature, entitled "Mérette," follows Bille's story (and the historical source) in essence, but the script reverted from a Catholic to the original Calvinist setting that appeared in Gottfried Keller's 1854 novel, *Henry the Green*. Bille herself only discovered the novel in 1974, in the French translation of 1946. According to Chappaz, she was so disturbed by the story that she went into a quasi-pathological creative trance. She projected a lot of her own childhood memories—motherly tenderness, simple life energy, natural children's games, fears of drunk horsemen and of fire—and dreams as well as her profound impatience regarding the rigidity of religious prescriptions. To close this window on film resources related to Bille's work, it must be noted that despite a television-free lifestyle, Corinna Bille and Maurice Chappaz gave several television interviews (1973 and 1974 in particular). A profile of forty-three minutes, "Corinna Bille (1912–1979): La demoiselle sauvage," was also released in 1994 by Pierre-André Thiébaud. It uses television archives, freshly captured natural sites and dwellings, and original interviews with Bille's survivors: husband Chappaz, brother René-Pierre Bille, a noted animal photographer, and one of her best friends, art photographer Suzi Pilet.

TRANSLATORS' NOTES

A few notes on the joys of translation and the difficult choices we made to compile the present volume seem a fitting conclusion. Several stories and novels by Corinna Bille have been translated into German and Italian, but only a couple of short stories were available in English prior to the present volume; they have not been included here. We selected the texts from ten volumes and decided to present them in chronological order of publication, which roughly matches the order of composition, excepting the posthumous works of course. The reason for this fact is that Corinna Bille and Maurice Chappaz, who at times served as her literary agent, did not usually have regular income. They were diligent submitting stories, poems, or essays to Swiss journals and periodicals when they were invited to write on specific topics, and so they earned stipends and minor or major literary awards. In other words, they kept busy preparing their writings for publication as much as they could. To structure our selected stories around themes was an option we discarded in order to maintain our full freedom of choice and not tailor Bille's achievements to suit our own chosen topics. Instead, we tried to strike a balance between the surrealistic mode and the mimetic, although the former clearly dominates our selection due to its enchanting virtues. Another consideration was the length of the full stories. Including the novella "Emerentia" clearly took up space that could have accommodated several more, shorter stories. Furthermore, one of the most powerful, tragic stories, a very early one, seemed too harsh to include alongside "Emerentia" on the same topic of child abuse and religion. Again, some excellent, and well-known eponymous stories such as "The Black Strawberry" of 1968 were too long to be included.

We spent many exciting working days arguing about the connotations of words or the reader's degree of tolerance for uncommon words. The toughest challenge was the incredible range and specificity of Bille's vocabulary—a trait she shares with Colette. It demonstrates her love of words, her erudition, and especially her familiarity with the natural world. Electronic mail proved incredibly helpful as did the gigantic encyclopedia we call the Internet. We experienced special excitement in discovering photographs of plants, birds, and flowers we did not know existed. But the most resilient challenges had to do with cultural details such as the front flap of a child's trousers before zippers existed, references to the history of Valais in the eighteenth century, or the likelihood of peasants using coffee in 1713. This is how we discovered, after several hours of web-ferreting, that even though coffee had been introduced to Europe for a couple of centuries, the popular French expression "sock-juice" for watered down coffee bordered anachronism: the coffee filter in the shape of a knit sock was invented in Paris in 1710. It is therefore highly unlikely that Valais peasants were already using it three years later . . . but not impossible. On one occasion, we had essentially given up upon the failure of SOS messages to French scientists and to our Swiss consultant. The word "prisope" (in the Tiny Love Tale entitled "Gorée") did not appear anywhere on the Internet nor in the best translation tools at our disposal. We decided that it must refer to dust specks in the sunrays and we considered the case closed. Then, two months later, came the answer: a "prisope" ("prisope" in English as well) is a phasmid, a large "stick-insect," and not an acarian nor a speck of dust. Where on earth might Corinna Bille have dug up such an exotic word? Two emails almost simultaneously enlightened us: the word, and an illustration, appears in a nineteenth-century two-volume edition of *Dictionnaire Larousse*. And, yes: there are prisopes in West Africa, so we could not fault the author for her choice of words. What joyful relief!

BIBLIOGRAPHY OF CORINNA BILLE (2005)

1. **Autobiographical Works and Miscellaneous Essays**
2. **Novels**
3. **Poetry**
4. **Short Stories and Short-Short Stories**
5. **Stories for Young Readers**
6. **Theatre Works**

1. Autobiographical Works and Miscellaneous Essays

Abîme des fleurs [1953]. *Trésor des pierres* [1948]. *Récits du Rhône à la Maggia* [1957]. Briançon, Ed. Passage, 1985.

Correspondance 1923–1958 / Catherine, Edmond et S. Corinna Bille; edited and annotated by Gabrielle Moix. Cossonnay, Plaisir de Lire, 1995.

Deux maisons perdues. Boudry, La Baconnière, 1989. Introduction by Maryke de Courten.

Finges, Forêt du Rhône, photographs by Suzi Pilet. Lausanne, Ed. du Grand Pont, 1975.

Le vrai conte de ma vie, Itinéraire autobiographique établi et annoté par Christiane P. Makward. Préface by Maurice Chappaz. Twelve photographs. Lausanne : Empreintes, 1992. 554 pp. Préface—« Gestation du Vrai conte, A la recherche d'une voix »—Chroniques d'un paradis—Maisons d'apprentissages—Le mariage blanc—Le journal de 1937—Epines noires, belosses ou prunelliers—L'année 1942—Le roman des enfants—Deux passions de Blanca—L'Aventure fantastique—Les années difficiles—Gloire et transparence—Hors temps : Le voyage sous les cils et Pensées aux quatre vents.—Repères biographiques—Index—Eléments bibliographiques

2. Novels

Deux passions, romans. Paris : Gallimard, 1979. 208 p.
   I. Emerentia 1713
   II. Virginia 1891

Forêts obscures. Préface de Maurice Chappaz. Vevey: L'Aire bleue, [1996], 136 pp. « Fuite de l'âge et malice d'un conte ». Prologue: Qui a tué Blanca ?—Les terres—Le chalet—La source—Guérin—Mayens—Le tour du propriétaire—Les signes—Seule—La troisième promenade—Fabienne—Le repas—Les champignons—Retour de Guérin—La cour des miracles—Brouillards—Les enfants—Le bel automne—Un visiteur—Epilogue : Le petit serpent noir ?

Les invités de Moscou, roman. Lausanne et Vevey : Bertil Galland & Ex Libris, 1977

Oeil-de-mer. Preface by Christiane P. Makward. Vevey: L'Aire bleue, [1996], 206 pp. « Oeil-de-mer ou la vie n'est qu'un roman » I. Le double II. L'amour III. L'ombre.

Le pantin noir, roman. s.l. Editions de l'Aire. 1981 [includes the rewriting titled *Jours de foehn*]

1ère partie [15 chapters, c. 1931]: Une fugue—La famille Alvaine—Ce mois de mai qui est si long!—L'Etrangère étrange—Les petits comédiens—Les Marquirotte—La dame sur le cheval blanc—La foire de printemps—Le montreur—Une série de mystères—Le pantin noir—Le secret de M. Alvaine—L'autre ville—Celui qui emporte le vent—Les fiançailles.

Deuxième partie, où l'histoire recommence . . . [15 chapters; rewriting of the preceding, c. 1936]. Le retour—Le foehn—Villa paradis—Le démon de Pagane—Une visite—Le mandarin—La tour de Romana—Les marionnettes—Gel et clair de lune—Papillon de nuit—L'invitation—Le bal—La surprise—Le coup de feu—L'aube.

Le sabot de Vénus, roman. Lausanne, Rencontre, 1952.

Théoda. Porrentruy: Portes de France, 1944 [etc.]. Albeuve: Castella, 1985.

3. Poetry

Chant pascal des cent vallées et *Dix poèmes d'amour*. Saint-Maurice: Saint-Augustin, 1997. Postface and notes by Maurice Chappaz.

Chants d'amour et d'absence. Lausanne: Empreintes, 1996. Preface and notes by Maurice Chappaz.

Le fleuve un jour. Genève: Slatkine, 1997. Preface and notes by Maurice Chappaz.

Un goût de rocher preceded by *Le lys a blanchi sous les pins noirs*, preface by Sylviane Dupuis, notes by Maurice Chappaz. Lausanne: Empreintes, 1997. 110 pp.

La montagne déserte* [1978]. Sierre : Monographic, 1997. Preface and notes by Maurice Chappaz. Five illustrations by Edmond Bille.

Le pays secret* [1961]. Sierre: Monographic, 1996. Preface and notes by Maurice Chappaz. Five illustrations by Edmond Bille.

La Rus, Russie! Lausanne: Empreintes, 1995. Preface and notes by Maurice Chappaz.

Soleil de la nuit* [1980], preceded by *Je n'entends plus battre mon coeur derrière la porte*. Sierre : Monographies, 1999. Preface and notes by Maurice Chappaz. Five illustrations by Edmond Bille.

Vignes pour un miroir. Lausanne: Empreintes, 1997.

* New, boxed collection of previously published volumes

4. Short Stories and Short-Short Stories

Le bal double, Vevey: Bertil Galland/Paris: Gallimard, 1980. 3rd edition, with a postface by Gabrielle Moix : Lausanne : Empreintes, 1990, 260 pp. Le bal double—Les insectes flamboyants—Un mariage pas comme les autres—Ainsi meurt ton regard—Angeline et Roberta—La rêveuse—Le clown—Ce sentier comme un tunnel—La vache—Le baiser—Une histoire qui commence quand on n'en connaît pas la fin—Le printemps fou—Fille ou fougère ?—Elle est tombée d'la lune—Voici venu le temps des parents maudits—Les fiancés de la Toussaint—La neuvaine des cloches—Mardi gras—L'amour de vous—Le cargo fantôme—« Un monde ambigu »—Biographie—Bibliographie.

Cent petites histoires d'amour. Vevey: Bertil Galland, 1978 and Paris, Gallimard, 1979.

Cent petites histoires cruelles [1973] followed by *Trente-six petites histoires curieuses*. Foreword by Maurice Chappaz, postface by Marguerite Saraiva-Nicod. Albeuve: Castella, 1985, 226 pp.

La demoiselle sauvage. Vevey : Bertil Galland, 1974. Paris: Gallimard, 1975, 216 pp. La demoiselle sauvage—Le garçon d'aurore—Le noeud—Carnaval—La jeune fille sur un cheval blanc—Le rêve—La petite femme des courges—L'envoûtement—Le nain et la vieille—Les fêtes du fleuve—Le lieu—La dernière confession.

Douleurs paysannes [1953], Albeuve, Castella, 1978. La sainte—La fille perdue—Celui qui ne savait pas son catéchisme—Elle ne reverra plus sa petite chambre—L'enterrement—La malade—Celui qui attendait la mort—Agatha—Le miracle—Reniement—Elle était allée gouverner—Le grand tourment—Clotaire—Vendanges—Le feu [these last "Four Valais Stories" were first published in 1951].

L'enfant aveugle. [1955] followed by *Entre hiver et printemps* [1967] Albeuve, Castella, 1980. L'enfant aveugle—Nativité—Donnez-moi un peu à boire—Les morts—La bête—Les oeufs de Pâques—Le brantard—Le propriétaire—Ulysse—Les poupées de maïs—La jeune fille transparente—L'homme qui retrouva le premier jardin. Le chat—Antonin—Le visiteur de la nuit—Qu'est-ce que tu es, toi?—Les gisants de Pâques—Le hameau dans le lit d'un torrent—Herbes de neige.

Juliette éternelle. Preface by Pierre Jean Jouve, drawings by Auberjonois. Lausanne: Guilde du Livre, 1971. Albeuve: Castella, 1983, 248 pp. Préface—Juliette éternelle—Mordre à l'églantine—Journal de Cécilia—Histoire d'un secret—Masques—Le passant de Dieu—Les jours les plus longs—La fuite de décembre.

Le salon ovale, nouvelles et contes baroques. Vevey: Bertil Galland, 1976, 186 pp. Albeuve: Castella, Postface by Jean-Paul Paccolat, 1987, 226 pp. Le salon ovale—Les étangs de brume—La chambre déserte—Le taureau des sables—La montagne qui était un château—Etrange—Les Léonore—La maison bizarre—Rose-de-nuit ou Le sursis—Quand les habits se mirent à courir—Dans le filet—Le vallon des hommes sauvages—La bergère—Le fauteuil rouge—L'île—Le poète, le vieux violon et les ciseaux—L'amour fou—Les jeunes filles dans la forêt aux mille miroirs—Une grande vallée rocheuse barrée de cordages—Danse macabre—Le garçon nacré—Villa des roseaux—Le caillou pesant—Le chemin des falaises—Postface : « La séduction de l'étrange »—Bio-bibliographie.

5. Stories for Young Readers

Oeuvres complètes pour la jeunesse. 3 vols. Genève: la joie de Lire, 1999.

1. *Martine et la princesse Onétropti.* 304 pp. Martine et la princesse Onétropti—La petite danseuse et la marionnette—Marietta chez les clowns—La vilaine comédienne—Le parfum de Mademoiselle Personne—Le berger et la marmotte—La perle rose du Lac Noir—L'ours rose—Le masque géant—La sirène turque—La dame qui voulait redevenir enfant—Le mystère du monstre—Monsieur Tuuuyo—Madame Rondo—Le sourire de l'araignée—Coco, le singe aventureux—La statue du lapin de Pâques.

2. *Les Métamorphoses.* 230 pp. Les Métamorphoses—La crèche de verre—Les deux Marie—Fleur de givre—Un écureuil tout blanc—La petite chèvre de Noël—La balance en traîneau—La surprise—La poupée qui ne voulait pas rester dans son carton —Le pauvre Père Noël et le méchant Robert—Le rêve endormi des faubourgs fabuleux—Le chat qui désirait trop de choses à la fois—La petite maison—Le petit cavalier vert—Histoire de Charmant—Un garçon vêtu de noir dans un paysage blanc—Le coffret—Les trois roses—La chatte—Messieurs les livres—L'arbre—Eugénie la petite marmotte.

3. *La maison musique.* 328 pp. La maison musique—Le violon de verre—La chaise à porteurs—Le messager—La tour—Le beau jardin—Le pantin noir—Jours de foehn.

6. Theatre Works

L'Oeuvre dramatique complète I. *L'Inconnue du haut-Rhône.* Preface by Maurice Chappaz. Paris: L'Age d'Homme, 1996, 164 pp. « Adam et Eve au village »—L'étrangère—Le diable et la mariée—La bague à ton doigt—L'inconnue du haut-Rhône—L'insomnie—La tendre acrobate.

L'Oeuvre dramatique complète II. *Les étranges noces et autres inédits.* Texts established and presented by Christiane P. Makward. Paris : L'Age d'Homme, 1996, 328 pp. Introduction: « De l'autre côté du rideau »—Les étranges noces—La chemise soufrée—L'avalanche ou La chouette—Au pays de l'est nous voulons aller—Halevyn—Les soeurs Caramarcaz—Les fifres et tambours au Grand Jugement—La pauvre petite alouette—La poupée ou l'enfant—La géante—Notes de travail et autres fragments.

"The Scent of Sulfur," *Plays by French and Francophone Women, A Critical Anthology,* edited and translated by Christiane P. Makward and Judith G. Miller. Ann Arbor: Michigan University Press, 1994.

Christiane P. Makward

• 1 •

The Transparent Girl

A young man lived in a bright little seaside town. Everyone found him strange. He didn't like people, or animals, or flowers: he only liked the dead.

They certainly returned his affection. They visited him joyfully. It's not always easy or pleasant for the dead to go on among the living. If he notices that his presence inconveniences or frightens, he becomes sad and withdrawn. But the young man devoted a real tenderness to them, and summoned them without fear. The dead were grateful to him. For his sake, they braved their own prejudices, which included a preference for dwelling in abandoned homes, narrow gorges, or fogbound harbors. They would rest in that town despite its disrespectful sun and its rough winds, ready to sweep away any troubled soul.

One evening, a young woman drowned while she was swimming, and her body drifted out to sea. No one cried for her, because no one had learned to love her. She felt very unfortunate, not being missed by anyone, and for several days, she wandered over the waters without knowing what to do.

Soon, the young man learned of her disappearance. He called to her. She heard him right away and came to the square little house; it was whitewashed with lime and had round windows that made it look like a single die.

"Your house is pretty. It's cheerful here," she said, smiling.

Her host stared at her. He found her so beautiful, he was speechless.

There was a strange depth to the young woman's eyes. And the more he looked at them, the more he felt that vertigo you sometimes get leaning over a well when you cannot see the bottom no matter how clear the water is. Her silvery-gray face and body had the softness and the sheen of sea-polished pebbles. Her hair, so blond it was nearly white, fell down to her shoulders in uneven strands, and two pink dots brightened her cheeks.

1

The young man lived very happily with the dead girl. He enjoyed listening to the stories, stories with no beginning and no end, that she told him in a monotonous voice. She also did his housekeeping, and prepared his meals, which he alone ate. She seemed content, and didn't know how to thank him for having called her to him and kept her.

One day, she remembered and recounted to him the final moments of her life:

"I was swimming, the water had turned black. It frightened me, but I pushed myself to keep going further. I wasn't alone; I could hear the other swimmers' voices, and that encouraged me. Great light rays fell on the ocean's smooth surface, surprisingly calm that evening, and they broke there, like bits of glass on cobblestones. . . . It was then that I felt myself caught in a current. I tried to fight it, but the water paralyzed me; it had suddenly turned ice-cold. I cried for help, and I felt a violent need to call out a name, but I couldn't think of a single one. I never knew my father or mother, and I had no friends. I died, and, for a long time, I cried out on the waters without knowing where to go. . . ."

So she spoke, with her back turned to the open window. The young man forgot to listen, so he could look at her better. He held his arms out toward her and said:

"You'll never leave me, will you?"

Then he noticed something extraordinary. Little by little, the girl was becoming transparent. The trees and roofs in the landscape could be seen through her silvery body. Filled with anguish, he examined her small face; the sky behind it was visible, too.

He said nothing. He knew that his immense love would not prevent the dead girl from dissolving, and then disappearing. All of his visitors left the same way. This time, his excessive happiness had made him forget that.

He was able to keep her for one last moment. He dared not breathe, for fear of breaking her fragile form. He closed the windows, afraid the wind would sweep her away. . . .

But it is given to no one, not even the dead, to stay forever with those who love them.

• 2 •

The Cat

They were a little old couple. Two eccentrics. Two railway workers. They had lived for a long time in a little house between the asparagus fields and the Simplon rail tracks. Nearby flowed the waters of the Rhone. But the last bell for railway gate-keepers rang a long time ago.

The house was destroyed to widen the road. The poplars were all cut down. But the two little old folks still have their hands and feet. It's funny though, they don't know what to do with them. They have retired.

So they could be closer to their nephews, their brother, and their sister-in-law, they came to live in the city. They have no children of their own. That was not given to them. But they have a cat. A very beautiful black cat. There is a tuft of white fur on his chest, just over the heart. A target. "Jump! You're in my sights!" shout the little nephews on Sundays. But the cat dilates his yellow eyes and flees. He doesn't return until evening, when all is calm in the apartment.

The woman has grown some parsley and basil in little boxes in the kitchen window. The man has set up a ham radio. They're bored; they miss their former worry: the train schedule. They still wake up at night. They listen closely: "Is that the express?"—"No, it's the local." They can still hear it, but not so well. And then it's not really the same train.

As a consolation, they bought a cabin in the gardens near the Rhone. Around it, they grow some strawberries and some corn; they have three apricot trees. But they can still see their cherry trees of days gone by, with cherries that glowed red against the gray of the Rhone and the dusty foliage. Those cherries seem to need the huff from the trains to be so beautiful, and the smell of iron even more than the sun. The travelers would reach their arms out without ever reaching them. "Yes, we were happy then."

They go often to their little cabin; they take the local train. It's at the next station. They walk a moment through the reeds, and then *voilà*. They turn the key, and there's the house again. Against the wall, the red flag is idle.

The cat always comes along on these excursions. In a double-topped wicker basket that pops open on each side of the handle. Dance, my basket! The cat is so used to it that he is no longer frightened at all, and only occasionally does he barely show the tip of an ear, missing a bit lost in a battle over love. Indeed, this black cat of ours sleeps out every night.

But this winter, the cat died. The cat died on Christmas Eve. "No, no, it's not true!" Struck by a car in the road. "That can't be true!"—"But yes it is, look. . . ." There he is, his coat as beautiful as ever, but the two gold dots are gone.

"He must be buried," says the man.

"No, no, it's not true!" the woman says again.

"At least he wasn't killed to be eaten," the man remarks.

"Christmas day!"

"We'll bury him tomorrow, at the cabin."

The woman still holds him on her lap; she caresses him, calls him:

"My piece of velvet, my live fur muff, oh!"

This load, so light, oppresses her. Where is that purring warmth that filled his stomach with music? And that damp truffle that would suddenly wet her finger? There is nothing left of it now.

She gets up and looks for a box. She places her small burden inside it. But he's not comfortable in there like that! He, who so enjoyed his cushion, but the cushion is too thick.

"Ah, yes. I'll give it to you."

The woman opens an armoire. She takes down something that is all the way at the top, wrapped in silk paper. It's some sort of garment made of white wool. A baby's top? No, a vest, a shawl; let's say a bed-sweater. A bed-sweater made of daisies. Yes, it's made of a hundred wool daisies all sewn together. At the heart of each daisy shines the yellow eye of the cat.

She crocheted it, evening upon evening upon evening. She crocheted it, but she never wore it. "It's for when I'm dead," she used to say.

The husband looks away. He doesn't like to see her show off this piece meant for the coffin. It was as if she were unfolding her own shroud. But she says:

"It's for the cat."

She puts it on the table: a big blossom. She lays the cat on it and folds the petals over him.

What beautiful, clear weather the next day! The sky and the mountains are blue; the earth resonates like a drum. The little train is full of people. Holidays. . . . But in the basket today, there's a little bit of bread, eggs, and dried meat that they will eat at the cabin. Today, it's the man who carries the basket. The woman carries the box.

There are families on the train. Those who are leaving with skis, those who are going to visit relatives. Voices buzz behind the tall wooden seat backs. Up above, in complete disorder: the wicker basket, a suitcase, one white box, two white boxes.

Everyone in the car seems happy. But the little old couple, they are not happy. They blow their noses. Tears, or a cold? No one is paying attention.

"What a Christmas we had!"

Their Christmas Eve: a wake at the side of the light catafalque, with Christmas candles burning at the four corners of the box. A blue one, a red one, and two green ones. That's not sad, for the deceased.

They got off the train. Red basket, white box, the two old people clopping along.

"Look!" Calls a happy traveler, "Look at them, with their little basket!"

But the reeds have hidden them. Now they can let their grief show. At the cabin, they have lit the fire, and the water is already boiling on the stove.

"When will we bury him?"

"Wait," said the woman. "I want to look at him again."

She undoes the knot. It's terrible to untie what one has tied forever.

"I can't get it," she said.

"Leave it be! Come and eat."

"I'm not hungry."

"Me neither, but it will be good for you."

She gets up and makes the coffee. They have eaten a little. He has taken the pickaxe and the box.

"I'm going."

"No! I want to look at him again!"

She has leaned over. With the tip of a fork, she has opened the knot.

"It makes me cry."

"I'm taking him," the man said. "We can't wait; the ground will be hard!"

"It's sand," she murmured. "And besides, I still want to look at him."

"But. . . ."

Inside, nothing is as it was before. Inside, there is paper. Underneath, there is a goose, a beautiful golden goose!

"We made a mistake!"

"The people talking on the train, who were saying, 'We're happy.' They were thinking of their dinner!"

She can't say another word. The man says: "We'll still have to eat it."

• 3 •

The Saint

*H*er eyes were the color of water and just as cold. Like water, they changed according to what lay underneath and what the sky was like. . . . Her hair was red, and too long, falling all the way down to her feet. It took her an hour each day to braid, but she refused to cut it. Arranged in a bun, it looked nothing like other women's; the bun was so large and so heavy that it completely covered her neck and the top of her shoulders. She had a straight nose, pure features, and skin so white that it surprised everyone. But her thin lips, always tightly closed, made people feel uneasy.

Her village was in the Conches Valley—a valley that, like her hair, was too long. A very dark village, with houses huddled close together and squirrel-like eyes staring up at a mountain that also turned very dark when the weather was bad.

As a little girl, she was nicknamed Will-o'-the-Wisp. No one dared to say that anymore, and everyone called her by her real name, Flavie. Nevertheless, she still lit up the street when she walked by. . . .

She went to mass every morning. The parish priest held her in high regard, citing her as an example. She had five brothers and two sisters. The oldest was a missionary; the second a Carthusian monk; another was a parish priest in the Lower Valais; the fourth was a Capuchin friar; and the last was still at seminary school. The two sisters were nuns. One taught the deaf-mutes at the Geronde monastery; the younger one was cloistered in a convent in Brigue. Apparently, Flavie had pushed them all to enter religious orders. She exerted a strange influence over those in her entourage. There was such certainty within her, such force of will allied with great gentleness; one could only submit.

"And what about her? Why isn't she a nun?" asked some people, those who always have embarrassing things to say. Some replied: "Her health is too delicate." Others said, "It's good for the laymen to have a saint among them." Spiteful tongues hinted, "It's to keep the family inheritance all to herself." And so she stayed at home with her parents, who were already old. The father and two servants looked after the property and the animals; the mother sometimes followed them to the fields and prepared the meals. Flavie did nothing, or next to nothing. They wouldn't have thought to ask that she do any manual labor. A surprising thing among the peasants: they were content with her beauty, her knowledge, and her wisdom. Maybe they remembered the story of Martha and Mary.

She never danced at the village fairs. But she always went, standing a little bit off to the side, on a hillside overlooking the festivities. The young men, tired of being rejected, had stopped inviting her. All around her, there was a void, an empty, taboo space, as if she had drawn a magic circle around herself. In the center of that circle she remained, standing straight, her head held high, and her lips tightly shut.

But the men looked at her anyway: she couldn't stop them from doing that. Was she aware of it? . . . Even as they waltzed, they would cast strange glances her way, forgetting about their dance partners. There was one who watched her the most, a young man with rough manners and eyes full of tenderness, Germain. He had loved her for a long time already, and he spoke to no one about it.

In the beginning, one is happy to love, even without hope, or almost without it; it makes your soul and blood burn with a good kind of fire. You don't recognize yourself anymore: the mountains have changed color, and the sky, too; the village starts to seem like Paradise because She lives there. And every time you meet her, it's as if you were receiving a beautiful picture. . . . An image you hide carefully in your heart, the better to contemplate it later, just as you did when you were a child, with those pictures of angels with shining wings and saints in golden clothes, given away by a wandering Capuchin monk. But soon, you realize that you can no longer tear out this love rooted in the very center of your being. Then, it is no longer happiness, but a great torment. "Ah! If only I could have that woman, every day and every night, just to myself." And this great torment gives you an unfamiliar courage.

At the April fair, Germain had the audacity to invite Flavie for a polka. On Sundays and feast days, she was even more intimidating than usual. On those days, all the women of the village seemed taller because of their furbelows, hats like precious towers wrapped in ribbons that conferred upon them the dignity of statues.

The villagers were quite surprised and interested when they saw him walking up to her; even the music faltered for a beat. Some of them laughed: "He'll never get her." Others admired him: "At least that one's not afraid of her!" Justine turned somber, because Justine loved Germain. And when he returned with Flavie, everyone was astounded. The couple stepped up onto the dance floor. The musicians stopped playing for a moment, then began again, forcefully. In Germain's arms, she, who never danced, was more supple than the branch of a larch tree.

"Will-o-the-Wisp!" someone said out loud.

And the others repeated, "Will-o-the-Wisp!"

At first, Germain was very moved; his eyes were blinded, and his ears became deaf. . . . He didn't know how he had been able to walk over to her. But now that he was holding her, his beloved, against him, he was filled with joy and courage all over again.

He looked closely at her as they danced. His eyes, starved until then, took from her all that they could take. He had never seen her so close. He made several discoveries: her cheeks had several freckles like the first stars in a still-bright sky; there was a small crack in her lower lip, and a dimple in her chin. And he saw that her eyelashes were neither red nor blond, but rather like those shiny specks of crystal sometimes mixed in with the sand of the Rhône. . . . That's why, instead of making her ugly, they lent a supernatural expression to her face. An angel's, or a devil's? Germain didn't ask himself that question.

★

From that day on, they strolled together every Sunday. "He's managed to tame her," people said. But the wedding wasn't going to happen so soon. She couldn't decide and found a thousand reasons for pushing back the date. Germain was growing impatient: he had waited so long for her!

"Do you love me, yes or no?" She answered yes, looking him right in the eye, but it seemed to the young man that she didn't see him at all. "You always seem like you're thinking," he humbly reproached her, ". . . and it's impossible to guess anything about you." To quiet his worries, he kissed her; then, he forgot about everything.

During the week, he would glimpse her in the street or behind a windowpane. She would signal mysteriously to him with her head, which she covered with a large, brightly flowered scarf knotted under her chin, as the other village women did. In those harsh regions where winter lasts a long time, people need to see flowers on their fabrics, embroider them on aprons, and put real ones on the windowsills. But for Germain, there existed none more beautiful or more real than Flavie.

"Either love will change her completely, and make her able to be a good wife . . . or else he is marrying an image," speculated the more thoughtful ones. These remarks involved a bit of jealousy from the men and from the women, too. Justine the abandoned cried into the red roses of her scarf, going out of her way to avoid Germain.

Flavie still wouldn't decide. "You'd think she was afraid," thought Germain. "What a strange woman. . . ." He was completely disconcerted. One evening, he went to see his uncle, the village priest, who had always shown affection for the young man. "He'll be on my side," he hoped.

"You're here to publish the banns?" asked the priest, with a wide smile.

"Yes. . . . No. . . ."

The fiancé didn't know how to broach the subject he had come to talk about.

"What's wrong?"

"Well. . . . It's about Flavie."

"You've chosen well."

"Of course. . . . But her mother has been sick."

"But as of now, she's well."

"That's just it. . . ."

The priest didn't understand.

"Oh!" exclaimed Germain, with an uneasy laugh. "This is all Flavie's idea, maybe it doesn't matter at all, but she is stubborn!"

"All women are."

"Well, so. . . . So her mother would get well, she made a vow."

"What did she promise?"

The young man drank in a big gulp of air and admitted, "She's made a vow of virginity."

The uncle guffawed.

"Ah! So that's why you look so pitiful! Don't you worry about it, my boy, she made that promise carelessly, without thinking ahead. We can give her a dispensation and send her on a pilgrimage, to make up for it."

"Good," said Germain, but he wasn't completely reassured. "The problem is that she holds to her vow!"

"Does she mean to break her commitment to you?" asked the priest, suddenly worried.

"No. . . ."

"Then maybe it's to make you angry." And the dusty cassock started shaking with laughter all over again.

★

The wedding was set for the last day of July. On the morning of the tenth, before the sermon at High Mass, the banns had been published for the first time.

After the service, the betrothed pair went to sit under the larches. Flavie murmured, "The forest smells so good!" Germain replied, "Yes, but I like smelling you even better." He bent over her, his nostrils flared. And he bit her a little on the cheek, just to frighten her. Next, he took hold of her lips. She pulled away, a droplet of blood at the corner of her mouth. Then, he pushed aside her bun and bit her on the neck; she let him do it, but while he did, he couldn't see how the color of the young woman's eyes grew darker.

Suddenly, he felt joyful again: "Flavie," he shouted, "Flavie, you are my wife!"

"Not yet."

"It's been recorded now; you can't go back anymore!"

And, carried away with enthusiasm, he overturned her on the russet carpet of larch needles. Furious, she got back up. "She's stronger than I expected," he thought, and he was happy.

She spoke: "You know about the vow I made. . . . Well, you'll see! . . . When I make a vow, I keep it."

"But since you've been absolved."

"What do you know about that? A vow is sacred."

Laughing, and sure of himself, he said:

"You'll change your mind soon enough. Come on, you're like all the others. . . ."

She replied:

"You'll see. Remember my words."

Right then, Germain started feeling very strange, very sad. He sat there in place, mute, blind, hands against the ground, dry needles pushing into his palms. But when he got back to the village, when he saw their marriage promise posted on the front of the Village Hall, he stopped thinking of what she had said. He was a strong man once again, a man who held in his hand all the mountains of the valley.

And the wedding day arrived. Flavie had had an outfit in beautiful black cloth made for her, with much gathering on the sleeves and skirt. On her head, she wore the furbelow, adorned with a wide black velvet ribbon embroidered with gold and sprinkled with pearls, jet beads, and little round bits of metal. She had no scarf around her neck: her red chignon, arranged in the shape of a fan around her shoulders, was more magnificent than a silk scarf.

Seeing her like this, Germain exclaimed:

"You are more beautiful than a vision!"

He thought about the church statues, draped in the splendor of their heavy robes, and about their faces, illuminated by halos and tiaras.

The priest was beaming: Flavie, such a serious girl, who would raise her children in piety and instill in them the love of God! He could already

imagine them as altar boys, with their skullcaps and their lace surplices. . . .
And there would be many of them: one every year. She would be the model;
she would be a fertile mother; she would put the stingy couples to shame!
Yes, it was a blessing. She had done well by not entering the convent like her
sisters. Her destiny was here. And Germain, well, yes, Germain seemed a little lukewarm on the subject of religion. His wife would know how to convince him and oblige him to come to mass more often. Yes, everything was
for the best.

When the couple emerged from the church, the mowed hay lit up the
fields all around the village, and waves ran through the fields of rye. Germain
leaned toward his wife and, circling his arm around her waist, spoke into
her ear:

"Tonight, I will harvest you."

And his arm became cutting like a scythe.

That evening, Justine the abandoned had such a heavy heart that she went
out wandering through the little back streets. She would have preferred to walk
through the fields or at the edge of the forest, but she didn't dare to, all alone
at night, despite her distress.

The wind had picked up, and roamed the streets, almost without sound,
with the uneasy style of a thief. In the sky, somber flocks departed toward a distant exile. The village had loosened the moorings holding it to the earth and
was set adrift. And Justine walked as if she no longer had a body, as if she were
only a soul, because that soul hurt her so badly. She said, "What good would it
do to be dead, if you carry the weight of your unhappiness with you? . . . Then
nothing would be different, nothing."

All the windows seemed dark, but two or three electric bulbs revealed
certain sections of the village. And Justine realized that she had arrived near
Germain's house. Why couldn't she go any further? Why did her feet remain
stuck to the ground? She wished that she could be off with the wind, be nothing more than a soul in the wind, but suddenly her body had come back, ever
so heavy . . .

So they were living up there, the young married couple, on that third
floor overhanging the second, and which she could see in profile: a black ship
sailing in the night. A staircase, half wood, half stone, led up to it. Justine's eyes
were fixed on a door up there, and the door opened slowly, cautiously, but
creaking anyway. A man appeared and leaned on the railing; for a moment, he
didn't move. Maybe he was looking inside himself and trying to recognize the
man he saw there? Then he came down the stairs, softly, but his hobnails
scraped the last few flagstones. The young woman didn't dare believe what she
was seeing. She waited for her vision to vanish. And suddenly, Germain was
right in front of her. He hadn't realized she was there. He let out a curse.

"What are you doing here?"

She tried to continue on her path out of the village, but he caught her.

"You're here to spy on us!"

Justine said nothing; she didn't know what to say. She saw only how the locks of the man's hair fell over his face and how lost he seemed. Germain understood that she saw all these things, and he grew angrier. He shook her by the shoulders.

"What's that to you?"

And because she remained before him, without fear and without a word, he began to beat her. And so that she couldn't flee, he grabbed her by the arm and held tight. . . . She didn't scream; but she uttered "Germain, Germain!" very quietly, as if calling for help.

He let her go and went off toward the mountain.

He didn't return home until the last hours of the night, when it becomes gray and ice cold.

★

Life in the village returned to its normal flow. Nothing seemed changed. The hay was almost in, and it would soon be harvest time. Justine had kept quiet. When people ran into Germain, they asked him, "Hey! How goes it with the newlyweds?"

He replied, "Of course it's going well!" And he laughed loudly.

As for Flavie, no one saw much of her. She didn't follow her husband into the fields, which was the custom. She came at mid-day to bring him his meal and sat for a few minutes on the embankment, silent and distant; then she returned home.

People criticized: "He'd rather see her keep her white hands than make her work. She'll cost him plenty in the end!" Once, they had even seen Germain carrying his wife in his arms like a baby doll, across a mountain stream. They made fun of him. "Ah, he'll get over that, just like we did," predicted the old couples, confident of their wisdom.

But Flavie still radiated such authority that no one dared to say anything in front of her. Her eyes had kept the transparence of water, yet the bottom of that water remained undiscernable. What was it made of? Fine sand, polished pebbles, or mud teeming with serpents? . . . Germain looked at those eyes and begged them for a response, but they would not speak to him.

No one knew, except perhaps Justine, that life had become a hell for him. Worse than a hell, even, because in hell, at least, you can let go and moan, you can scream—you have the right to be unhappy! Not in a village where all the windows are spying on you. . . . If only he could beat her—Flavie! Hit her, and then subdue her. But he could clearly see, now, that she wasn't like other women. Even in his most violent outbursts, his arms remained paralyzed before her, and his tongue failed to find even one insult. And worse still: she was always right; he felt guilty about her, and he went so far as to ask her forgiveness!

But when he was alone again, a great sense of rebellion built up in him; the blood in his veins turned to poison, and no matter how hard he worked from morning till night, his only thought was this: "I will cut her down like a stalk. It's my right!" But he always heard her crystalline voice respond, "Not before you have harvested every other blade, every other stalk on earth. . . ." Which meant: never.

When he walked by the church, he thought of the words the priest had said at their wedding: "*They are no longer two, but a single flesh. What God has joined together, let no man put asunder!*" He knew perfectly well that they were not united, and that nothing—not heaven, not hell, not men—could change that. And a bitter taste filled his mouth. One evening, he even began to murmur, almost out loud:

"Life is unfair; life is unfair! Can a person still believe in God after that?"

But his eyes happened on the crucifix, and he quickly crossed himself with an ample gesture.

There were days, however, when he found hope again, days when the air seemed full of joy. "No," he thought, "this can't go on forever. Surely there will be a miracle. It takes patience." The torture returned without delay. So his whole life would be like this! If he could at least confide in someone, but these were things impossible to say—one would rather die—and even in his prayers, he didn't dare speak of it.

The summer went by, then the fall, then the winter, and the spring came. And since people hardly ever saw Flavie anymore, they began to ask Germain, "Is there a little one on the way?" or "Might she be expecting?" Which meant the same thing. But his face grew somber and he looked away.

Behind his back, they whispered:

"He keeps her locked up, he's so jealous."

And they laughed.

★

The month of May arrived, the month of Mary. The Virgin's altar was decorated with geraniums in pots, paper lilies and roses, and lots of candles.

And then one evening, going into the church to say the rosary, the villagers were shocked to see the Madonna's altar stripped of its flowers and candelabras. They ran to alert the priest. He knew nothing about it. Everyone assembled under the porch. Someone had desecrated their church! Embers glowed in the eyes of the men; the women crossed themselves; the children cried in the forest of skirts. They were all very upset, but little of their emotion was expressed in words and gestures; it remained within, as do all the violent passions of mountain people.

A little girl ran to her mother and pulled her by the hand:

"Come see! Come see!"

"What is it?"

"Come see!" the child kept repeating.

She said it with such insistence, and her face shone with such a strange light, that the woman yielded and let herself be led along. And seeing this, the others followed along, too.

"What did you see?" they asked her.

But her emotion was so great that she could not explain it to them. Her impatience proved contagious, and the procession grew, led by the little girl, walking faster and faster. Justine joined them, sensing a disaster. They walked down a street, across a square, went around some barns; in the end, they stopped in front of a house. Germain's house.

"It's there!" And the little girl pointed to the door at the top of the stairs.

"What did you see?" the mother asked again.

At this point, she remembered that, a little while ago, she had sent the little girl to Flavie's house.

Several people had already rushed up the stairway. They pushed open the door, went into the hallway, and opened another door, the bedroom door. Those who arrived first stopped at the threshold. At first, they could see only a sparkling wall of candles, and they breathed in the smell of incense. Then they saw Flavie, stretched out on a table.

She was motionless in her best festive dress, and her hair, all undone, surrounded her body like a flamboyant mandorla. With her head crowned by the furbelow, her eyes wide open, her hands joined together—pale hands, where her wedding band shone—the artificial flowers and the candles devoutly arranged before her, Flavie looked like those wax figures laid out in glass coffins, deep in their crypts.

And in her breast was buried a dagger.

The people looked upon her with amazement, overwhelmed by fright. Others came in behind them, pushing them forward, and soon the room was full. After a while, they noticed Germain kneeling before the table. He seemed to hear nothing, but suddenly, he turned around. And in a rough voice that no one recognized, he said, pointing to his wife:

"She's a saint."

It was then they understood that Germain had lost his mind, and they led him away.

• 4 •

Grape Harvest

At first they didn't notice her at all. Then it was her silence that made her presence more real, just as another would have accentuated it with her laugh or her voice. Not so different from her companions: a beautiful girl with eyes that don't offer themselves and a rounded chin; her mouth, the only thing in her face that allows itself to dream.

"She's not from around here," they said. She shrugged off her torpor and began to speak. She lived in a village in Lower Valais; she had come to Sierre for the grape harvest. . . . They left her alone. A good worker. She would break off the cluster of grapes with her fingernail and cradle it delicately in the palm of her hand. Always fragile, a cluster of grapes. When the stem was too hard, she would cut it with a little knife that she sharpened every day before starting out. That year, there were hardly any spoiled grapes; they revealed themselves intact in the hand, icy and covered with droplets at dawn, hot as lamps at noontime. If a grape fell, she picked it up quickly and put it in the pail with a bit of earth. Nothing must be lost.

The bucket filled, she would go and empty it into the main basket. For a moment there was, between herself and the man pressing the grapes, a faint mist. For that moment, she looked at him. The man was amazed by those eyes fixed on him. She left. The leaves jostled against her apron; she turned at the waist; she rejoined her companions.

They often spoke in patois around her, which isolated her even more. But she listened with the same grave attention that she put into the work of harvesting, and when she knelt before a vine whose grapes trailed in the dirt, it was with a strange sort of fervor.

The carts made an immense noise as they passed by on the road, a noise they didn't make the rest of the year. The carts of the *Last Judgment*. They were

17

weighted down by the vats and the barrels. She would watch the man who led them, then turn her head away.

In the morning, the vineyards on the plain remained in the cold and the shadows for hours, while those on the mountain were all bathed in a light that advanced by descending toward the harvesters. They finally received it over themselves. The light reassured them, as if they had suddenly learned that they were among the chosen and not among the damned.

In the evening, when they returned, the young woman walked alongside the others, her cheeks powdered with sulfate, and in her body the dancing movement that she had had all day while circling around the vines. Sometimes, they came back through the town. They felt proud. The main street was filling with shadows and fire, but the sky to the west was still clear, like a cluster of grapes.

She was staying at Muraz with one of her mother's sisters, who regretted having taken the girl under her roof. "She's making money in the vineyards, of course, but it's still an inconvenience," the old woman told her friends. Fortunately, it would only be for three weeks.

The girl spent the evenings standing in the doorway, observing all the motion in the street, with the dignity, the assurance, that come with a long day of work. She stared at the passersby. "She's an insolent one," thought her aunt. The aunt was afraid of everything, those nights. "People aren't their usual selves. . . ." They were living another life, nocturnal, full of passion and mystery. That was easy to see, just from watching the men march by with their shining faces, moving like sleepwalkers. And the racket they felt free to make, as if it were the middle of the day! They pounded on the staves; they washed the barrels with buckets of water. And that girl, her niece, who stood there enraptured, her eyes growing wider from the effort of keeping them open. It's true that they were beautiful, those eyes, and unblinking, despite her fatigue. And when the moon rose over the cliff of the Corbetschgrat, because the moon is always there for the grape harvests, but larger this time than anyone remembered ever having seen it, the dazzled old woman hid away.

The girl, too, also eventually went back in. Once, her aunt caught her by surprise, crying in the kitchen.

"What's wrong?"

"Nothing."

"When a person cries, it's because something is wrong."

"I'm discouraged, that's what."

The next day, she went off to the vineyards again with the same élan as the other days, the joy that made her seem taller than her companions. With deep breaths, she took in the cold air of this autumn country, happy to be there, to have before her a whole day that might bring her what she wished for. On the road, near the orchard, some nuts had fallen. She crushed them with her heel, then ate them, taking care first to remove the skin. "Nuts that fall in the road belong to those who pick them up," the women who worked the harvest always said.

But the girl saw all the vineyards of Sierre around her and was seized by anguish: those of the Noble Country, terraced and spreading out like fans, those of Bernunes, facing the forest of Finges, those of Planzettes and of Géronde, those of Pradegg, and those of Saint-Gignier. Never had she imagined that there were so many. So many hills, and on each hill, a vineyard! She wasn't used to that, she who lived near Fully, with the mountain so close and a plain that kept back no surprises, but laid itself out in a single glance.

She went through nearly all of them: she harvested for merchants, for people unknown. Now, in the mornings, the fields and the vineyards were covered with white frost. She had put a heavy sweater under her gray apron; on her head, she wore a blue serge scarf knotted under her neck. The leaves crumbled to dust in her hands and the withered grapes were no longer so transparent.

One night, it snowed. She saw an extraordinary landscape, white and gold, as some of the leaves had not yet fallen. That day, she was sure that something would happen.

But that evening, she returned disappointed. The snow was gone from the roads, leaving only mud. She murmured: "I'll never find him again."

She thought about going back home. But she stayed on. The harvests were coming to a close. She offered to help a neighbor woman who had a vineyard on the mountain. She climbed up a very steep path, full of pebbles, walked through two villages, and then arrived on the main road. There, by a wall, a cart awaited her. And the man who held the mule by the bridle—it wasn't she who looked at him, but rather it was he whose eyes first lighted on the girl.

She jumped; she hadn't seen him. She had stopped waiting for him. Confused, she was amazed to find him so like when they first met.

"Hello," she said.

Like the first time, they had no need to explain themselves: each immediately trusted the other. They had met on the road, in Lower Valais, a year ago. After having spoken for a moment, they had parted. Later, she realized that he didn't know her name, and she didn't know his. He had told her only that he was from the central region, and that he worked in the vineyards. He spent the winters poaching. "Someday, I'll send you a fox fur, or a marten. . . ." She had laughed. She no longer felt like laughing, now.

"I knew I'd see you again," he said.

"It wasn't that easy," she thought, and she was angry at his stupidity.

• 5 •

My Forest, My River

August 17

I have a true passion for the forest. I am in love with the forest, and with the river, too. It's a violent, absurd love, because, after all, what can my love mean to the forest or the river? A willow branch pulled by the current, a pine tree motionless against the sky; these things almost put me in ecstasy, and it makes sense to me that, in the old days, people worshipped the trees and the waters. But they worshipped everything, the sun, the stones. Perhaps they just reacted simply, as I do. They must have felt that infinite well-being, that friendship, all that I feel in the woods on the banks of the Rhône.

August 18

This morning, after a night of rain, I breathed in the forest. In some spots, now, it smells like wet hay, but in the thickets I am always surprised by the fine smell of bark and plants.

I saw a big brown butterfly with two little blue moons ringed in black on its front wings. I looked it up in my book afterward; it's the glacier Erebus.

August 25

The days are very hot and the nights are cool. At dawn, the forest, drenched with dew, takes a while to dry in the first rays of the sun. A little steam rises among the pines.

I left for the ponds that are an hour from here, across the fields and the alders where a wide gray brook, heavy with silt, prowls in silence. There, it's full of blackberries, brambles, and broken branches that fly up underneath your

21

feet. It is dark and damp. Then I went through a very dry and sunny region, the Redsands, which is no longer forest, but rather the Rhône's old riverbed. Pines and junipers grow there on stretches of white pebbles and reddish lichens. Long tracks were laid out there by the military for their tanks, but they fled the place; the sand from the river, composed mostly of flint, was ruining their machines. All that's left are these tracks that I use with my horse to dash through the open spaces where a blonde mane of steppe grass floats.

Today the cicadas were singing. Well, just two or three, actually! The first was in a grove of poplars. I tried to spot it; I stayed and watched, looking up into the branches. It seemed so close, but I didn't see it. Lin tells me that they are smaller than the ones in the south of France and that they sing only when we have burning hot summers.

Once again I entered the dark, aquatic light, between the thin trunks and the rotten roots of alder trees. Spiders' webs gagged me; there were some on my tongue. I led my horse into a thicket of reeds that he split apart with his chest, as if it were the hull of a barge. But then he reared suddenly: there was opaque, green water running by. It's the Big Farm's canal. I followed alongside it, struggling with the brush that engulfed us. We managed to cross two bridges of boards over tiny streams, one transparent and the other completely black. The differences between these waters that end up mixing in the canal remain a mystery to me. The passage opened onto a marshy trail where my mount sank in sometimes all the way up to his thigh. I lost my footing, too.

Finally the ponds! I watched the fish. The tenches swam toward us because of the sun. Fascinated, I contemplated the stripes of their translucent, golden gray bodies and their waving fins outlined in orange. There were four very fat ones. The rest of the pond was already in shadow, and the water was ice cold. I found that out by swimming in it. The dragonflies above me flew as high as the tops of the pine trees.

On my way back, around six, I was struck by the scent of the Redsands. Very particular and delicate, less resinous than that of the forest, it was the scent of warm pebbles, of grasses, and rushes, almost a flowery perfume.

August 26

I live with my mother in the northeast corner of a little eighteenth-century French castle, in a land where people speak the old German of Niebelung, with its harsh sounds. It's a pretty castle, well-proportioned and pathetic, gray like the rocks that crop up everywhere on this dried-out soil. My father, a lawyer inclined to take on lackluster cases, had hands that always rembled, and a humble demeanor at Mass, but a proud one when hunting. (Then, he didn't tremble.) When I asked him for a horse for my fifteenth birthday, this man who could offer us neither a servant nor a Mercedes, and who had long since buried his own horses, said yes. "But you'll have to be the one to take care of it!"

That was two years ago. My father is dead. I took the rotten hay and the disgusting rags out of the abandoned stable, and I brought in a beautiful chestnut horse, half Arab, that I groom and ride every day. His coat is so shiny that I called him "Brilliant."

It's hard to be an only child, to speak two languages (French at the table, Tudesque at the stable), to be poorly taught, to have no friends because the people here, ah, well, they don't like what I like, they like what I don't like. (Except for Lin. He's my cousin who lives in the big southwestern wing.)

Yes, it's hard to be a girl, to be poor, to be alone.

I don't get along very well with my mother. I don't think she's ever loved me. (Perhaps I'm wrong; I'd like to be wrong.) I think she wanted a son. My earliest memory is that of a noise rising from the wooden floor of a vast room, stopping and suddenly starting again. My mother was a men's tailor. My mother knew her trade perfectly and had four women working for her. She couldn't give up this work during the first years of her marriage, and still spent a large part of her time in that low-ceilinged, stifling room that hummed with sewing machines. Me, I was one or two years old, the age before memory starts. So nothing unfortunate could happen to me, they would hang me on a big nail against the wall, like a laundry bag or a puppet. I was both at the same time. I opened up my arms; I closed them again, I laughed, I cried. Sometimes, someone would come and take me down. Having married a lawyer, my mother thought it would be better to forget the sewing machines, little by little. When she wanted to get them going again because her husband hardly earned any money, it was too late. In the meantime, ready-to-wear clothing had already seduced the region's male population. Without the help of her workers, she began making dresses, but she followed a stern cut, and had already acquired a displeasing haughtiness. Poor mother, she now lives like a needy aristocrat, after having been a well-off woman of the people. . . .

My father, I did love him. It was from him that I got my flax-colored eyes, but my physical strength I inherited from my mother. He was always good to me. He tried to explain what our nobility consisted of, since he had given me a nobleman's name. It dates back to the time of Louis XV. My favorite ancestor is the captain of the Swiss Guards who were killed for the sake of the king. We have his portrait; he holds a heart in his hand. When I was little, I called him "the red grandpa." He told me many things, and certain feats of arms that I make myself remember. But history is not my forte. Aside from his very blue eyes, what I recall best about my father is his hand. Perhaps because it trembled. As a child, during Mass, I would keep my cheek right near it, feeling its vibrations, but my eyes rested on the other, wooden hand, rising from the pulpit. It held a crucifix and it did not tremble. "It's not alive, it's not alive," I thought, until the day when I saw the crucifix hand tremble. I didn't dare look at it again for the rest of the Mass. Now my father is dead.

His family never supported him: it was a misalliance to have married my mother. The nobility of this little country marries among itself. His brothers were very hard with him and forced him to sell what he owned for derisively small sums. That's also why we live in the darkest wing of the castle. My cousins have a terraced garden with sculpted bushes where roses and lemon trees flower. They scorn us a little, except for Lin, the youngest, who is sweet and intelligent. My girl cousin is going to marry a count soon. The boys are in school far away; when they come back here for their vacations, they loll about in a garden hammock, on garnet-colored cushions, or else each one drives around in his own sports car. The only thing I envy is the view they have from their windows. Our little town sits on the flank of the mountain, and it dominates the whole plain of the Upper Rhône. But I can have that view, too, each morning and evening, by standing straight up on Brilliant's back in the stable, like a circus equestrian. It's to my forest and my river that I blow a kiss.

August 27

I went back to my pond. It's still very hot out, although the light is beginning to look like it does in the fall. On the way back, amongst the debris of the reeds and the willow trees, the mosquitoes feasted on my bare legs. (In the summer, I wear shorts when I ride; the rest of the year, it's thick, gray canvas pants, fairly supple, which I prefer to jodhpurs.) Once I reached the trail that leads up to the big tower, I decided to return by the new dike that was built ten years ago or so. It's already sprinkled with plants and dwarf pines that rise up from the white gravel. On either side, large blocks of stone are crudely stacked up. I had some trouble getting Brilliant to climb up there; at first, he refused. But right near the row of birches, I happened to notice a sandy slope that led gently to the dike. The sallow-thorn, almost as tall as the trees, are covered now with orange berries. Some of them don't have any at all. Why not?

I noted the stumps of the felled poplars. (Yes, I can remember huge foliages shining in the sun here.) They were savagely overturned, and their bases sit there, earthy roots in the air. Lined up alongside one another, they act as a canopy for the water which could scarcely have overflowed this year: we had a snowless winter. The sound of the Rhône is fainter; I miss it. I used to like listening to it all night long in my room.

I breathed in a smell that I at first I thought came from the water, but it grew more and more sour and disagreeable; it was actually coming from one of the Big Farm's garbage heaps. If I avoid using the road to the farm that cuts the forest in two, which would certainly be easier, it's because it used to belong to my grandfather. Now it belongs to the Bomboli Stores of Zurich, and they've put their insignia at the entrance! The farm has grown three times larger. From town, you could see the clearing grow wider, and I wondered if we would have a bit of forest left. . . . Their northern boundary passes through the shady underbrush I mentioned, which lines the edge of the Redsands. I don't much care to step inside this domain that, on principle, is off limits for us. They also have some very mean dogs that could frighten Brilliant. And it makes me a little sad to think that all that no longer belongs to us.

Tall brown butterfly orchids were invading the dike, except for the two ruts, and I was back on the wide stretch that I call the steppe. There were fresh prints from other horseshoes, and I said to Brilliant, "In the old days, only my grandfather, my father, and his brothers rode here. I'm keeping up the tradition, but you can see we're not the only ones anymore."

August 28

Today I have something important to put in this secret diary. First of all, it's my birthday: I've ended my sixteenth year and am beginning my seventeenth.

Soon I'll be twenty! "It's the most wonderful time of life!" say the married ladies I know, as they swoon. I think they're stupid to say such a thing because it is quite the contrary: it's the age when you have the most to worry about. You have to choose. And if you make a bad choice?

But it's for certain that, by that age, I will have left my mother and the village. I want to live a new life, far from here. However, I could never completely abandon my forest and my river. I still haven't dared to tell what is happening to me. It's going to take a certain amount of courage. . . . How strange.

And here it is: my glorious day. First, I must be honest. I never thought this would happen to me so fast. All at once, just like that. And so violently that it . . . yes, it took my breath away. I have to stop writing at times; I hear my heart beating all the way to the top of my head. I'm even trembling.

No, I never would have believed that I would be caught this completely unaware. I had always imagined that love came to those who really wanted it, who thought about it all the time. Me, I always turned a deaf ear to love.

I had gone back to my favorite pond. To tell the truth, it's off limits to everyone, except for the people from the Big Farm. They built a little pier there and two wooden cabins, with a sign that says: "No swimming or fishing." But I know there's no one there at certain times of day. And these days, they've got far too much to do, getting their hay in with their red machines, etc.

I get undressed up above, in a hollow between two hills. I tie Brilliant to a pine, and I steal quietly down to swim. It's the deepest of the ponds, and the cleanest. It's almost round, and a very golden green; the reeds have their funny little brown, dry flowers. To the west, the forest stretches out all in hills, black and mossy, under a sky that grows clearer as the day wears on. Like the other afternoons, I lay down on the pier in my bathing suit and watched the fish. There was one following a dragonfly in his flight from under the water, ready to pounce on him at the slightest show of weakness. That made me laugh. Minuscule speckled gudgeons circled in the weeds. Suddenly, I heard someone coming. I didn't move. A young man in blue jeans and a gray sweater. At first I thought it was someone from the Big Farm, but, since he didn't say anything, I wondered if he might be camping. He was watching me. I continued to observe the fish, as if nothing were happening, but I could feel his eyes on me, which made it difficult for me to breathe freely. He sat down and kept his eyes riveted on my person. So I decided to dive in, and swam to the other end of the pond. The water was so cold in that shaded area that I came back quickly. I climbed up the little wooden ladder that comes down from the pier; it slants a little, and the steps under the water are very slippery. I almost fell over and hurt myself; fortunately, I caught hold in time.

He was still sitting, but he wasn't watching me anymore. I saw that he had a book in his hand and was reading. That took me by surprise. . . . I lay back down on my stomach on the pier, and just enjoyed feeling the sun on my body. I didn't worry about the young man anymore. I rested my head on my folded arms and, through the cracks between the boards, peeped at the fish underneath me. A multicolored frog jumped into the water; a duck glided into the darkest corner of the pond. Time went by. When I looked up again, the young man wasn't there anymore. "Maybe he's hiding somewhere, watching me. . . ." I don't trust boys.

But I was neither annoyed nor worried. I was very relaxed, dulled by a sense of well-being, and happiness, too. I am always happy in the forest. And then a strange metamorphosis took place. I became an other; I divided into two, yes, my usual self went to sleep (I wasn't sleeping), while a second person was born from me, someone who was still me, but a little girl. I was eight years old.

It was a morning in March. There was a touch of red in the willow branches, and a touch of madness in us. . . . I was running. It was cold out. But I had left my mother and her sewing machines behind for hours, and that school that I didn't like, too! With other girls and some boys. Our shoes were already covered with white dust. We went all the way down to the Rhône and followed the path that cuts its way beneath the boulders. The river was still transparent. We walked for a long time; an older boy was leading us.

"Where are you taking us to, the Promised Land?" we asked him.

"Yes. You'll be amazed."

"How do you know?"

"I've heard about it."

"But what is it?"

He didn't want to say.

And we kept on going, not running now (we couldn't anymore), under a March sun that was already warm after a winter that had made us suffer. We had all taken off our sweaters and wore them over our rear ends, the sleeves tied around our waists. On the younger children, they trailed along on the ground. And when we arrived, we saw, below the boulders, a great waterhole, surrounded by blackthorns.

"That comes from the Rhône?"

"No, from there!" the older boy said, showing us the tall granite wall above our heads. And we understood at once, because we had all heard about the warm water springs. The little rack-railway train that came up from the plain and crossed our little town led through a vast amphitheater of mountains and meadows where there was a thermal station as old as the world, or so we believed.

A light steam floated over the violet water. Then, in front of all of us, the older boy undressed. Bathing suit on, he threw himself into the water. We all squealed in chorus. But after snorting and splashing us, he waded about peacefully in the water, which reached up to his armpits.

"You still don't understand!" he shouted at the rest of us, seeing that we were still openmouthed with astonishment. "You still don't understand: the water's warm!"

Yes, we had understood. Yes, it was warm, as it can be in a good bath in a good bathtub. We yelled, "Well, then! If that's how it is."

The boys took off their pants and emerged from their little heaps of clothes in underpants, which were varying shades of white. They joined in the dance one after the other. The girls stayed at the edge and whispered, "Let's go in, too!"

That was nine years ago, since I am beginning my seventeenth year. Finally, they were all in the water in little knickers and undershirts. Everyone was laughing and splashing around. I had stayed alone at the edge. I don't know why, an irrational fear prevented me from joining in their jubilation. I didn't dare to get undressed. "That," I thought stupidly, "is a sin." And already the dread of having to confess it deadened any impulse within me. The others did not care one bit. What would they say in confession? Would it even occur to them to confess it? One thing was certain: it didn't trouble them in the least. And they were right. When they got back out of the water, they were all basically naked on account of their light cotton underclothes, except for the oldest boy, who was wearing a real bathing suit. They shook themselves and ran into the magnificent stretch of sand behind the blackthorn bushes. I don't remember anymore if they managed to get dry, or if they just put their clothes back on without worrying about it.

I had stayed off to the side, observing them. I was a lot slower to feel that joy, but I had finally decided to get in, too, once they were all ready to leave. I let them disappear on the path. Believing I was alone, I showed an audacity that far surpassed theirs. I got completely naked and placed a large stone on top of my little pile of clothes. The warm wind, the *foehn*, was picking up. I took my turn getting into the water and nearly cried out with pleasure, because the cold in the air had at first seized me and slapped me, but now—oh! now—I was rocked by a warm, maternal wave. My feet pushed down into the sand a little. I closed my eyes and buried myself in water up to my chin. The risk of drowning was very real, but it wasn't on my mind. I was dizzy with pleasure, and the blood buzzed joyfully in my ears. Then suddenly it was completely extraordinary: I thought I saw my double coming toward me; yes, I believed that the water had become a mirror or a mirage, and was sending my own image back to me. But that naked body, just as white as mine and scarcely deformed by the water, was not mine. That head wasn't mine, either, that severed head set on a tray of water. "Ah!" I said, and stopped.

The boy, for it was a boy, stopped also. He burst out laughing.

"You thought you were alone?"

"Yes," I answered, and suddenly I was shaking.

"You see" (and this he said in a calm, authoritative voice), "you and me, we are Adam and Eve."

I must have looked very worried and imploring. He let out another burst of laughter.

"There's no wrong in it, because this is Paradise here!"

He helped me out of the water, but my feet were unsteady, and I swayed. I was back on the sand where, very quickly and without looking at him, I put my clothes back on. He did the same. I could hear his little suspenders snap. Like me, he had put his clothes under a rock.

"I don't know you," I said. "I've never seen you before." (My dress had returned to me the capacity to speak.) "You're not from the town?"

"No, I'm from the forest."

An incomprehensible tenderness for him dawned at that moment in my heart. But I thought I had better keep it under control.

"You followed us?"

"Yes. . . ."

"And why didn't you swim with the others?"

"Because they're from the town, and I'm from the forest."

I didn't know what to say in response. I understood, obscurely, that he considered himself in some way inferior to us.

"And you?" he went on.

I looked down. The boy smiled. He must have been ten or eleven, and had strong teeth. His eyes, tilted toward his temples, were magnificent. He pointed to a blackthorn bush.

"Hidden!"

I looked, and I saw something that filled me with boundless wonder and amazement. The blackthorn had bloomed! Thousands of little white flowers had just opened in the warm *foehn* of the first spring.

"The crown of thorns," the boy said gravely.

He, too, was surprised.

~~~~~~~~~~~~~~~~~~~~~~~~~~~~~~~~~~~~~~

I put in this dotted line because so many years have gone by since then. And now I'm lying here on the pier, over the pond, watching the tenches. And all of a sudden I know. The young man who was sitting over there, who has just disappeared, and who watched me so intently for so long, that was him! He's the boy who swam naked with me, in a sulfur spring, ten years ago.

I love him. I don't know why. I love him, I love him. . . .

September 2

I've started school again. Home economics courses, along with some stenography and accounting lessons. I don't much enjoy these subjects, but it is a way for me to go and earn my own living one day, far away from here. I still think of leaving, but first I want to know; I want to see *him* again.

September 6

It's been cold and nasty out. I haven't been able to do anything.

September 11

I'm in a bad mood. I'm bored at school. I won't repeat here the conversations of my classmates or the remarks made by the Sisters. They no longer interest me. I do try to learn something, though, so that I can go to work in another year. Papa would never have wanted me to work, but you have to be able to make it on your own in this world. I want to be independent and live in the town on the other side of the forest. We see its lights at night. I'll put Brilliant in a boarding stable (I know there is one), and I'll come back with him often to these woods: people say they are even more beautiful to the west.

As discreetly as I could, I asked some questions about the people at the Big Farm to one of the girls who lives there with her family and comes here every day for classes. I will become her friend if I have to. I absolutely must know.

September 15

I haven't learned anything thrilling. On Sunday my mother had some visitors; I stayed home to help her. I hope I can get all the way to the ponds on Thursday. Will I be brave enough to go swimming again? Although the weather has cleared, there's a chill in the air. The herds came down from the mountain pastures today, and the fields are full of autumn crocuses.

I saddle and ride Brilliant for an hour each morning. Grooming him, cleaning out the stable, and going to school take up all my time.

September 16

Today, Sister was teaching us "artistic fruits and vegetables." After explaining to us all that food can gain when well presented, not just in beauty, but also in flavor, she taught us how to cut turnips and carrots in slices, stars, cubes, and triangles. This is what we get for geometry lessons. . . .

"What a waste of time!" I sighed. "I'll never go to all that trouble!"

"True enough," said Sister Bertrand-de-Jesus. "You'll buy cans and dry packaged soup, dead foods, and your stomach will be the first to suffer for it."

There was a brouhaha and some laughter. Among the pile of vegetables that we had cut "artistically" (I had tried to make a horse, but the legs had broken), there sat enthroned a little woman with a fishtail, sculpted from a carrot. A mermaid! She had minuscule, curiously pointed breasts. Sister got very red in the face and snatched her up with a nimble hand, hiding her in the shadows of her heavy skirt.

"Are you the one who did that?" she asked me, furious.

"No." I was stunned by so much anger. My astonishment made me look guilty, and I didn't know how to defend myself. The other girls watched me with malicious merriment.

"Of course it was her!" affirmed several voices.

"Me? But you could all see that I was sculpting Brilliant."

"Ah! Yes, Brilliant!"

I could feel their jealousy. Not one of them would defend me. They were put off by my solitary wanderings so deep in the forest, ignorant as they were of its beauty. No, they didn't understand me; they were thrilled to have caught me in the act. What act? A trivial insolence I hadn't even committed.

These Sisters entrusted with our education? They have only two words in their mouths: *pure* and *impure*.

On the way home, I felt melancholy. And the shortcut that goes up, paved with blue and reddish stones, seemed so steep that I held on to the old wooden rail that runs along the wall, attached by rusty iron hooks. But from time to time, a gap in the wall would show me my realm: my forest, the Rhône, and its sands.

September 20

Held here by force, I am enraged.

Sunday, Sunday. . . . A sermon about death. I've never liked thinking about death. I don't think of it as nothingness, but it is far less than life. I see life after death as a faded existence where human love no longer plays a part. That's why such an altered state hardly interests me. I have no real passion for God. I am sorry about it; it would make everything more simple, or perhaps more terrible. But nothing on earth seems simple to me. However, the idea of sin, at this point, no longer torments me. What I sense, rather, as the fatal corollary of an overly intense happiness, is an intense pain that feeds on that very same happiness, but is not a punishment. And what if God and the devil, Good and Evil, were just a single being with two faces?

What I'm writing is probably nonsense. In any case, that's what Sister Bertrand-de-Jesus would say if she could read it. But she won't read it, nor will anyone. I have a safe hiding place for this notebook.

I believe I'm endowed with a mind that's quick enough (that's intelligence, perhaps?), but I admit that I'm incapable of reflection. If I try to reflect on something, I soon find myself with nothing but fog in my brain. Whereas if I allow thoughts or images to arise freely, they appear to me in stunning clarity. But they are fleeting, uncontrollable.

I'll admit there's one image that keeps coming back to me. It's that of a man's sexual parts. Actually, they're not a man's! All I ever see is a little boy's wobbling penis, and I don't dwell on it, because it seems a little ridiculous and far from seductive. But this shapeless organ, I can't help but see it grafted onto the body of the one I am searching for. At such times I feel a great tenderness and pity. Of course, I'm aware that the root of the world is there, and that's why, I suppose, boys are so proud of it and women are so impressed.

(That must also be why, in the church, on an old fresco that I find quite homely, the penises of all the chosen ones are erased, and those of the damned disappear underneath the devils' torches.)

September 27

Finally I made it to the ponds again, and even further. *I did not see him again.* But a curious thing happened that I'd like to tell here; I believe it must have come my way as a sign. And yet! A rather sordid sign it is. Before I made Brilliant enter the thicket of reeds, I was surprised to see a trail waving through it. There was no wind. "So it must be a duck hunter," I told myself. I waited. As I didn't see anything else and was afraid of being late, I used my legs and heels to spur Brilliant on, forcing him to speed forward. He suspected something. Along the marshy trail, I took great care to make him step where the ground was firmest, but he suddenly shied away, and his back end fell into a mud hole. We had a hard time getting out. My pants and boots were covered with mud, and I looked around for something to explain my animal's fright, since he usually isn't skittish. Suddenly, there was the steady sound of a little sickle cutting back branches. At the same time, I could hear someone breathing, very close by. It sounded heavy, almost animal-like. I spotted a back: an old reddish sweater. A face turned toward mine. A cretin! He opened his wide, toothless mouth and mumbled a few syllables, a compliment, no doubt. (Young girls put them in ecstasy.) To tell the truth, this one wasn't particularly frightening. Maybe my horse was scared, not of this poor creature, but of the sickle, which gleamed.

We continued along our way, happy to be back on solid ground and the path lined with tall Queen Anne's lace that leads to the ponds while circling about the hills. I saw my pond again, and the grass where *he* had sat. Which way had he gone? Toward the east and the Big Farm, or to the west and the other ponds and the little farms? I decided to push on to those.

Why haven't I gone there more often? It's an admirable spot, and peaceful, even though they turned an old hovel there into a restaurant with trellises and an orchestra. It's near the main road. My cousins come here to dance with girls and look at the way they display the roasted chickens, in long festoons. And to think that it used to be a poor little cafe where you couldn't even get a cold lemonade in the summertime!

The ponds haven't changed. I went around the largest one, fringed to the north by pines, to the south by silver birch and ash trees. I watched their foliage quiver in the sun, and some wood pigeons take off in flight. A water hen swam along the rings of reeds. I will never know the pond in its entirety; I would have to have a canoe. . . . No one swims there; the bottom is unpredictable and there's not much water. In some spots, it's very green (the rest is beige); I don't know if that's due to the depth, or maybe to some invisible algae. At the end of this vast pond stand two tall stone columns. Long ago, they supported an aqueduct. They make me think of the stylites—those men, touched by God, who lived for years on top of columns, with no fear of vermin or excrement. I am always overcome with astonishment at their story. But I admire the people who dare to take on such follies; at least those men didn't bother anyone!

The third pond is full of a yellow moss that floats on the top and gets dried out. The fourth one pleases me almost as much as the first; you can swim there, and the water isn't as cold. There is a little island in the middle. The slopes of the hills reflected there have been taken over by bearberries beneath the pines. I like trees with leaves, but I like pine trees even better, especially here, with their round foliages that push into the sky like bunches of balloons.

Over there, toward the Rhône, are three or four little farmhouses, hidden and poor, with coxcomb cactus taking over the nooks and crannies. In front of us, I was surprised to see the cretin again, with his little sickle and his bundle of sticks. He must have taken the path that goes through the hills, while I had lingered on in the water's company. Brilliant no longer even flinched, on the contrary, he steered straight toward the farms, playing his ears about and letting out joyous whistling sounds.

I had gone past the last farmhouse, which is all white and sad, and has a staircase with a wooden rail, and still the cretin kept walking. "Where can he possibly be going?" I followed him. That's how I discovered another farm that, until then, I hadn't known existed. On the outside, it seems both shabby and cheerful. In a circle of sparse grass surrounded by the forest, it looks like the caravan of some bohemians who have given up traveling. The roof and walls are partly covered with the rusted bottoms of gasoline cans, assembled skillfully, even artfully. On its peak, I noticed a weathervane with several arms, each one adorned with an egg; they must be the shells from chickens' eggs. There are about a dozen brown and white pigeons flying around it.

I'm giving all these details because I observed this farm carefully. For what reason? It interests me more than the others. The cretin went in there. And right away a little boy came out, ten or twelve years old. He reminded me of the young man I saw on my birthday, at the edge of the pond, who watched me so intently . . . but mostly, he reminded me of the boy who had swum with me in the hot spring. They are certainly somehow related, unless my imagination is going completely wild.

The little farm boy, his brother, no doubt, wears the same blue gray pants. Of course, he is dirty and quite unkempt. He hardly paid any attention to my horse or to me. Besides, we drew back discreetly. I've seen enough today. I came back by the main road to save time.

(About the ponds, Lin revealed to me that there is yet a fifth one, hidden amongst the hills, but it's almost dry.)

September 28

Half asleep last night, I had a vision of a gigantic tree, whose trunks and branches were very thick. The main trunk didn't go up very far, but new trunks started up from it, and then branches. I hardly remember the foliage (maybe it existed way on top), but mostly the impression of force and power radiating from the tree. And also of coarseness.

Does our family tree hanging in the corridor have anything to do with this? They hardly resemble each other, though. It's rather the condensed image of all the trees that passed before my eyes yesterday. . . .

Then I fell asleep for real, and I had this dream. We were on the outskirts of Paris (many of my relatives lived and still live in Paris), and we marveled at living on a mountain where the houses looked like fake Swiss chalets, surrounded by vast evergreen forests, and all so close to the capital. From there, the waters of a river rushed into an artificial lake in which I claimed I was dying to swim. "But it's freezing cold!" they told me. It was winter, and I was bragging that I could even throw myself into the waterfall!

Then I saw myself talking to my father. I was explaining to him *what a girl is*. "You can't know what they are! But I am one, and I know: girls are tiaras, they feel beautiful like tiaras, and they want to be admired. It's their reason for living. And that's why they will go where there are people to see them."

There's what I was telling my poor father. And now I tell myself that, even in the most deserted spots in my forest, I have a chance of *being seen*.

October 8

It's the grape harvesting break. I went back to the ponds and the farms. I didn't see anything. My cousins are out hunting roe deer. I wouldn't want to run into those boys who kill out of boredom.

October 11

Today, Sunday, I saw him again. I spoke to him. He spoke to me.

This time I wandered around the little farmhouse. Before getting there, I tied Brilliant to a tree down between the hills, in front of some nice grass. I kissed him between the eyes and said to him: "Be good now; wait for me patiently." I don't usually make such a fuss; I think I must have been nervous. Then I stayed, half-hidden, in the pines. I was watching the house. I could see the fountain, the cornfield, and the garden with sunflowers, which were already dry, and some beanstalks. In the back, I could see a shed full of scrap iron and a tractor. To while away the time, I was singing to myself:

Madness may one day come to me.
Until then, dear, it's with you that I'll be.

It's a song that's popular this year, and I quite like it. I kept waiting. Not a single sound nor soul came out of the little house. I had sat down in the grass, and then, I was terribly thirsty. I was dying of thirst. Going to the nearby restaurant was out of the question; I didn't have a penny. I can stand being thirsty, but just over there, the little fountain was running . . . I listened to it; I watched it. Then, since I still didn't see a living soul, I came out of the forest and walked toward the fountain. I was just about to reach it when, out of the shed, a big German Shepherd pounced at me, barking. And suddenly, the whole family stood on the doorstep: women, men, and children! The dog was almost on me, and I had the time to feel, rather than see, the smiles of the women. There were even sparks of malice and victory in the old woman. But I'm not afraid of dogs, because we used to have some. I didn't move. An authoritarian voice called him, and he stopped cold. It all happened in the wink of an eye: the beast that dashed out, the cruel pleasure of the women, the call to order from one of the men. There were three: an older one, the retarded one, and the disheveled boy, and then two sloppy little children. We looked at each other. I caught a real hostility in all of them, mixed with a little astonishment. They had expected me to be frightened, and they certainly would have relished it.

"May I drink?" I asked.

"Ja."

I drank eagerly, right from the spigot, under their mocking, disapproving eyes. I was fully aware of all of this while the water went down my throat, spilled over my chin, and down my blouse. I savored it, feeling out the strange family with my antennae all the while. They seemed to have calmed down; the old man had tied up the dog in the shed; the boy had gone to sit down on the staircase; the cretin and the little children had disappeared. The two women, who were still watching me, had gone into the little garden.

"Well, that's fine," I said to myself. "Now I've seen the household, but *he* doesn't seem to live here. And how could he be one of them? He is neat and refined. He reads." I had a hard time imagining the uncouth boy reading under the pines. And yet my instinct told me I wasn't mistaken. "That must be a brother or a cousin; the resemblance is too striking." Especially the resemblance, as I've already noted, to the boy I met ten years ago, who must have been roughly the same age then.

I drank one last gulp and left. I went back up the hill, but couldn't yet bring myself to leave. The watch began again. Fortunately, they couldn't see me from the house . . . but it was there through the branches for me as through a pair of binoculars. No, I hadn't renounced meeting the one I had come for.

Madness may one day come to me.

I kept repeating. Yes, I like this sad melody, even that phrase whose meaning escapes me. Is it about real madness, or simply the madness of love? I don't know the rest of the song.

No, no one could see me from the little farmhouse, but . . . *he* was behind me. When I realized it, I blushed so hard that I could feel my neck burn. Instead of being vexed at my own agitation, as would have been natural, I was almost happy about it. He greeted me politely, "Bonjour, mademoiselle," in French that was unexpectedly smooth, and plunged his dark, rather hard, prying eyes into mine. Then he walked by and disappeared into the house. I was so surprised and embarrassed that I didn't make any response. I got up and took off as fast as I could. In the hollow of the hill, I found Brilliant, who was a little anxious. Someone must have spotted and then circled around him; I thought I saw some footprints in the grass and pine needles, but maybe they were mine.

I took off at a trot, trampling on the Big Farm's alfalfa fields without remorse, and then got back on the road. I have absolutely no memory of how I got home afterward or unsaddled Brilliant.

I was excited and disappointed.

October 18

I don't want to ever go back again. At least not for a long time. I know everything about him now. And also that he doesn't love me, that he can't love me. For days and days, he had been my sole preoccupation. There I was, sitting on the edge of the forest, waiting for him, so full of him that I was becoming more him than me. And he passed by me with indifference. Worse yet: politely.

Night of October 25–26

I went back. Ah! So many things today! I'm dead tired, but I know that I won't sleep all night: I feel crushed by a frightening happiness. This is the first love I've ever had. And it's so strong, I can feel it, it's more solid than a rock. It will last forever, because it's impossible for it to be any other way. Christofer, Christofer, do you hear me? I'm calling you! I listen to you; you respond to me. How have we managed up until now to live parallel existences, without seeing each other? Our existence is now *one*.

Let me tell it all, quickly.

First I warned my mother that I would be gone for the whole day. She wasn't happy about it: "Why do you always go into that forest? There are other places to go out wandering. . . . It has a bad reputation. In my time, a young girl would never have ventured in there by herself." She forgets that she used to go pick dead wood there, while her mother and father (my grandparents) went down to the riverbank with an old wicker stroller to collect the flotsam.

It was the Feast of Christ the King. At Mass, the altar almost disappeared under the red branches of the logwood that grows here on the rocky slope. (The farmers call it Brazil wood.) The branches formed a huge burning bush around the tabernacle, and through the dust and the incense that I detest, I thought I could discern the deep, harsh scent of leaves. But it seems to me that there is a profound sadness in Christianity, a sadness I can't comprehend from the teachings of Christ.

When I got back to the house, I took some bread and cheese, then pilfered a handful of figs from my cousins' garden. They just let them rot. With all this in my pouch, I impatiently mounted my horse. But he was skittish, since he hadn't gone out for a week, and it was with a great deal of nervousness that he went down to the bridge. The combined roaring of the Rhône and a passing train frightened him. I was really afraid that he would bolt, and I barely managed to keep him in step. I could hardly wait to reach the forest. There, instead of going around the ponds, I decided to take the short way, through the hills. It was difficult for Brilliant, who is certainly no mule. I bent over his neck to clear the branches. Sometimes I had to jump down and pull him by the bridle. By the time I got to where you can spot the small farmhouses, I was all scratched up and my hair was a mess. (My toilette is the least of my worries, but I'd rather have people find me pretty and tidy, than slovenly.) But never mind that, what matters is that *I saw him*. He came out as I was passing in front of the little house. So I got Brilliant to turn and circle in my own way. He watched me coming toward him and said:

"Are you thirsty again, mademoiselle?"

I answered no.

"Maybe your horse is?"

"There is always the pond."

"It's no good to drink from; it's full of frogs. Come to the fountain."

We went to the fountain. The dog was tied up; he didn't even bark.

"You go out riding by yourself?"

"Yes."

"We don't see many women riding around here."

"I know."

"I saw a lady last month. She was with two men. They made their horses get into the pond, but the woman's horse almost tumbled into a mud-hole. He reared, and she very nearly fell into the water."

Suddenly looking concerned, he asked me, "Is he yours?"

"Yes, I got him for my fifteenth birthday." Then I added, "That was two years ago."

"Myself, I'd rather have a motorbike," he said with a funny kind of pout. I was offended. Preferring a motorbike to a thoroughbred!

"Well, of course a motorbike is less of a bother!" I retorted. "You can put it in the shed, even outside—anywhere at all."

He raised his eyebrows, which are very thick and very dark (mine are blond, like my hair), and looked toward the house.

"Next year, we'll enlarge it, and then. . . ."

He gestured, as if he were sending these poor material goods to the devil. Nothing was moving behind the red curtains, which half-covered the windows. Two hens and a rooster began circling around us.

"Would you like to see the rabbits?" He was pointing to a huge box with compartments. It smelled bad. "I also have a beehive near the pond."

"I have to go back."

He suddenly looked so unhappy that I took pity on him. I got down off my horse and drank a little water. I didn't do too well at it, because I felt the icy water run down my neck, all the way to my stomach. An idea came to him: "Would you like to have a cup of coffee, at the house?"

I was very surprised. I said yes. Alas, I noticed I was trembling with emotion, but he must have thought I was cold.

I saw the inside of his house. The old people weren't there; neither were the children, nor the idiot. Maybe they were sleeping. The woman, the young one, put a big iron coffeepot and two cups on the table after a moment. She looked at me with fear and curiosity. She said, "Who are you, young lady?"

I told her a fake name. Why? It was instinctive; I can't explain my reaction very well. Natural reserve? People's tongues in town are very malicious. But that's not the main reason. There is another: maybe this woman, who is *his mother*, frightens me a little bit. She has a prying way of looking, and yet she seems submissive to her son, who speaks to her as if she were a servant. She left us alone in the kitchen. I felt good on the bench, almost wedged between the wall and the table. Christofer had sat down across from me. I had heard his mother call him by that name. I asked, "And what's your last name?"

He told me a name that is very common around here. I drank the coffee, which was delicious, although I think it was reheated. Christofer spoke in German dialect to his mother, who returned with walnuts that were still fresh and some very dark red apples. (Ah, those apples! There are hardly any left in the country. It's a very old variety, which I prefer above all others.) I unpacked my little bag of provisions. "If they only knew," I thought to myself, "if they knew that I sometimes go hungry at home. . . ."

Then he accompanied me back into the forest, all the way to my pond, where we had seen each other again for the first time. He was holding my horse. I spoke to him of the warm sulfur spring and the blackthorn that had flowered. He remembered it very well. Before I left him, I said,

"Christofer, you must forget the name I told you." (I was ashamed of having lied.) "Forgive me, but you must forget it."

"Forget mine, too!" he said abruptly.

He looked serious, but not at all angry.

"Well then, we won't have names!" I said.

"Yes, we will. I thought of one for you right away."

"Which is?"

"Forest."

I smiled.

"And me, I will call you River."

We looked at each other. He took me in his arms, held me very close without kissing me (I didn't know a boy's body could be so hard), and took off at a run.

October 27

I hoped that he would venture all the way out to here. I was so sure I would see him again . . . but nothing. Will I have time on Thursday to go as far as the little farms?

October 30

I didn't see him again. "He's in Brigue," they told me. With a painful, almost lecherous insistence, the old man stared at the turquoise necklace I was wearing over my black sweater. I worked up the courage to ask a few questions. When I asked how many brothers and sisters Christofer had, they smirked, as if I had said something out of place. Somewhat irritated, I pointed to the young boy.

"Are you his brother?"

"Nein, Onkel."

"Christofer is your uncle?"

"Nicht. Ich bin Onkel."

I no longer tried to understand. The women remained distrustful, but the idiot spoke to me (in a stream of unintelligible sounds). I was so disappointed that his pathetic good will was a comfort to me. It seemed like he wanted to explain something to me, and he, at least, wanted to help me. What a family!

November 3

Yesterday evening, I went with my mother and Aunt Sigeste to pray at my father's grave and to light the candles planted in the ground. From time to time, a chrysanthemum or a branch from a fir tree would catch fire.

I watched the men in the procession, without being too obvious about it, hoping to catch a glimpse of Christofer among them. But how would I recognize him in the shadows that a few scattered flames only made thicker? His relatives must be buried here; I read his family name several times. That night, I had a nightmare. It's left me with a painful sensation of vertigo and horror that I can't get rid of. It took place by a river, and I remember very clearly the ground, covered with oval pebbles, some black, some white, all the same size. A mysterious body entwined itself with mine, suddenly becoming part of me with an intensity so violent that I could not bear it. And both of us, but we were *one*, we fell, we consented to fall, into the abyss of the waters.

November 5

I galloped over there this afternoon. The first frosts have hardened the silt, which resounded a thousand times over with the muffled blows of Brilliant's shoes. The ground is now a drum that nothing can puncture.

The old woman opened the door to me with a grimacing smile and devoured me with one little black eye (the other one hidden beneath a bruised eyelid). Her hostility vanished. In a half-French, half-Tudesque gibberish, she conveyed to me that she was home alone. Her old man works at the electric plant. Irregularly, at that, she explained. I brought the conversation around to Christofer. At that point, her face took on a solemn expression and she announced to me:

"Christofer? Oh . . . ! Student, Advokat!"

I was afraid that he might be involved in a lawsuit, that he was in trouble over God only knows what stupid thing! Not at all; the old woman told me he was studying to become a lawyer.

I was stunned. I thought I must have misunderstood, but she kept on telling me a whole bundle of stories: that he had always been first in his class, that the teacher was very proud of him, etc. She let out forceful, *Herr Gott*!s, and *Nicht dumm*!s that were among the most guttural I had ever heard. I was listening to her. I found all of this very surprising and pleasant. But I might have enjoyed it just as much had she described Christofer in the midst of spreading manure over the fields or collecting a swarm of bees. Someone was talking to me about him!

She also showed me a postcard-sized photograph of him in the company of other students wearing caps. I had to control myself and make a fist in my pocket, not to snatch it out of her hands and take it away. I was thinking, "How could I buy it from her? Steal it from her?" The craziest ideas were going through my head. But I took my leave of her respectfully and set off again.

I had asked her, "When will he return?"

She answered, "Next *Zonday*."

November 6

Yes, I realized quite quickly that he was no country boy like the rest: his way of speaking French, of remaining unflustered around me, and that unexpected grace throughout his perfectly muscular but refined body. And his paleness still amazes me: his skin is whiter than mine. Maybe it's that he studies too much, stays up late at night. . . . He used to be sturdier.

To tell the truth, even if he worked cutting down the forest, as his parents do, I would happily live with Christofer! I wouldn't mind having a shack and a few acres to ourselves. I have no social ambition whatsoever, only that of love.

November 8 (Sunday)

He was waiting for me at the fourth pond and stopped me from going all the way to the little farm.

"The grandfather's sulking; he's shooting at the pigeons. Let's walk toward the Rhône. . . . You know, we have a vineyard over there, over the cliff."

We walked side by side, without touching each other. The earth felt good underneath our feet; the grass was still green, and we passed by a cherry tree that had lost half its leaves. "There are five here, in the forest," he told me. "You'll see how beautiful they are in the spring." There exists in Christofer, in spite of himself, a strange gentleness, precisely the gentleness I lack. People have always told me I was a boy.

"Your mother? She doesn't seem happy."

"No," he acquiesced, suddenly distressed.

"And your father? Is he dead?"

"I don't have a father."

We had now arrived at the vineyard, his vineyard. The shoots were bare and rust-colored.

"Oh!" I said, stupidly. "It's in a bad spot! It doesn't get enough sun. You should see how it beats down on our vines. They cling to the rock, facing straight toward the south." Alas, I realized I had hurt his feelings.

"I found out that you belong to the aristocrats. . ." he said. "I suspected as much."

"Does it bother you?"

"It would be better if you didn't."

"Kiss me," I murmured, and I wanted to say his name, but it had gone from my mind. "We adore each other and can't even tell one another!" I felt as though I were suffocating. He had turned even paler, and he was watching me. Suddenly I found him less beautiful, almost vulgar; his black hair, bulging with too much life, looked as aggressive as a coxcomb. Its animal vigor made me ashamed, and I wanted to run away, but he held my hand and kissed it. The sensation of his lips on my skin was so sharp that I let out a cry. I examined my hand and was surprised to see that there were no marks. I thought that a thick, hot flower had just burst open on it. Christofer was watching me still. The iris in his ink-dark eyes was turning yellow, and the pupil narrowed to the point that it looked like the slit in a cat's eye. I was losing all sense of time and place; I heard a drum beat in the distance. We fell gently to the ground and there we stayed, spread out, without saying anything, without moving, like two young dead bodies. My eyes were closed, and the sun was scorching my eyelids. I felt Christofer raise himself up on one elbow, and I raised myself up, too. Our faces drew closer together. They were strangely heavy; yes, they were going to fall; they would fall against each other. The rest of our bodies hadn't followed, not yet. And our cheeks brushed against each other. There was a black veil over us. For a moment, our heads were like two heads cut off and thrown in a bag, colliding, and then sticking together. And then it was as if a new body was being born from them, an immense body. I noticed I was crying.

"Don't cry, don't cry!" he was pleading.

But the river had flowed over me.

November 12

And now there are days when I am taken by so strong a desire for him that I feel pulled apart, split open. My arms and legs grow long enough to stretch around the world; my eyes see beyond the mountains. . . . Yes, I'm becoming excessive in my happiness, but deaf, too, and blind to all that is not Christofer and me. I had no idea of love's power. It anguishes and disconcerts me.

Christofer has left again, but his face draws near mine and looks even more real to me than if it were truly happening. Sometimes I try to surprise *his gaze* in my mirror. I don't succeed.

November 14

Lots of wind and rain, but it's mild again outside, even warm, amazingly so for the season.

I must not forget my horse. He's had his ration of good oats and a long currying session. I gave the stable a thorough cleaning. It's a man's work and yet, underneath my coarse clothes, I hear more and more the beating of a woman's heart! I'm afraid of becoming too soft, weak. . . . But my need to love and be loved is so violent that it also gives me great strength. I will overcome every obstacle.

This morning at Mass, I gave thanks to God. It's the only prayer I know how to say. The others bore me so completely that, when I begin one, my mind escapes and feeds on whatever it can find, a memory, a project, a ray of light coming through a stained-glass window, a mouse walking through the transept. (There actually was one this morning.) I thanked God for giving me this love, for allowing me to find once again this love I believed was lost. But I am rushing toward it with such deliberate haste, such blindness, that I can scarcely see where it will end. I cannot believe in a happy life. . . .

November 15

Christofer was working in the bee-house.[1] "I've got a lot to do today." He seemed worried, and as I stayed there, mute, he said to me in a very low voice, "Come here." Serious and proud, he was watching me, more conscious of his own power than I was of mine. "They've already gotten sluggish. . . ." But I didn't fear the bees for even a passing moment. I slithered in through the narrow opening. His gestures were almost maternal as he helped me, and so slow that I was astonished. Inside, there was the sunshine illuminating the red wood, which, heated, gave off a strong perfume; and it was full of resonances, muffled tapping sounds. Mixing with these was the sound of our blood. My body was now lying on the floorboards against his, against the very body I had so desperately cherished. From my own, a chant was rising, as if from a thousand birds and plants and leaves, a formidable joy running all the way through me and invading me, enveloping my head and veiling my eyes with a fog that grew more and more dense. I murmured, "I'm lost. . . ." And suddenly, roughly, underneath Christofer's almost feminine appearance, the milky whiteness of his student's chest, I submitted to the implacable sharpness of the male.

~~~~~~~~~~~~~~~~~~~~~~~~~~~~~~~~~~~~~

There I was, wounded and whimpering, in the center of the crimson-colored bee-house which continued to vibrate. He had gone out again and left me by myself. I groped around for my jeans, which were wadded up in a corner, and rolled them into a ball between my legs to stop the blood from

---

[1]The bee-house is a small cabin with a door and a central passage, holding honeycomb compartments.

flowing. I breathed carefully, sparingly, and sank into a smothering half-sleep. I was *given*, I no longer belonged to myself.

The idea of sin hardly troubled me at all. Not even for an instant did I feel as though I had done something wrong. What we had done was right. The wrong, in fact, would have been not to do it.

I must have fallen asleep because his touch, so tender all over again, woke me up. Christofer had gone for a dip in the stream, and his ice-cold body brought a coolness that was soothing to mine. He also offered me a bowl with a little water and wine. Gently, he lifted up my head and made me drink, as if I were ill. The two eyes I raised up to meet his were no doubt filled with a childish gratitude. But his face seemed so serious that it worried me.

"Aren't you happy?" I asked him. (I had heard praise of the happiness a virgin can give a man.)

"I love you too much," he said.

I closed my eyes again; I was pleased with his response.

"We'll have to see each other often . . . and in secret," he added.

I could feel that he was afraid. What was he afraid of? Just then, we heard someone call.

"My mother!"

Christofer rushed back out. I got dressed again and waited. There was no other sound. No one was coming back. I might have fallen back asleep. When I came to again, it was already dusk, and it was cold. I struggled out of the bee-house and went to untie Brilliant, who was trembling. I had forgotten him!

November 19

I find myself waking up at night to savor this disturbing happiness: someone loves me; someone wants me. I also think of all that they've told us about the evil of the flesh! At church, at school, at home, in books, everywhere! Poor flesh! The whole process distorts and belittles it, making it uglier. We've been fooled. If I ever have children, I will never, ever denigrate it to them! There are sins against the flesh . . . but people only tell us about the sins of the flesh.

Yes, I have a lover. I'm not ashamed to write it; I'm proud of it. But sometimes I'm also afraid of growing too attached to him. I realized this the other day, with the deathlike split I experienced the moment he left me.

Why didn't he come back to the bee-house?

When will I see him again? I have run out of patience.

November 22

I went back there. It left me so unnerved that I'm still shaking. From a distance, I heard shouts and gunshots. The old man was putting on a show again. No doubt he had been drinking and gotten angry at the women, so he was shooting at the pigeons as a way of getting even. When he saw me, he pointed the barrel of his gun in my direction. "Shoot, you fool!" I shouted. Then he aimed at the weathervane and broke one of the eggs: he had already killed all the pigeons. . . . From a ways off, the old woman gestured at me to run away.

I've lost hope.

November 24

Still no word from Christofer. Not even the slightest sign, the slightest breeze of his love. This is as heavy as death. What has happened to him? Has he stopped loving me? No, that's not possible.

Alas, even if it makes me feel a little ashamed, it will still be up to me to take the initiative. Next Sunday, I'll go over there. I'll convince my mother I'm going to visit my cousin in S. But in the end, she'll find out everything. I don't really have any illusions about it. Then I will announce to her that I want to be Christofer's wife forever. I belong to him. He belongs to me. And if my mother gets angry, I'll leave; I'll go and work in S.

Five days from now, I'll know what I must do.

November 29

Now I know. I don't know how I can go on living after this. I'm afraid I might not be able to hold up. The most unjust, irremediable thing has happened to me, someone who believed, with good reason, in the innocence of love. . . Just when I discovered the wonder of it, I had to discover the senseless misery and blame as well. It makes it that much more cruel.

This is agony.

November 30

I knocked at the door and within myself I heard the soft, mysterious, *Knock, and it shall be opened to you.* But what a revelation that door was opening for! Christofer's mother greeted me with a bizarre little laugh.

"Ach! It's you again!"

"Yes," I said, looking friendly in order to hide my anxiety.

"Why, young lady!" she began again, scandalized. "You're so cozy up there, with sunshine all winter long. . . Why do you keep coming down to this cold, nasty forest?"

"But I like it; it's wonderful, even now!"

"Yes, yes. . . ." (She sized me up with an arrogant, ironic look.) "The forest isn't the only thing. . . . That's not good for young ladies. Especially like you. . . ."

I continued to look her in the eye. "What is she getting at?" I wondered in anguish.

"You, always wandering around, doing nothing. You, you're rich. . . . You have nothing to worry about! When I was your years, it was a different life, always *slaving* away in the cafe where I did nothing but serve and eat bad food. And one day. . . ."

She watched me now with a humble, almost tender hatred. I stayed mute. She was about to tell me things I was afraid of guessing.

"In those days, I knew your father well." (She glanced at me in a way that was both troubled and triumphant.) I was your father's girlfriend. . . ."

"Oh!" I said, without batting an eyelash, but my hand was groping for something to hold on to. I felt as though I were falling into a black hole.

She kept going, "Your father's lofer." (She had trouble pronouncing the word 'lover'.) "What a man he was. . . . He gave me ten thousand francs. All for Christofer, so he could be advokat . . . just like him. But me, I wasn't good enough for your father."

I was so stunned, I hadn't yet begun to suffer. She continued: "The boss was jealous, so he fired me. . . ." And still this feeling of falling, falling into the very depths of the earth. But I still didn't accept it. I was clinging to life, to the smell of that kitchen, the smell of Christofer's home, to that light there in the little window. Was there any reality in the words I had heard? The only reality was in the smell of the kitchen, the sun, my love. Perhaps she thought I still hadn't understood, or maybe she took pleasure in torturing me further.

"Didn't you see?" she hissed. "Didn't you see? You have the same eyes."

She went to take down a mirror that was cracked from top to bottom.

"Didn't you see?"

"No! No!"

I pushed her away. Now I was overcome; I had fallen to the bottom of the abyss. But there, at the bottom, our eyes were open, and *I saw that they were alike.*

"Not the same color . . . ," she admitted. "His, black. Yours, gray. But the same long shape, the same expression. Yes, it's better for morale, better you never come back down, never come back here."

She was going to talk to me for a long time; she was never going to stop. I ran off and fell onto Brilliant who brought me back home, almost numb. And I was thinking of how, in the old days, people would tie corpses to mules to take them across the mountain. You could see them go by in the night.

· 6 ·

The Little Girl and the Beast

In the entrance hall of the Benjamenta Institute, the old maid who was knitting night and day so that she could keep an eye on the comings and goings, dropped one of her needles under the table. She bent down, but saw nothing. The needle was hidden between the larch slats. The old maid rose from her chair and got down on all fours to retrieve it from the crack using her other needle, which she first had to free from the knitting.

The little girl chose just that moment to slip out. She closed the door gently behind her.

The valley already lay in shadow. At first she took a little alley covered by thick layers of ice, which made it terribly slippery. She, too, had to get down on all fours, but she was wearing heavy woolen gloves and sealskin boots.

She arrived very quickly at the street where the wood was stored. Ah! This street! Is there anything like it on Earth? Made of so much piled-up wood? Wood burnt by frost and sun, and which will be burned again in the fire. Logs, sticks, trunks, and rough-sawn boards? They were piled all the way up to the second-floor windows, and the little girl was looking at this heap of pink moons, red moons, amber triangles. The baroque frieze sculpted into the façade could hardly be made out. Sometimes, between two chalets, a very dark, narrow passage would open up, suddenly illuminated by the white arch of a sleigh's rails.

That street—of how many forests was it made? Very old forests where bears and lynx roamed, as did the men who killed them with arrows. In the display case of the Benjamenta Institute, you can see two or three bows found on the glacier—a bit twisted, a bit broken, but still smooth to the touch at the precise place where the hand grips them.

Such are the thoughts of the little girl who has just run away from the Benjamenta Institute, built of concrete and lacquered yellow wood, down below the village. She is eight years old and has such delicate skin that her mother has sent her some face cream from Paris. Her face is already golden with freckles, which makes her gray eyes seem even more gray. Her long hair emerges from under her knit hat and falls over her shoulders like a cape.

"We will braid it," said the headmistress, "and it will look like the braided bread we eat on Sundays." But the little girl said no, so they left her hair in peace.

For the first few days, they gave her a sled, because she couldn't yet ski. And she followed other children, younger than herself. They crossed the bridge over a very dark river, watched over by a sparrow hawk, and the snow sparkled. They went sledding on the slope, but these little children bored her, all screaming in languages she didn't understand.

She began to see some masks. One, at first. He was running in the street and when he saw the little girl, he hid himself behind the corner of a barn. He has a yellow cane. With the other hand, he holds his wooden face by the chin. His sheepskin is belted by a cow's collar, complete with the bell. The little girl draws near, but he runs from her again, and the bell rings. She can see the floating mane of blonde goatskin he wears; his legs and feet are wrapped in old floor rags. She waits for him around the corner of a house across the street, wanting to see that black face again, with its two rows of painted teeth. He's coming back! She laughs, unafraid. But he turns around and takes off running.

"He is the one who is afraid of me. . . ," says the little girl.

She meets another one. This mask seems to be more ferocious; its face of Arolla pine is even bigger than the first, with a long Roman nose, round white eyes, and a mouth that grins all the way back to the cheekbones, with real cow's teeth planted inside. He, too, holds his chin in a woolen-gloved fist, and he prances to make the huge bell behind him ring. This one has a hump on his back, but you can see an old raincoat underneath his sheepskin; the belt dangles about and he is wearing boots.

With a very attentive expression, the little girl has noted every detail. She feels a bit afraid because he suddenly starts jumping savagely in the snow in front of her, and his badger-skin hair begins to flap and fly. This one is not shy like the other; he accepts her presence, and she doesn't really know what he wants from her. But suddenly he looks discouraged and slowly mounts some icy steps. She follows him. Some snowflakes hesitate in the air; she puts out her tongue, and they end up settling on it. She tastes: "That's good."

She has trouble following the mask, but does not lose sight of it. It is *her* mask, and she gets angry when other children climb to the barns' upper levels to watch it. She would like to be alone with him, even though he frightens her. Whenever he turns around to look at her, bends over, and cries out strangely, she stops. But now he has disappeared. He's gone into a stable.

She pushes open one of the half-doors, revealing a warm shadow, a foul and sweetish smell. The mask is standing before her; he lifts up the huge wooden face and uncovers his own. Now she can see that he has a charming face, blue eyes full of kindness and with a slight squint, a small nose, and a strangely cut mouth, a mouth a bit like a wound.

"How old are you?" she asks.

"I'm eighteen."

Now he has put aside the mask, and he takes off the animal skins, then the coat, and she can see that he has used a bag of hay for the hump. On his bare hand, she also notices that he is wearing a chiseled ring of fake silver.

"I have to milk the cow," he says.

And he hangs all the clothes on a nail. He is still wearing a knit sweater and a pair of serge trousers, and he sits on a strange little one-legged stool.

"Is that your cow?"

"No, she belongs to my aunt. Me, I just come here in winter. In the spring, I go down to the valley, where I work for the French as a gardener."

He smiled at her and his skin wrinkles prettily under his eyes.

"Do you wear a mask very often?"

"Yes, when I have the time. But the men here are getting lazy; they don't put on their masks very often anymore. They say it wears them out!"

"Is it heavy?"

"Yes, it's heavy."

"I would like to see more of them."

"Soon, they will come down from up there," he said, and he pointed his finger toward the forest, which was now very dark. "But I have to milk the cow."

He pressed his head firmly against the cow's flank and started squeezing the teats, which shot white into the bucket.

"Do you want to drink a cup?"

He pointed to an aluminum cup hanging on a nail beside the cast-off mask, and filled it for her.

"It's sweet," said the little girl. "There is no skin on it. The milk at the Institute always has a skin on top."

"They let you go for a walk around the village?" asked the young man, surprised.

"Yes, to see the masks."

"Hurry up then, before it gets dark. Go to the square over that way. They're coming for sure."

She rushed back down the alley steps and found herself in the main street again, which she followed for a bit. It was almost empty. Only a few boys smoking cigarettes had hoisted themselves atop some sleighs, backed up to a wall. "They are waiting for them, too. . . ," she thought. A woman fetching water at the fountain looked at her inquiringly.

The girl raised her head and saw them coming down. Three of them! She holds her breath: a red mask! The other two that accompany him resemble those she's already seen in the cities, but the one in the middle has a huge red face and a billy-goat skin over his body, a black and white skin with long hair, and he does not have a bell. He is right near her; he bends over. . . .

She tried to see the eyes, but there was nothing behind the little openings. Maybe he was peering through the two holes underneath the nose? The nostrils seemed like two loopholes, but there again she could see nothing. This one does not hold on to his wooden chin; his hands are free, emerging from the sleeves of a jacket turned inside out, with a ripped lining. He holds one out to her and moos softly. She is scared by the big paw covered with rags. She backs away.

"Nein!" she says.

But he is still holding it out, and so she understands that he wants to say hello to her. So she gives him her hand.

"You are handsome! Schön! Schön!"

He bowed, then threw his arms open with a sigh.

"Schön!" the little girl repeated.

She raised her finger to touch his nose, a hooked nose and blood-red. He bent over once again. She was fascinated by this nose.

In the meantime, the other two were banging their canes one against the other and were swaying their heads, which looked small on top of their long, skinny bodies, decked out in steel gray raincoats and tight, wine-colored running suits. On their cardboard masks, bought at a store in the valley, beamed an expression of stupidity so intensely immobile that it contrasted with the agility of the bodies.

But the little girl was not interested in their country clowning. She only had eyes for the red mask. He made a bow for the second time, then abruptly turned his back to her, and remained there, staring at the street they had walked down.

Only then did she look at the other two. They pirouetted, fell down in the snow, and stood up again, noisily crossing their canes. Their faces, jovial with smugness, remained dolefully stupefied. She returned to the red mask.

He was still watching the top of the street. She saw that he was wearing a pair of black corduroy pants and heavy shoes with cleats. A young girl, lending her arm to an old lady, passed near them. The red mask rushed toward her, brandishing his chewed-up woolen glove. Trying to shield herself behind the old lady, who pulled her away, she screamed, but she had only a mark of soot on her cheek, light as a shadow under the eye.

He turned toward the little girl and let out a dull groan. She was marveling at this wild face, enchanted with the humble, ceremonial attitude he was showing her. He pointed to the ground before him and drew a little circle in the air.

"Yes," she said.

He took her hand, and they walked up the street. It, too, was covered with ice and even looked phosphorescent under the electric lamp that had just been lit, hanging on a chalet wall.

Disappointed, the other two masks watched them leave. They crossed the square and disappeared into a little café.

The red mask was still climbing up with the little girl, and she was having a good time, slipping along behind on the ice. He was holding her tightly (he is so strong); he even was lifting her, and then she wasn't touching anything anymore, or maybe just a pile of snow with the curved tips of her boots.

"I am flying," she said. "I am an angel."

But now they have arrived in front of a three-story wooden house, and they climb yet another flight of wooden stairs. They enter a room. There, accordion music is playing and couples are dancing; when the music stops they all go and sit on the benches along the walls, girls on one side, and boys on the other.

The red mask stands with the little girl in the middle of the room. The accordion plays out of tune, then starts to play faster, and everyone starts turning around, stomping their heels on the floor.

Then she felt herself lifted up in the air; her head brushed a paper garland. She dropped down a little and he held her tightly against the rough billygoat hair of his chest. She saw the underside of the man's real chin and the skin of his neck, a bright, young, pink skin, hot, flushed, and covered with a thin down, almost red.

But the waltz is over. The accordionist wants a drink! The pitcher carrier[1] walks over to serve him, then approaches the red mask with another glass. At first, the mask signals no, but the server insists, so he grabs the glass and puts it to the girl's lips. She drinks. He takes it back from her, turns to the wall, lifts his heavy wooden face and empties the goblet in a single gulp.

---

[1]The pitcher in question is a *channe*, a specifically Swiss-French term for a tin pitcher with a cover. Made to serve wine, it can hold several liters.

Back to the street, where it's now dark. He still holds her by the hand. She takes off her knit hat and lets it trail behind her in the snow, on the side. He laughs. He bumps into a very dark house, shakes off his cleats, and walks through the door, pulling the little girl behind him.

A tall, elderly woman, her face half hidden by a fringed purple scarf, sits near the fireplace.

"Is that you? And who are you bringing along?"

She speaks in a language that the little girl cannot understand, and looks at her fixedly with hard eyes that do not see properly. An acrid smell rises from her steaming skirts.

"One from the Institute?"

The mask gives no reply.

"Hurry and take her back where she came from! Hurry up, you fool!"

She waves to chase them away. The mask squeezes the little girl's hand more tightly; he still does not move. His mother eyes him sternly. There is a silence. She rises to reach for the little girl, but the two of them leave.

They walk out, away from the village, on a path through deep snow. It's snowing again. You can't see it, but on your cheeks and nose, you feel the touch of its cold little wings.

They walked for a long time, or rather, he walked for a long time because he was carrying her in his arms. She wanted to thank him with a kiss, but where? On his wooden cheek? She gives up and falls asleep.

She awoke when he put her down in the hay. She inhales a stifling scent.

"It smells like summer here. Is this your house?"

But he is singing softly in the dark, or rather, he is humming, because his song has no words. He digs in the hay, then shapes a cave and spreads a blanket at the bottom.

"What are you doing?"

He is still humming. The tune was sad, then became gay; now it is sad again.

And suddenly he grabbed her and rolled with her into the hollow.

"You hurt me!" said the little girl.

He puts her on top of him, encircles her with maternal hands, wraps her in a fold of the blanket. She feels better; she even feels very good. He lifts his arms and pulls a roof of dried grass over them.

But where is that warm breeze coming from? The breath that smells like wine? She no longer understands what is happening: the red mask didn't breathe. She tries to touch him, and touches a face made of flesh.

"Oh," she says, "it's not you anymore." He moans dolefully once more. She fingers the plaintive mouth, she touches the teeth, a man's teeth.

"I don't know you."

But he pressed her against his chest, and she recognized the billy-goat fleece that gets into her eyes and nose. And him, he has taken the little girl's hair, lifted it up, and covered his face with it. He remained like that for a while, then began to moan again.

He slides two fingers down the little girl's collar; they creep in between the blouse and the shoulder blades (also called *angel's wings*).

"But you're tickling me!" She laughs and squirms. "I'm too hot!"

He helps her take off her sweater and starts pulling at the zipper of her ski trousers. But he is very clumsy and the little girl does not want to take them off. Then he turns quiet again and kisses the girl's cheeks and shoulders. She is surprised by the rough, almost sharp lips that weigh upon her, though without really hurting her. But she turns away: "You smell bad!"

Then: "Where did you put it, the red mask?"

The hands go down the length of her back (and her belt digs into her belly). It feels like a beast crawling on her buttocks, a strange beast. She started to laugh again. But then she screamed: "Leave me alone!"

The belt is cutting even deeper into her belly; she kicks to free herself. The hand leaves her, but the man beneath her groans, as if he were gasping for air.

She is scared. What is happening to him? He is shaking, and now, is he dead? And she is afraid of dying, too.

Eventually she fell asleep, and he did, too, because now he is snoring. Where is she? A grayish glow seeps through the straws of hay.

At that exact moment, she heard a bell ring, always the same bell. The man sat up beside her. He was listening. "What is it?" asked the little girl. She recognized a dried flower nearby, a sweet scabious that was still mauve, and at the same time she looked at the man. She did not know him. She could see his profile, his reddish hair and milky complexion.

But he turned his head toward her, and then she froze with panic: the man had only one eye. She stood up to run away, but her legs sank into the hay. He was looking at her strangely with his single eye and without speaking. The little girl wanted to scream, but she swallowed her saliva and felt her throat aching.

The barn door opened.

A peasant came in first, cautiously, then a solemn-looking man, dressed like a city type, and finally, a fat lady.

"She's alive!"

All three rushed to grab the little girl. Again she tried to speak, but she could only cough vaguely and point to her burning throat. They covered her with a shawl while the constable started searching the hay, growing angry because he could find nothing.

"He must be gone. . . ," said the lady, who was the headmistress of the Benjamenta Institute.

But, oh! (They raised their heads.) Over there, they could see something. "He's hanged himself!"

There was a mass of white and black hair swinging from a roof beam; as if it had fallen upside down on itself, the red mask was hanging. It really was the death of the mask. But the peasant shouted: "Oh my God!" and tugged at a corner of the blanket.

"Get out of there!" he ordered.

And the man stood up in the hay, his snout as pink as a rat's. The little girl could not stand to see that face again and buried herself in the headmistress's frock, who was struck with astonishment.

"He was kicked by a mule, three years ago," said the solemn man. "They had to take his eye out."

The man was staring at them stupefied; only his torso was showing out of the hay.

"They all drink too much around here!" the headmistress said sternly.

"You'll let me see her for an examination. . . ," whispered the doctor. And, turning toward the little girl: "Did he hurt you? What did he do to you?"

"Nothing," the little girl answered.

Outside, the landscape was not glittering like it had the day before. A fresh blanket of snow, fallen during the night, was covering it now, and on the matte whiteness, the chalets studded the slopes like black stars.

· 7 ·

Eight Tiny Cruel Tales

#2 The Bird-Woman

The bird-woman—and beautiful she was—surveyed a great concha of rocks and pines above the valley.

She took wing and glided gleefully, drawing circles. Her body, burnished by the wind, was that of an earthbound woman, but it was perfect. Her two wings were linked to her arms by a thin membrane, and covered with long, shiny black feathers that glimmered green. She waved her arms slowly, flapping her wings open and closed.

A warm stream of air, laden with scents of resin, mother-of-thyme, and bearberry pressed against her tender breasts, her belly and legs, while her useless feet dangled in the air.

"How delicious!" she thought, but a different hunger was pulling her down to the ground.

She landed in a little field of broad beans where a peasant woman was digging.

"Do you know if there are men around here?" she asked.

"Yes, four woodcutters in the forest."

The mountain-woman strangely curled up her lips to bare a set of pointed teeth, as she chewed on some rye bread.

"You like men, too, eh!" The bird-woman faltered. Would she invite her to join the feast? But she left alone. Now a walking woman, she approached the woodcutters.

"I'd love to have a taste of you!" she said. She soared into the air above them, swirling around and flapping her wings.

It is not known whether they were frightened, but all four of them made love to her.

#5 The Horse

The girl strolled across pastures without bulls: they were horse pastures. The horses had been romping about since dawn and now were resting.

The girl walked from one fir tree to the next, her arms stretched out like theirs. "I am looking for my love," she said, "but I am alone in the world."

She stopped. "I am alone in the world; my love is dead." A horse drew near. He rested his teeth on her hair. "Hey!" she screamed. "That's not hay!" She stroked his forehead. "Horsey, horsey!" His huge eye was set upon her, shining like black oil. In it, she could see her own face, a frightened face.

She stepped forth; he followed her. She wanted to run away; he followed her still. He put his neck around her waist. "Where are your arms, my love?"

Wouldn't leave her till evening, once the dark had set in.

#13 The Mother

Made so that flowers fall from her mouth, and birds bloom from her fingers.

She had to bend her back; empty out; wash whatever was dirty. Dust was her rice powder, and spit her stars.

Still she smiled, she so loved life. And to thank her, *they* said strange things to her.

Which she didn't understand.

"Pardon me?" she said. Then *they* shouted in her ears: "To hell with you!"

#45 Agony

I was lying in a bed and about to die. I could hear all the words whispered round me in low voices. My mother and another little old woman were by my bedside.

One said to the other, "She has entered the final stage."

Maybe I should have signaled to them that I had understood. But I was so weary.

"At long last, I'm going to know what it's all about. . . ."

#63 Don Juan in Heaven

He sits at a table, writing. Love letters, no doubt. . . .

But these days, he receives none. Women no longer answer him. The angels are so heartbroken for him; they feel terrible that Don Juan is aware of it. They try to hide the truth from him.

The truth is that he can no longer *love himself* as he used to; he can no longer *adore himself* as he used to. That's the reason why women no longer write to him.

#68 Lovesick

My beloved is asleep in a house made of snow. I hate that white; it's killing me. But what can I do against such high walls? I can't open those frozen doors. How I wish my body were made of brambles and thorns, with wildcats resting inside, with nails like knives and eyes of glowing embers.

Lo! I'm but a stark naked man with pale flesh, crying and shivering, crouched at the bottom of the stairwell.

#73 Mourning

I was in mourning for my lost loves.

I put on a crepe veil and went out in the country. There, too, was nothing but shrouds and funereal draperies. The earth had stopped breathing; the leafless trees knocked together; the black pines wore crowns of pearls, but the violet of the dead remained underground.

The wind dried out the roads; it sharpened the mountain summits, blue as a knife. And the grass shifted under the snow. I thought my lovers would come alive again. But I saw them lying, pale and stiff, in their little iron coffins, and I heard a voice tell me:

"You will not find them again in the next world. They have forgotten the color of your eyes, the honeysuckle of your breast. And you yourself, you will no longer have even the memory of their shadow."

And I cried.

#100 Parabole

I have no name, and I am part of the infinite. Give me a name! Then I will be created.

I, light and shadow; I, the canopy of cascades, streaming with loves and with tears.

I, who make man turn like a top and then even whip him to lessen his pain.

I do not believe in the evil that is done on earth. It is only the other side of your suffering.

I am rocked in the trees, and I walk across the water of ponds. But round-bellied spiders climb all the way up my arms.

Mechanics tear out my hair, heavy with potatoes they have planted. They burn the reddish hairs between my thighs. They breathe their foul fuel into my mouth.

The architects of the universe used my legs for a compass and broke them while they were spread wide apart. They consecrated the host of the new world on my worn-out back.

But a day will come when I will be alive, my hands scattering flowers and my chest decorated with ribbons. The dove will coo on my shoulder; the dead prairie will be filled with grass; springs will bubble up from the sand, and the forest will rise up to walk.

· 8 ·

The Knot

*A*ll I could get from L. to C. was a local train and what had once been a first-class compartment. Its wide, deep benches were covered in red velvet stamped with Venetian motifs, double arabesques. The corners of the little windows, half-covered with curtains in an old-gold color and already edged with frost, accentuated this strange atmosphere of refuge. A young couple got on at one of the larger villages; they shook off two identical, luxuriant fur coats and uncovered two faces hidden under caps made of wolf fur. Laughter and snowflakes sprinkled two heads of hair.

This tore me most disagreeably from my torpor. And yet, both of them were of a beauty . . . not so unusual today, when youth triumphs, but of a beauty both frightening and discreet. And what struck me more than their fine features and clear eyes: their complicity. They cast a single look my way, furtive but piercing, and then a similar one at the man across from me, a banal gentleman, an invisible man. That was all the attention they gave us! They had seen that we were unable to harm them. Harm them how? Completely reassured, relaxed, they took a deck of cards out from I don't know where and began to play.

Still a bit sleepy, I observed them through my eyelashes. The game only intensified the complicity they radiated. They certainly couldn't have had any idea just how much the nice, harmless lady I was in their eyes was subject to their charms and measuring the width of the glow surrounding them.

The young man had the shadow of a moustache, sideburns, and a blondish crop of hair. She was without shadow: her hair up high, the arch of her eyebrow a clean line, and her face a perfect oval. I listened to them without understanding a single word. There, too, I told myself, even in the most insignificant of their words, there was such a perfect correspondence, an understanding

61

so complete that it could only have entered the world at the same time they did. And beyond that, which is already quite something, already bizarre, there was love. I couldn't be mistaken about that. "But a forbidden love!" I thought. With newlyweds, even on their honeymoon—and this couple carried no luggage with them—with a young married couple, despite their joy, some flaw would have been visible, a lassitude, a thin, ominous ray of boredom. Not with them. They lived an intense happiness, incommunicable to others, probably dangerous, and at the same time so simple, so childish. Yes, their game was a game, not for adults, but for the nursery.

They laughed a lot, without a touch of vulgarity. They seemed to take a lively pleasure in these cards that were surely no more than a pretext, like things without importance but used in a ritual that momentarily masked, like scaffolding, the construction of a terrible reality.

What mattered for them were the bonds formed by their gaze and their language. But what language was this? I still couldn't identify it and decided in the end that they expressed themselves in words of their own invention.

Completely indifferent to this magic, the old gentleman across from me slept. So he was out of play. But I, who wasn't sleeping, was also completely out of the game. And I accepted this rejection; it seemed normal to me.

Without loving them (I love or do not love other beings, entirely without measure), I was subjugated. It would be too much to say I was fascinated, since I didn't lose my critical sense.

Lovers, forbidden. Without a doubt. But why forbidden? What law were they transgressing with so much impertinent civility? Neither of them seemed very likely to be married to someone else. They were too close to adolescence! And, at the same time, so old. Yes . . . what knowledge, what troubled wisdom there was in their childish ways. Of course, I thought of a possibility . . . but I was wary of my imaginings.

What seemed beyond doubt—but did I have the slightest proof of it?— was that they must have, just moments ago, emerged from a castle, and a large castle at that. In this prince-less country, their ancestry was so princely that it made me feel, almost touch, enormous rusty stones, sprinkled with lichens, surrounding them, protecting them, and imprisoning them. Stones from ramparts, towers, and battlements, and sepulchral stones as well. Not to mention the oak trees, centenarians five times over. But what power could their shadow have over this couple? They were too luminous, translucent. They had just left drawing rooms where they had laughed, surely less than they did now, where the furnishings weren't necessarily beautiful or precious, but where the other guests *existed* for them, and still passed before their matching eyes. They must have been laughing about these people unknown to me. Yes, I believe they were mocking them, musically, cruelly. And all the while with the aid of this secret language that didn't bother me, that I judged natural. What was less so, and intrigued me above all: their joy. Irrepressible, reckless, and monstrously innocent.

At the train station at C., we all got off except the old gentleman, now awake but absent.

On the platform, I noticed that the couple hadn't simply separated: they no longer knew each other. Not a single sign of understanding between them, no good-bye, no more laughter. Two strangers, two creatures at opposite ends of the earth, unaware of each other even to their souls. And I, so near them, no longer daring to look at them or even to experience their presence.

Dazzled, yes, I was dazzled, and I understood nothing, or rather, I understood everything. In any case, it was too much. I forgot them.

The truth is, I didn't forget them. I thought about them from time to time, still marveling at the perfection of their understanding, at their gaiety, and at their youth, nonetheless slightly tainted by an intimate irony and the dark phosphorescence of their secret, by what was already overripe in their splendor.

And about what, about whom, could they have laughed so much? What visions did their eyes, their bodies hold?

At C., I visited some friends, but hadn't the courage to breathe a word of all this to them; restrained perhaps by modesty, I returned home. And some time later, during an important ballet performance in L., suddenly thinking I heard the couple's voice again, I turned around. It was only to find a pale moustache, a blasé expression, or a playfully joyous one, but never the complete pair, never their glory or their virginal wisdom.

And I had lost all hope of ever seeing them again when, during the summer, I took the same local train with the seats of crimson velvet to the lake at N. I got off at the same village C., which I knew was close to a spot where the lakeside was still wild and overgrown, a spot I had often seen from the train. This spot had long tempted me, and I had brought along my camping gear: folding tent, sleeping bag, and witch's cauldron. The weather was just the sort of heat I like, with light wafts of cooler air.

I found a taxi driver willing to transport me and my baggage over the porous sand paths; beyond that, we trekked on foot to a drier clearing, the kind foxes like. I thanked him much, paid him well, and began laying out the plans for my canvas home, where I slept without dreams until the next day. I was quite hungry, which I settled without even taking the trouble to cook anything, except a bit of water for tea. And quickly, wearing my bathing suit, I went to the edge of the lake whose strong scent I had been breathing in since the night before. I dove in, laughing, all alone.

But I wasn't alone.

I guessed it immediately, and yet I saw no one and not the smallest square of blue or yellow through the leaves. No smoke, either, and no one calling. But the birds were so silent.... I knew that my presence never frightened them this much.

The waves covered the freshwater mussels with a soft lapping sound, and there was no trace of footprints in the mud. It was while returning to my campsite, as I walked around a thicket even more dense than the others, that I spotted them.

Her and him! That diaphanous couple, silvery-white, intertwined, sleeping —but were they asleep?—and I felt anew that same sense of amazement. That was him, that was them! I recognized the milky texture of their skin, the mystery.

I didn't bother to hide, to walk without making noise; I knew that I scarcely troubled them at all. I didn't exist, and they were untouchable. So I continued swimming, cooking, daydreaming. They went for walks, chased each other; they were alone, too. But they didn't swim much, didn't sunbathe on the little sandy bank, preferring the underbrush, the thickets of willow trees where marsh plants abounded. And when I saw them pass slowly by, hand in hand, I was watching Adam and Eve in the Garden.

So all was for the best. Perhaps I would even become their protector.... But what dangers were they facing? Why my inexplicable anxiety about them? So few people came out here. You had to be as odd as I was to live out here, as unreal as they were, to survive here. Far from everything, without drinkable water, pursued by swarms of mosquitoes, surrounded by stretches of reeds and mud like traps! And our feet, already wounded on the sedge and the broken bits of old earthenware, were often at risk of slipping on a cold grass snake.

But on the little islands, where that rigid grass called "choin" grew, orchids also raised their heads. But water lilies lit up the dark creeks; but the moorhen and the coot, the heron and sometimes even a scarlet pheasant did us the honor of being our neighbors.

And there, alone and never alone, I deployed my daydreams. I had two skies, the lake and the azure, and both gleamed with the same fish-scale gray, exhaling the same scent. We renewed the alliance the first creatures had with the world. That marshy forest was alive; it was breathing. I even thought I saw eyes opening in the leaves; I felt vegetable breath upon me. I was at ease.

I don't believe the couple was unaware of my presence, but we never spoke. The silvery quivering of their bodies, so beautiful among the brambles, always took me by surprise: man and woman united in the happiness of Eden. He had fun, carrying her on his shoulders, and I heard his companion's cries when a pine branch blocked her way.

Certain evenings, the lake appeared so pale that its reality faded away; at such times, it was no more than an immense void. We kept to the edges of this void as if the earth, here, had ended. But suddenly, the insistent deathly smell of the water invasively reminded us that it was there. I was surprised to find I loved it so much, I who prefer the sea! But I had come to know the sea rather late, whereas lakes, their muck and their transparence, were part of my childhood. My earliest desires had been to bathe in them, to disappear among reeds through which a bottom of infinite purity could be glimpsed, while feeling my ankles gently sucked downwards.

Here, nature rejoined the limbo of those early years: the tangles of roots and tree trunks that changed color, their reflection ash-colored or greenish on our skin. Despite the sun, the couple's skin had stayed curiously white, and I could only admire from afar the fineness of their ankles, the animal quality of their hair. Did they eat at all? They appeared with flowers in their mouths, it's true, but I never saw them occupied with anything but themselves or their famous game of cards, from which they one day lost an ace.

It was the ace of clubs, and I found it by chance. I didn't want to return it to them; I was determined never to break, with a single gesture or word, my beautiful friendship of feigned indifference. I could just as well have left the card there, but I wanted to keep it as a souvenir of them. And they could do without it! If they had invented a language, they had certainly invented their games. And if I ran into them on their wanderings, always completely naked, I smiled to myself: their proud freedom was so real.

But I couldn't smile for too long. I soon had to fold up my tent and leave.

And perhaps I would have forgotten them a second time, without forgetting them, preserving the ace of clubs, smooth and clean, between two pages, smelling faintly like a talisman, when an article in the newspaper caught my eye. It mentioned the drowning death—suicide? accident?—of a young man and a young woman whose names were withheld, on the lakeshore I had left the week before.

I tried to find out more about it, calling around to a number of people. No one knew anything. Finally, I saw once again my friends from C., whom I had not contacted during my vacation, due to my inexplicable need for secrecy. They told me, "The family hushed up everything; they bribed the doctor, the police, and the journalists. The whole truth will never be known. But we have found out the basics."

"And so?"

"It's worse than Mayerling."[1]

---

[1] A hunting lodge in Austria where the double murder or suicide of Crown Prince Rudolf Habsburg and his young mistress took place in 1889. Films, shows, ballets, and books have diversely treated the unresolved mystery, sometimes referring to kidnapped corpses or unearthed remains.

"Nothing can be worse than Mayerling, if you believe certain details!" I shouted. "The self-castration, for example. . . . But there, too, we'll never know. The witnesses were frightened."

My friends fell silent; they looked heartbroken, worried. Thinking it through, I asked another question. "The couple from the lake, our two lovers? They were brother and sister?"

"Twins."

"That's what I guessed."

"They were found tied to each other, near a small island of reeds."

I still couldn't understand. "Tied together?"

"You've never heard of the *Gordian knot?*"

"Ah! Yes, I have. . . ."

"That's why they preferred the water. Witnesses frightened them."

And, as solemn as a minister, a student opened a book and read: *"Crimson fish devoured their eyes, and an animal shredded their silvery bodies; the blue water braided a crown of nettles and wild brambles around their thick hair."*

· 9 ·

The Last Confession

$\mathscr{I}$ had them drive me up the hill in the black church car that reminds me of a hearse. Then I asked them to leave me at the bottom of the estate, as I wanted to walk the rest of the way up to the house. I had never been there before. The owner, whom I had been requested to visit, was hardly better known to me than was her home. I had occasionally seen her during our services at the cathedral. She had been pointed out to me as a solitary and charitable person whose fortune might, upon her death, end up in the parish coffers and be put toward good works, perhaps even toward the construction of a new church that monseigneur planned to build above the village. Naturally, this possibility was of greater interest to my colleagues than to myself. To tell the truth, I've never developed much enthusiasm for this sort of activity. I already have enough difficulty trying to decipher the poor human soul that reveals so little of itself to us, even under the light of confession, so banally cruel.

Through the fields and vineyards, I took a shortcut that vanished into the tall wormwoods and the cones of purple flowers whose name I don't know. I startled some lizards; it was just after noontime, the hottest hour of the day, and I was really suffering under my long cassock. To top it all off, I was still carrying my black cape over my arm! Alas, we quickly become like old maids, distracted or frightened, fearing everything and nothing.

The path followed the edge of a rèze vineyard, and I was seized, almost suffocated, by the smothering smell of the sulfate thickly coating the leaves and the bunches of grapes, each hard grape already well formed. But suddenly, I found myself in an orchard that felt divinely cool. The thick grass, in the shadow of the fruit trees, seemed cold to me. To better refresh myself with its touch, I sat right down on it, even lay down over it, my arms out, just barely moving my hands, like a swimmer floating on his back. Soon I had to start walking again. After having climbed a few tiered fields, I was surprised to find a rectangular pool blocking my path. There was an amber tint to its cement bottom, underneath water whose complete transparency was, I believe, the result of the excessive light that fell there, and was further enhanced by the sunflowers, two feet tall, surrounding it on three sides.

I went around it and soon arrived in front of a low house that I recognized from the description they had given me at the bishop's palace. In the courtyard, a serving woman who was feeding an enormous mastiff; she shook her head.

"Mademoiselle isn't well; in fact, she's doing very poorly. But you can see her. She's waiting for you."

They let me enter alone, through a maze of corridors filled with shelves of grayish books. I knocked on the bedroom door. No answer. I pushed it open.

The mistress of the estate lay on a bed surrounded by curtains that were as dusty as everything else. At first I thought she was sleeping, but she had clearly seen me enter, and said, "Sit down."

I leaned toward her. From her face, I thought I understood everything, right away.

"Is it time?" she whispered.

"Ahh . . . yes," I stammered. I had no idea what to say, and yet this was hardly the first time I had been sent like this, by surprise, to see the dying.

"I want to make my confession."

And, as I said nothing at all:

"It will be long. You will have to hear me out."

I thought, she knows how to talk, like so many of the women around here, and she'll do it in a way that's not wanting for salt. My own needs tended more toward fresh water at that particular moment.

"I'm suffering. . . ," she said again. "Oh! I don't like to suffer."

"Don't they give you any sedatives?"

"Sedatives don't sedate me. On the contrary, they get me excited."

"It's true," I acquiesced. "On certain strong temperaments, they produce that effect. Above all on those who are imaginative, intellectual. But you are surrounded by such peace here; your estate is so lovely!"

She raised herself up a bit on her cushions.

"This estate that my father created, that he organized so well, just like God-the-Father invented the world—me, I let it return to nature. True, the workers tried every year to keep going through the motions he had taught them, but I didn't watch over them anymore, and after a while they learned how to take their time—and good times they had, too. The moans of lovemaking filled the irrigation ditches in the springtime, and the loose tendrils in

June hid a few things, too. At harvest-time, things really got underway. The men stamped the grapes or pressed them on the girls' chests. That was the game: you eat the grape from one side, and I'll finish it from the other. The little birds were frightened, but in the end, they let themselves be caught. That was the season where I made my selection: weighed down by the men's lechery, they lost their sense of mistrust. Me, I was only a woman. But what a woman! Ah! If I could have, I would have fucked the whole earth; I would have put my arms around it, and my legs; I would have split its bark wide open and made its roots and springs flow; I would have bruised myself with joy on the boulders. Ah, yes! I would have devoured the world."

She stopped talking. She was panting softly; suddenly, she sat back up. "You hear!"

I heard nothing.

Speaking like that must have exhausted her, for she sank back into her sheets and groaned, "You hear the girls? They're shouting."

"What girls? Who?"

"Yes, they're shouting, they're shouting. . . . Ah, my little loved ones."

I stopped talking, taken aback, looking hard at her. The dampness of her skin gave a shine to her bony face, where her black eyes were as hard as nails. "She's going through her crisis, a moribund old maid. . . . I must try to reassure her."

"God's mercy knows no limits," I said. "There is greater joy in heaven for one repentant sinner than there is for ten just souls."

"You are aware that I was forced to live too much alone. My mother was dead and my father kept young men away from me. Was it from jealousy? From fear? I don't know. But at the age of fifteen, my shapely body took on a disproportionate importance in my life. I felt it grow and breathe, as if it were outside of me. My body! I thought only of it, and I felt a strange pleasure in seeing it claim for itself a sort of nourishment that had, until then, been distant and unknown. I became a giant woman, swollen, hollow with desires. My spirit grew heavy with lazy voluptuousness. I would spend entire days lying on a divan, or underneath some bushes. I had a real religious devotion to my body. I adored it, I consoled it, excusing it, admiring everything about it, celebrating its delights, because naturally, I learned quickly how to satisfy it myself. I nearly fainted, practically done in by that superhuman sense of well-being I thought I was the only one to have discovered. I invented a thousand ways to reach that bliss. I would gallop naked and bareback at night on my horse. His animal heat rose up through me, filling me completely. It seemed to me that my blood and his were the same, flowing from one body into the other. From time to time, I'd come across a farmer who, not recognizing me, would cross himself. I'm sure they never thought it was the young lady from the estate that they were seeing. They all believe in visions, ghosts, and the devil."

"And you? Don't you believe in Evil?"

"Oh, yes, I believe! If anything, I believe too much. That's exactly what kept spurring me on even further. Those who don't believe, they experience more joyful pleasures. There was no joy in me, but a dark rage, so intense that it destroyed me sometimes, completely sapped my strength for hours. But I came back to life quickly. My secret life out here in the country allowed for that. In fact, this solitude only made my senses ever more feverish, more greedy and demanding, and so the yield became even more pronounced."

"If this is a confession, finish it up! Don't tire yourself unnecessarily." I lifted my hand, but did she still even see me?

"My desires were married to nature. Not knowing how to put out this fire inside myself, I would open my legs to the grass; I coupled with the earth and the trees. One day at dawn, I even believed a cherry tree had come to life; it wrapped its limbs with their bitter leaves around me; it had a soft skin and a thousand cool nipples. When the sun came up, I found myself at its feet, impaled, bleeding. But I never returned to that again; an event so extraordinary doesn't happen twice."

I, a priest, was telling myself: "This is the wild, primeval forest that the Church Fathers had to clear, that their firm grip bruised. . . ."

"The oozing mosses of the underground garden or the rough gravel in the vineyards matched my ever-changing desires. What did I not put inside myself? Shells, pebbles, ears of corn, pine cones all sticky with sap. And flowers! I crushed purple buddleias and hard black tulips against my breasts. My fingers became tentacles of extraordinary perfection and precision. I pillaged flowerbeds, taking only the strangest of flowers. The gardeners were stunned: 'Mademoiselle likes only the exotics!' But they were happy: those were the most expensive ones. I was also tempted by cats, by their obscure sovereignty and their agate eyes, but I quickly learned to fear them, because of their claws. As for dogs, I found their slobber and their fidelity repulsive, and above all, those beasts felt nothing the way I did. Already, all I wanted was myself, my own double! I pretended I was a statue. At night, I would go and stand on a pedestal on the side of the road. I managed to remain still for hours. I shivered with joy when a couple would stop, late at night, and contemplate my nudity in the starlight. Once, I was pinned by the stubborn headlights of car that couldn't get enough of blinding me. I didn't dare to move. What was he doing, that man I could vaguely make out behind the steering wheel? But the car took off again, and I used that moment to slip away. My final experience as a statue was so painful that I gave it up. A drunken peasant climbed up with me and began embracing me in a way that I didn't find at all thrilling. He fouled me with his vomit and insulted me as he pulled away. Yes, the long summer days were much more favorable to my bacchanalian dances. And, as a projection of myself, I began to imagine feminine forms coming to join with my own. Nymphs like the ones you see in museums made their way through my dreams. But the procession of beautiful young women, nude underneath the trellises, was well within my grasp! I realized that soon enough. As you know, ever since the end of the war, thousands of workers from Spain and Italy have arrived in the country. Those women came onto my estate. . . ."

What a woman! Ah, what a woman! In another time, she would have ended up at the stake. I should have ordered her once more to be more concise, not to dwell with such satisfaction on a life of sin that she hardly seemed to repent. But she went on.

"I began to look them over, to choose among them. These pickers and swineherds had thin, brown bodies, or else they were fatty white heifers. I let them bathe in the big reservoir of irrigation water where the sunflowers and reeds would hide us, along with the quince trees whose branches reach all the way down to the ground—did you see them?"

Yes, I had seen them, and had myself shivered in the coolness of that summer grass.

"And those little cabins covered with ivy, where the tools are kept—when the cold came, they became precious shelters for us. Diversity in all things is love's best companion."

I couldn't restrain a gesture of impatience, which she noticed.

"I know, I should say, 'the love of the flesh,' because you men, and you priests especially, you separate the two loves. But they are inextricably mixed in us women, the two loves, and that's something you men never manage to understand."

I muttered a phrase that she didn't hear.

"My father having been dead for years, no one suspected anything, aside from my ever-silent accomplices. I was respected. People thought I was wisdom herself. But an old man accosted me one day and said, 'Mademoiselle, there is a sort of glow about you now . . . (he was searching for words), something that shines too brightly.' And he added, to himself, without looking at me, 'An evil glow.'"

As for myself, I was wondering: did she really do what she said? Or had this happened to her once? Perhaps it is all imagination.

"So," she began again, more slowly. "I realized that I was both man and woman. I was filled, and I filled. I was at the same time both the weapon and the victim. How amazing! I had felt and contemplated my own self so much that I recognized in *the other* each shiver, each vibrating response. She was my reflection. I knew her pleasure, I knew what she was feeling. A man doesn't know the pleasure women feel. I had caressed myself too much not to desire caresses from hands similar to my own. It's masturbation that creates homosexuality. It's a game of mirrors."

"The origins of homosexuality are far more profound and mysterious, and all excuses for it are false excuses."

But she didn't hear me.

"The best of all those girls, I took her right from the nest. She was living with her mother. She still smelled of milk and the warmth of her mother's skirts; she didn't dare to call me by my name; she called me 'Madamoiselle.' I spoke of adopting her; she was ready to disown her childhood, sniffling with happiness: she loved me. She wasn't afraid of Evil; she was so natural; all that came from me was Good. I brought her to life; I made her feel death."

"You'll keep talking until the end of time!" My impatience was growing.

"We would take long walks together. We would go so far, so high up on the mountain; I didn't want men to see her; in the fall, there was no one on those wide, high mountain pastures. I would undress her under the blueberry bushes that had turned red, where the grass was already frozen. Her body was without a shadow; it was rose-colored, her entire body would blush; the tips of her breasts were an even darker shade of rose, like a real raspberry. I would suck on it."

That was something. It was too much for me, despite my experience with the sacrament of Confession. It seemed that she had had me come there, then, for the final joy of telling me all about her turpitudes!

"I can still hear her mother saying, 'You'll take good care of my little one.' And me, answering her, 'Such a beautiful child.' 'Not just beautiful, but nice, too,' the mother insisted. 'We'll see about that!' 'You must keep her out of bad company. At least, since she's with you, I can rest easy.' 'Oh yes, I swear to you, I'll never let her go out alone!' 'Oh, thank you, miss, you are too good.' And really, I was good; I was going to give only happiness to this little one . . . aside from a little teasing, and maybe she even enjoyed that. Spoiling a girl too much just makes her life monotonous!"

I was taken over by a great lassitude. I began to pray, but where to find the calm necessary for prayer, in this woman's company? Her wan face tilted forward; her brutal chin, her thick hair, still curiously black, divided into two serpents around her, Mademoiselle was belching up her life. Obscene words, glowing red, emerged from her mouth. I could see them flame, then go out like embers.

"I'm confessing, I'm confessing. . . . Why? I'm not afraid any more. . . . I don't repent."

"You are dedicated to sin."

"Oh, no!" she protested with a childish sweetness. "Oh! No . . . but I know very well that I cannot suffer any more. God can't make me suffer. God doesn't want to make me suffer."

"You still believe in God?"

"Yes."

"But it doesn't occur to you that you have offended him!"

"God understands," she murmured.

And, for the first time, she was quiet. The odor of an anthill rose up from her bed, painfully strong, a smell of burning. I heard her laugh:

"He was put to death by me, and now he's putting me to death in turn."

"But afterwards?" I asked. "Do you believe in the immortal soul? In life beyond this life? You will have to account for even the smallest things. You will have to answer for everything!"

"The body no longer exists."

"The spirit survives, and if the spirit survives, then the body, which is a part of it, survives also, in a certain way. You were taught the resurrection of the body. Even though the new school. . . ."

"That would be lovely!" she said naïvely.

I thought she was going to fall asleep, that she had fallen asleep. I wished for it only too much! Over her, I made the gesture that unbinds, and I silently withdrew.

But she gave such a shout, truly begging me, both of her arms outstretched.

"My Father, deign to hear me! I haven't been to confession in so long. . . . I must tell you; I must tell you everything; I'm going to die."

She didn't do what she's telling me; she didn't do the half of it, I told myself, but in fact *she thought it.* And I stayed.

"You have claimed to believe in Evil, but you have no sense of sin! Of fault. It's contradictory."

She looked me in the eye. "No. I believe in original sin; I believe that we are made of mud. But God doesn't judge us the way men do."

"Yes," I agreed. "Christ had another language."

"I believe in his Goodness," she sighed.

It was the dying one, now, who was offering reassurances! But she returned to her obsessions: "The last girl, the one I killed! There was a slate-colored light in her eyes, and she had a lovely pug nose, a little chestnut-colored bun on top of her head, and that air of distinction that peasant women from the mountain have when they come down to town. And she was so fresh, so innocent, after all those migrant workers whose skin tasted like the tide.

'The flea dazzles me!' she shouted sometimes. I never understood what she meant; she had some strange ways of saying things. I would run my hand over her the way people do over a piece of fur. . . . One day, I said to her: 'Get up! Walk ahead of me!' She was a bit surprised, but she obeyed. Behind her, I honed my desire while keeping my eyes fixed on the dimples in her back. I ordered her, 'Turn around!'

" 'You'd think this was military service!' she said, trembling.

" 'Have you done any service?' I answered, rudely.

" 'No.'

" 'I have. During the mobilization, I was a truck driver. March, my little Cranach!' She thought it was a pet name; she was without culture, and it irritated me. 'You are too stupid!'

" 'I'm shivering,' she said again, and I could see that she was getting pale, no longer from happiness, but from the cold.

" 'Keep walking!' I was becoming cruel; it was the first time that had happened. I experimented with a gesture that she didn't see; I was practicing. For the first time, I took pleasure in tormenting her. We came to a brook. 'Walk into it!'

" 'Oh! It's frozen. . . .'

" 'Walk!' I pushed her. She fell. The waters flowed over her, like the transparent scarf, so beloved of that man who liked painting virgins. 'Ah, this time,' I shouted at her, 'you are even more Cranach, you idiot!' But I helped her get back up by pinching her little breasts. 'Your plums!'

"Then her coquettishness won out over her pain. 'Plums?' She was stunned.

" 'Peaches, if you prefer. . . .' And I pulled her again across the abandoned pasture, practically by the skin of her neck. She started to run, half crying, half laughing, and soon we reached a little shepherd's cabin, which was empty. There were a few logs, which I used to get a good fire going, but I wouldn't let her put her clothes back on. She accepted it, now that she was warm and happy again. It was at that moment I admired her most. I had gathered some little October flowers, and I braided them into the hair on her Mount of Venus; the hair was long, red, and curly.

" 'You're decorating me, just like the queen of the cows!'

" 'Like the queen, yes, but you are only a calf.' And I grabbed her by the shoulders, but just then a shepherd burst into the cabin. He was so stupefied that he stood there, open-mouthed, astonished by the sight of our two beautiful bodies offered up on that bed made of boards, two stories high, like on a platter. He passed his bovine tongue across his lifeless lips, his face as red as a tomato. We found him ugly and stupid, and I grew mean again: 'Go away!' But he didn't move. I thought I caught an air of conspiracy between the two of them. 'Go away!' I repeated. But he stayed, petrified and breathing heavily. I jumped down onto the floor, which was made of dried cow dung, took a beam from the fire, and threw it at his head. He ducked just in time; it only struck the wall. I picked up another one, and he scampered off, snickering, 'Pigs!' No one else bothered us after that, but I was put off by the strange look that my little Cranach had given the boy."

"You never loved . . . a man?" I asked.

"No."

"But you are one! Without even knowing it, you are one!"

Mademoiselle didn't deign to respond; she contemplated me with a look that was even ironic. Yes, me, there in my cassock, what did I look like?

"She died. . . ," she moaned, "because of me, up on that bed. I should never have done that to my little dog, my angel, my darling, my bride. . . ."

She began to cough, a very rough cough, and spit into a towel. It's the end of a life, I thought. . . . Tuberculosis? Cancer? Did she repent? Even she doesn't know what she is about. Most of all, she needs to tell her story. And me? Given the disorder the Church is in today, do I know any better what I'm doing? As if she has guessed what I was thinking, she said, "Only the false is true."

She shot a glance at me. Was that a question?

All of a sudden, I felt weak. I was a hundred years older.

The sun had been gone for hours. The dusk and its indecisive bits of dust invaded the room, the folds in the curtains, with a stench of incense. What religious ceremony was it we were participating in? Was I really in the process of giving the sacrament of confession to a parish woman in agony? I put my head in my hands to avoid seeing her anymore. Because of her, sensual images of the ancient practices of the Adamite sects had burst back into my head. Perhaps she had read some vulgar accounts of them. Poor woman! Maybe she had never approached anyone, never touched anyone . . . but herself. The mythical beast that devours its own entrails! But that allusion was unnerving; I remembered that she believed in original sin. In original sin only.

She gave a start: "Listen!"

I heard a nearly imperceptible sound, coming from underneath the floorboards.

"It's a mouse," I said.

"It's a smile. . . ," she corrected.

She pushed further into the sheets. For an instant, her wide mouth remained open, the lower lip and chin hanging down. This silent scream of the dying, I knew it well. And without demanding anything more, I administered the Last Rites to her. The servant came in with the doctor. I left the room.

Where is the truth?

Who will ever know?

Nonetheless, I discretely gathered some information. No one had ever heard any talk of young women workers disappearing, or of any scandals surrounding Mademoiselle. She died two days after my visit. Her fortune, in accordance with the bishop's wishes, will be dedicated to the construction of a new church on the hill.

One morning, as I was walking back up through these vineyards to see another invalid, I paused to contemplate the landscape. I threw out my arms, murmuring: "Go in peace!"

But alas, I had said it with irritation, just the way people say, "Leave me the hell alone!"

· 10 ·

The Wild Demoiselle

I

$\mathcal{T}$he man crawled through the ferns, feeling like a giant in a palm plantation, searching with both hands for the lost spring, when he saw. . . .

No, not the spring, whose moist presence he nonetheless felt on his fingers, but her, the wild girl.

She stood in the center of the clearing, her arms and legs naked. The skirt of a silky, reddish-colored dress that she had lifted up in order to walk was carelessly knotted between her legs.

But she wasn't walking now. She had stopped; she would stay here now. The man understood that something was happening. . . . An aura of despair around the young woman immobilized her, made her as absent as one of the dead.

He waited.

She was waiting.

She raised her face toward the sun. Her hair, gathered together on the side he could not see, tumbled down her back and brushed her calves, just level with the grass. But, as if this weight set her body off balance, she groaned and collapsed.

He stayed hidden. He could no longer see her, and he was already beginning to have some doubts. "You're in trouble, my friend, if you're having visions. . . ." Him, a man who was still young and healthy, solid—even happy! An engineer. But solitude is good for no one.

It was morning, and very warm, with smells rising from the earth.

He stood up straight, pushed apart the branches—sinking into the mud, but his leather boots crushed everything in their path—and those broad leaves, the wild arums or "pilgrim's chalices," with the dewdrops still on them. He emerged from the underbrush that the sun had not penetrated. Dazzled, he lowered his eyes. At his feet lay the young woman, her face in the mourning bride flowers, her hair like a black sheet carelessly spread over her.

So she existed. And he, of course, also existed. And he was endowed with the best of health, and intelligence besides.

He knelt down gently. He was afraid of waking her. And he was afraid of making her afraid. But she wasn't sleeping. He turned her head slowly, holding her cheeks as a priest does with the communion chalice. Her eyelids, shadowed in blue, remained shut.

He lifted her up a little. She was no heavier on his arm than a grown rabbit, and her head dropped backward. Her fine neck was twisted, and the line it traced was swollen. Too much, he briefly thought, the hint of a goiter? He put her back against his shoulder and bent down to listen to her heart beating. But he saw from the red stains on his own hands that she was bleeding.

He kissed her brusquely on the mouth, then looked toward the abandoned chalet: the center, the temple, and the raison d'être for a clearing now reclaimed by all the offspring of the forest. The door was gone, and the roof, made of coarse strips of larch, had caved in. But this summer cabin contained a wooden bed without covers. He placed her upon it, then went back out and plunged once again into the branches and soft plants by the spring, where he soaked his handkerchief. He returned. She had already opened her eyes and was contemplating him without understanding. He wiped the damp cloth across her forehead.

"Mademoiselle, mademoiselle!" he said, too surprised, almost angered by such uncommon beauty.

The girl's eyes were *smiling* so strangely that he found them unbearable.

"Close your eyes," he ordered.

He dabbed at her eyelids. Blue eye shadow stained the handkerchief.

"What happened to you?"

He was getting ready to preach at her: "What sort of foolishness have you been up to?" He belonged to an older, wiser generation, or so he believed. And this girl, where had she come from? From the bar at the ski resort across the valley, no doubt, where the police had once again picked up some drug dealers and some more minors drinking, not long ago. But here, on this face of the black mountain, all was deserted.

"What are you looking for in these woods? Are you hiding?"

She didn't answer. Her eyes were still closed.

"Don't worry; I won't say anything. I'm not even asking anything of you."

Her silence irritated him. Yes, he felt like shaking her, and it made him a little ashamed. But he continued stroking her face. She allowed him to do it; she allowed herself to be touched by his agile, flat-tipped fingers. What was she thinking about? She just enjoyed the fingers; their softness confused her.

"You're wounded!"

"I'm bleeding. . . ."

"Where?"

"Everywhere. I'm bleeding everywhere."

"That has to be taken care of! I'm going to take care of you. Get undressed!"

"We need some pure water," she said, looking at him (and her voice becoming clearer), "but I haven't been able to find the spring."

"I know where it is."

He picked up an old iron bucket that was nearby and disappeared. Still lying down, she closed her eyes again. For the first time in a long time, she felt well; in fact, she had never felt so well. "I'm happy!" she thought, and she knew there was no reason why.

But the man was returning.

"No water in the world is better than this!" he said. "I'd like to have it analyzed. We could put it into bottles and make a fortune. . . . Ah, would the scenery around here ever change!" he laughed.

"The chalet is mine; the spring is too. And I forbid you to meddle with them."

"Oh!" he said, uneasy. "You're Mademoiselle L.?"

"I'm no longer Mademoiselle L."

"I thought you had gone away."

"Sometimes people come back. I've come back forever."

She answered and he spoke to her while he helped her undress, but the clothes stuck painfully to her because of the dried blood.

"Am I hurting you? Tell me if I hurt you."

"No, you're not hurting me."

She was now naked and untroubled, trusting in the hands of this man who was cleaning her wounds.

"You didn't cut yourself on purpose, did you?" he scolded. All these gashes, and all of them identical. What were they made with?"

"A Swiss army knife, the practical little red army knife," she said ironically. "Blade, hole-puncher, and can-opener."

He winced slightly.

"We should put. . . . Wait a minute! I know a little something about plants."

In no time at all, he had torn off his white shirt and was placing it over the girl's body. His tanned chest was speckled with bran; it was his turn to be naked.

"It's clean from this morning. Excuse me. I'm going out once more and I'll be back."

The heat of the summer, a living heat, she thought, warmed her outstretched body. She shut her eyes again. "I am too happy... what's going to happen to me?" Anguish filled her once again. She had difficulty breathing. What if the man never returned?

He returned, his hands full of ribgrass leaves.

"I found some right near here. You'll see. Those old wives weren't so crazy after all. This will do you good. I'll stick some on you here, and here, like postage stamps. Turn around. My! Oh, you have scars, too."

She was now covered with leaves. She smelled like a field where a herd has just grazed. Then she got up to put on the man's fine cloth shirt.

"It's long enough for you—it works for a dress. I'm a giant and you're a...."

"Dwarf."

They laughed.

"You're the Good Samaritan."

"Thank you. That's kind of you."

He was becoming ceremonious. But his eyes were teasing.

II

"I'm the one who dealt this blow," she thought. "Now I'm receiving it in turn. Death given, death received. Precisely the same blow. But this blow, this monstrosity, today has turned into love. There is no difference between this monstrosity and love.

"I knead the silvery part of a chocolate wrapper. I roll it between my palms. It takes shape. It becomes a little silver statue. I stand it up and press it down on the table; it either stays up, or it doesn't. I press my fingernails into the sides: that forms the arms. I press my fingernails in again up higher: that makes a head, and suddenly I see his eyes, and even a nose. It's a minuscule Specter in silver. But it's a man.

"Yesterday, when he came back to the cabin, weighed down with blankets, a thermos, clothes, and a kerosene lamp, and when he leaned down over me, I got a good look at his eyes. They were like the café au lait he made me drink. It was the first time I noticed their color, but I saw something else along with it: pain.

"With a stone and some heavy nails, he hung the thickest blanket up as a door to my cabin. 'This will be your lair!' he said."

Distractedly, she rolls the little silver Specter, the little man, over her chin, over her lips.

"Yes, as he leaned over me, he surrendered his *gaze* to me. Him, too: he is miserable. All of us, we're all miserable. But we laugh."

She had told him about her escape: the car pushed into the Rhône, her climb up the slope on the left bank, the darkness, the interwoven roots, the piles of fallen rocks, the treacherous mosses, the black snow in the hollows where avalanches stop. And afterwards her arrival at the clearing, this spring cabin that she had inherited from her family, but which was now abandoned. And her exhaustion at dawn.

"I knew you by name, your maiden name," he said. "But not your husband."

He watched her closely. "He was the one who cut you?"

"Yes."

"Often?"

"Ever since. . . ," (she let out a single sob), "ever since our wedding night. At first, I rebelled. But he'd tell me, 'It's a pact, a love pact. We'll mix our blood together and drink it. Then we'll be linked together forever.' He put such passion into it; it troubled me; it attached me to him in spite of myself."

He asked severely, "You enjoyed it?"

"At first I enjoyed it. But later . . . "

He contemplated her disapprovingly. "I don't blame you."

"You think. . . . Oh no! I'm terrified of suffering—I could never enjoy suffering—it destroys all pleasure."

"No need to defend yourself," he said softly. "These things happen, and they are more subtle than most people imagine. But you should have filed a complaint, gotten a separation."

"He kept threatening me. I lived in constant terror up until the day. . . ."

"Cruelty is the best grounds for a divorce. Even the Catholic church allows. . . ."

"Bodily separation. Yes, I know."

"And annulment, in the case of insanity."

"But he loved me!"

"And you? Did you love him?"

She didn't answer. She wanted too much to say, "It's you that I love!"

"I have a friend who's a lawyer," he concluded. "You'll consult him."

"I can't."

He stared at her, curious. Would he guess?

"No one can know where I am." She was even more serious, even more authoritarian than he. "Don't you understand? I'm a woman who has committed suicide." She made a single sweeping motion with her hand. "I didn't just disappear in the Rhône; I committed suicide. I left a letter."

He narrowed his eyes. "And him?"

"I killed him."

So, Monsieur de A. was an engineer and not much inclined to having visions. His realist hands revealed all the active science of a man who has been obliged by circumstance to fight, no longer with a sword, but with today's weapons. And then, he was a Hercules, but supple, almost like a dancer, and the jackets that covered his strong shoulders always seemed on the verge of bursting. He lived for part of the year in an old tower, up above the forests, where he could monitor the dam. The young woman had heard of this tower, but she had never visited it and thought it had long been deserted. "It belonged to my family," he told her. "As far back as the twelfth century. It was burned. I bought it back, and we redid the inside but left the old stones outside intact. You'll see."

Monsieur de A. went down to the town, bought the day's papers, and discreetly gathered information. He came back up into the glen, his wife and children having left for the seaside.

"I've read the news. They're searching for you" (he set a stern eye upon her), "but in the Rhône, where they pulled out your car. As for the other one, your husband. . . ."

She hid her gaze.

"Committed suicide with his army-issue gun. They must have thought your good-bye letter to the world was from him. Besides, it's impossible to tell anything; the carbine was lying in *his* blood. That's what the papers are saying."

She looked serene, almost happy. He watched her.

"Did you really tell me the truth?"

"Yes. You know—people put the barrel of the gun under their chin, and they pull the trigger with their big toe. I gave a lot of thought to how to set up the scene."

He shrugged his shoulders and looked away. "It's the rifle's answer to the army knife."

And he went away. Several days. But he returned, and he asked her to come and live with him in the tower.

"You'll be better off there."

"I have to stay invisible. No one comes by here except you."

She was eyeing the gold ring on his finger.

"Up there I live alone," he said. "Perfectly alone, for the month of August, on this deserted mountain."

He was smiling again.

"Are your little wounds healing? Did you apply what I brought you? Take off your blouse."

"It's your shirt," she said, rolling up the sleeves.

He had also rolled up his, and she saw that his arms were the color of ripe apricots. The first day, she had hardly paid any attention to this body, sensitive then only to the aura of goodness emanating from it.

"You've still got some gashes," he said, "but none of the wounds seems infected."

He got back up.

Yes, his body showed an admirable balance, trained by all sorts of athletics, altogether solid and utterly refined. This fineness combined with strength stunned her. How she would have loved to take him in her hands, to knead those sides that were virile, but not coarse. Why, in that town where she had spent three years, had she met only too-feminine jackal-men, or those heavyweights who took pride in their genitals and their leather-ringed fists? Now, she knew a man, and he was light itself.

But she had chosen to remain alone in her lair. That night, she was awakened by the sound of a plane, and grew worried. They went by in the daytime, too. "A lonely land where only the sky is inhabited." These noises told her the time. "My roaring clocks."

Afraid of being seen, she rarely left the cabin, and kept plunging into sleep as if to drown. Sometimes, she talked to the man, who wasn't there.

"You have made me reconcile myself to life. Your golden glance, your wheat-brown freckles, your severity when I tell you of things that don't please you. . . . Your mature gentleness. So rare. You have to bend down to enter my lair, and always you must lean down over me. Sun-Man. In order to reach you, I traveled across the dirty snow and the slimy boulders. I hung onto the roots of trees, and I was afraid. In those black forests, there are as many snakes as there are roots; the fir trees are a green so dark they suffocate me; on this, the bad side of the river, they decay; their lichens stick to my mouth. I wanted to die. But you are here."

She recognized the humming of love inside her. She had singing hands, closed hands, full of bees and very warm. The beating of her heart pounded her chest, and she felt the thumping all the way to the top of her head. Her belly was tender, ready to open. She was created for marvels of levitation. But her eyes were becoming almond-shaped, strangely elongated by insomnia.

She ventured out to the spring, filled the bucket, and washed herself all over, surrounded by the strong scent of crushed mint. Her wounds were healing well. She went into the field, pushing aside the clumps of hemlock, the young trees, the sweetbriar. She gathered fresh grasses for her bed. She found the bleached skeleton of a fox in a hole. One day, she brusquely picked a daisy and began to pluck the petals: "He loves me a little, he loves me a lot. He loves me with passion. . . ." Turning the stem, she noticed she was forgetting the "He loves me not." Oh well. The last petal said, "He loves me a little."

"That's it. He loves me a little. But me. . . ."

The excess of her love made her fiercely reserved, almost haughty. How she would have preferred to laugh, she who was a laughing person by nature. But in front of this man, she laughed no longer; she could hardly speak.

"Last night I saw a white bird. You say that there are no hoopoes in these woods, and no collared doves either? Nonetheless, I saw it. Twice. At dawn, he hopped onto the window ledge. He grew so large that he filled the entire window. I saw very clearly his feet, covered with curled feathers, and his enormous claws. He has a round, very black eye. But I made a sign to him and he flew away."

"I've brought you a companion," he told her one morning. "You'll feel less alone."

"I like being alone."

The kitten he put on her arm was completely black.

"Silk velvet! I had a dress like that for my wedding day."

"Are you superstitious?"

"No."

"There weren't any others. He's as black as black crystal. And do you know what his mother fed him? A squirrel every day."

She was stunned to see that he was laughing. But the cat had hyacinth eyes and a flat nose. He was working his front paws.

"A boxer!" she said. "I'll call him Tuesday. We saw each other for the first time on a Tuesday."

"I found a very pretty name for you right away: the wild demoiselle."

She realized that she still didn't know his.

"Elysée de A.," he said. "They gave us peculiar names. It was one of our forefathers'. . . . I used to come here almost every day, because of the spring. You have to search for that spring among all the moss and the leaves; you can no longer see it; you have to search for it like you search for the soul in the body."

Suddenly, she understood from the mist in between them that she was crying. Had he noticed?

He was still talking: "These clearings, these shelters, they belonged to us, too, before they belonged to you, but all that we possessed was scattered and sold."

His voice became hard. "Don't cry! I don't want anyone to steal from me what you are, either. It's true you face a certain danger, but I'm here. Don't wander outdoors. Yes, I have to go away for two days, but then I'll come to get you. I want you to live in the tower, with me."

She didn't answer.

He gave her a quick, ironic look and took his leave, like a courtier, with an odd movement of his shoulders.

III

In love, she was capable of living on very little. As it might be said of a people that they are frugal, she was frugal in love. A trifle sufficed, a glance became a world and found infinite resonances inside her. So she waited, patient. And when he returned to tell her to leave the chalet and follow him, she made him ask several times.

"I like being here; I want no other paradise. I would like always to live in this cabin."

"Impossible. Hunting season is about to open, and there will be people walking by! And in November, you wouldn't be able to hold out. That little kerosene lamp won't do much to keep you warm. There's no way to make a fire here; everything would go up in flames."

He had led her outside. She observed his eyes. The field and the forest turned them green; they were mirror-eyes; the pupil was almost nonexistent, as was the white, but there were those large irises, gold or brown or greenish, and a gleam of malice, of anger. She had seen them be alert, honest; she had never really seen them be tender. Now they were tender.

"Come!"

They put the cat in a basket and left the cabin in order. She might need it again later.

The watchtower seemed enormous to her, and its rust-colored stones, cemented arris-wise, inspired in her more fear than admiration. But once they entered the reception hall and its heavy door was tightly shut behind them, she felt safe. Safe from what?

She stared at him once again. "Would you perhaps grant me a favor?" (She always addressed him formally.)

"Hurry!"

"I would like to put my head against your heart for a moment."

He said nothing. So, approaching him as if she were blind, she nestled herself against him. He stood there, as dead as a statue. He didn't put his arms around her, but he crushed her hair with his chin.

He wasn't touching her. Then he carried her to a cot, wrapped her in an eiderdown with a bold flower print, and left her.

She slept as she hadn't slept in a long time—without dreams, without anguish.

Each morning, he would leave for the dam. Each evening, he returned. The two of them ate at a black walnut table in the knights' hall, surrounded by silence. They sat in rough-hewn armchairs with sculpted feet, underneath a ceiling crossed by heavy beams of arrola pine, supported by beveled columns. The hall was scarcely illuminated by little iron-barred windows. As early as six o'clock, they would light the candles and play cards like two old war buddies. She often won.

"You're not bored?" she asked.

"No, I have my wild demoiselle."

"You're still making fun of me!"

"No, you're my distraction. I have something to think about. I think about the things you tell me; I think about you. I take a gun with me when I go out, but I don't even feel like hunting anymore."

"You've already got your wild animal!"

"Not securely enough...," he said sadly. "She's freer than she believes herself to be. She must remain free. I won't pursue her."

One day he questioned her. Did she have any relatives she could trust completely?

"I didn't have a mother," she said, "and my father died a long time ago."

She had been raised by an aunt whose austerity froze her, but who never refused her any "luxury" whatsoever. "And luxury," she admitted, "is all the same a kind of tenderness."

Brought up without defenses, without friends, distant with her schoolmates out of shyness and civility rather than pride, without curiosity, reading little, dreaming too much, what could she know of life?

Elysée de A. contemplated her and thought, "No one could want to be rough with her. She's too fragile, too skittish."

Up on this mountain where the herds no longer lived, the grass was already becoming dry. It turned the pale yellow of overripe wheat. "What an avalanche hazard," he said. "The snow will slide right over it." The moon further accentuated its sheen. From her little window in the tower, the damsel of the wilds watched it rise in the sky and bleach the dark forests as well. Sometimes, a muted huffing sound made its way up to her, almost a barking: the roebucks in heat. The black cat had left to rejoin its mother among the alders.

"Our family has always been careless. That's why we became poor," he joked one evening.

"Who was that over there?" She was pointing to a painting of a person whose attire was adorned with pearls and bands on his epaulets. He wore a blue satin vest and held a sword with a hilt in mother-of-pearl.

"One of my forefathers. He lived at the court of Louis XIV."

"And this one?"

"He was a knight-banneret at the battle of Marignan."

"And this beauty?"

"My great-grandmother. I met her. But tell me about yourself, how you played, where you went to school."

She told him of her father's death when she was ten years old: "It was as if God had died; yes, as if God were truly dead. And afterward, my aunt, his sister, was forever lost at sea. She threw me little life preservers, of course, as often as she could. It wasn't often. The tenderness of someone who's not there; a lot of toys."

She saw a set of garnet-colored jewels laid on velvet, inside a windowed cabinet: a necklace, a ring, and two drop earrings. The stones were mounted in the old-fashioned way, on filigreed little collets of red gold.

"Amethysts?"

"No. In daylight, they look green. They're alexandrite. They're probably from the Urals. I don't know how they ended up here."

"It's like the way the butterfly, the Great Mars, changes. Dark, and then, depending on the light, violet."

"But I think they must be fake. They're not locked up. Look."

He easily opened the little door and put the necklace on her.

"I'm too small for jewels like these," she said. "They're made for queens." But she joyously wounded her fingers on the prongs, and it wasn't without trembling that she hung from her ear lobes (which were pierced) the earrings' wavy stems.

"Twist them," he advised. "Gold can be twisted."

She wanted to keep them for the night. "I feel good with them on. They're not heavy. They protect me."

But at dawn, and without him seeing her—he slept far from her, at the top of the tower—she took them off and put them all away in the jewel case in the cabinet. On her left ear was a drop of blood.

IV

"I was hidden, lying down or kneeling. I don't know where. It seems I was surrounded by white cloths. And *he* had taken my head in his caring hands and *he* was caressing it. . . . He re-created my eyes, my nose, my mouth, my cheeks, my forehead. I remember even more particularly how he caressed the length of my throat, first down, and then back up my chin. But I woke up."

That very night, at dinner, at the far end of the long, smooth table, Elysée de A. was hardly loquacious and coldly polite.

"Now I know the desert of love," she suddenly complained. "The glacier of love."

"Me too," he said without looking at her. "And it's not because of virtue."

No, he knew that: he was hardly virtuous. He even belonged to a prodigiously gallant race—when it wasn't off waging war—and it had stopped waging war a century ago.

"It's not because of virtue!" he repeated.

Then why was it? An indefinable feeling held him back. He had had her too quickly, right away, naked in his arms, completely naked, but like a sick child. And he was not of the sort that rape children. Even if she had offered herself (and she offered herself, naturally, hardly even realizing it), he wouldn't have been capable.

Sometimes he would lie on a sheepskin near the cot and contemplate her. Sometimes they fell asleep together like two young soldiers.

"What can I do for you?" she pleaded. "I would like to do something for you."

"Nothing!" he replied. "I would even prefer that you not love me."

He insisted: "There's nothing more cruel to request, is there?"

"No."

"I'm not asking it of you!" he shouted brutally, and he turned scarlet.

At first she thought it was a reflection of the candles, but then he became quite pale again. She remained startled. "Does he really love me?" At midnight, when he left, he still had that half-destroyed face, that bizarre fold across his cheek and a reddish streak.

September was still very hot, but the valley was filled with a slight haze that persisted until dusk.

He was gone for four days and then returned, announcing to her that some of his friends were arriving that very evening for a hunting party. He asked her to put sheets on a dozen beds, and, because they were mostly canopy beds, she felt as though she had never worked so hard in all her life. Living as a recluse must have made her lazy.

But when the guests arrived, they were more numerous than expected. Slightly unhappy, he warned her that his wife was there.

"You'll stay in my room at the top of the tower. No one goes there. I'll bring you food. For now, no one should notice that you're here. Later, I'll see what we can do with you. For you," he restated. "I've already talked about it with my cousin, the lawyer, by the way."

They all ate in the dining hall, and the scent of venison in wine sauce rose up to the wild demoiselle. But in the little room, she had found the scent of Elysée de A. And it was well into the night when she heard a soft knock at the door. It was him.

"Oh!" he said, touching her hands. "You're frozen!" He took her in his arms. She curled up in this human nest, leaning her head on the man's shoulder. Her braid was undone; he clasped her hair in his hand.

"How strange. Your hair is hot."

She whispered, "You don't know everything. There is also. . . ."

He said with a strange slowness, "I know everything about you."

"No, you don't know everything."

"I know everything about you." He was overexcited, joyous. He must have been drinking. He knew everything about her, from her birth to her death.

Silently, he laid her flat on the room's narrow bed. And he placed his mouth on her mouth, and it was like a heavy stone that sealed her up.

"Yes, I'm sealed like a tomb," she thought. It was an immense, blissful repose.

"One time," he murmured.

He was undressing her now. Each of the man's kisses is like an exploding star that marks her skin with a cross-shaped burn. And she remembers a picture she received as a child, a picture of the Virgin outlined with silver stars bursting through the paper.

"I'm a virgin."

He was startled, but said, "I knew that."

He gently spread open her thighs, took possession of her little patch of dark moss, and lodged himself inside her. A long moment must have passed. Then it seemed to her that she was making a voyage in a storm, a terrible voyage on red waves that carried her away, only to drop her and pick her up again. One wave took her very high, so high that she thought she was dying. Then everything fell back into darkness.

V

The next evening, he returned. "I'm married, I love my wife and children. But I can no longer get by without you."

"It's an impossible love," she said, tranquilly.

"It's an impossible love," he admitted, just as tranquilly.

They were smiling at each other.

"Yes."

"We will smile at each other for as long as we live. . . ."

She remained wordless, too shaken to be able to say more.

"I brought you some funny clothes. With this beard, you'll disguise your-self as a coach driver. Everyone's going in costume tonight. There will be a lot of people, and no rules. You'll enjoy yourself, and I'll be able to watch you. I need to see you! And soon I will, in the knights' hall."

Worried, Mr. de A. was wondering, "Where is my wild demoiselle?" Would even he find it difficult to recognize her? ("You'll never know who I am!" she had assured him.)

She had arrived last, dressed as a boy, but not as a girlish boy—there is, all the same, a shade of difference—and she had certainly succeeded. There was no trace left of her small breasts, wrapped tightly with leggings underneath the thick jacket with the leather collar, and her hips were no wider than those of a bullfighter. She had cut off her long hair, leaving only a few blackish strands across her neck and forehead. But *him*, he felt a lump in his throat. He shot her a glance so unhappy, and with such a pout, that she regretted what she had done.

The women were dressed in extravagant hunting outfits. They wore jack-ets made of heavy tweed or striped cloth, puffy pants, boots, and berets topped with birds' wings.

That day, the ladies had killed a large stag.

Monsieur de A. had always preferred to hunt only with men, but the wives and their daughters had protested: they had the vote now, they had the right to voice an opinion on any subject, things weren't the way they used to be. And some of them were very good shots.

"But be careful tomorrow not to get taken for a flock of quail or grouse, with all your fine feathers!" he told them.

The hunters, who were already going gray, wore dark sashes and bright silk scarves. They cut a fine figure, but young faces were few and far between in the crowd. The berets soon flew down to the end of the room, and the jack-ets followed shortly thereafter, leaving the women guests half-dressed, with bare throats in choker necklaces. She noticed one wearing an aggressively em-broidered tunic, her face shadowed by a large, black felt hat. The lady turned her head; she seemed more kind than did her outfit. From the compliments the men were paying her, the demoiselle *sauvage* understood that this was the lady of the house. "His wife!"

"I've misled myself!" she raged, fleeing up a narrow staircase and taking refuge behind the first door she saw. It was a glacially cold bathroom, illumi-nated by an oil lamp. A curtain decorated with red lilies encircled the bathtub.

She creaked open the spigot on a tin sink and washed her hands. Then she pulled off the beard that had been pricking at her chin. She knew there was a mirror in front of her, but she didn't dare look at herself. Suddenly weak, she swayed, and closed her eyes. "Would I be afraid?" She was afraid. "If I'm no longer the same, he won't love me any more. If I'm ugly, he'll disown me. I won't be able to stand it." She felt that she could stand fewer and fewer things. But she forced herself to lift her face, keeping her eyes closed meanwhile. "I don't want to see myself."

Suddenly, she opened her eyelids. She was more than beautiful. She had never been so beautiful.

She returned to the room where the meal was being served and hid away in a corner. Lost behind a seven-branched chandelier, she limited herself to thanking her neighbors with hoarse sounds when they passed her a glass or a dish. People were talking loudly and drinking freely, exalted by the day out in the open air, the shots fired, the sparks, the dark that had grown thick so early, the unbelievable solitude of the mountains. But *he*, no longer seeing her, was looking for her. She smiled with her almond eyes and shriveled up even more.

"Have you noticed a little coachman?" he was imprudent enough to ask.

"All the way up here?" was the ironic response.

Someone had seen the coachman. They looked around toward to the bench at the end of the room, but the wild demoiselle had disappeared again. She was now in the darkest corner of the room, seated on an ottoman, to the left of the huge fireplace that gleamed with soot, where juniper roots were brightly burning. This brightness was precisely what prevented anyone from getting a good look at her. But, so disguised, she was watching, listening.

At the end of the meal, he discovered her and stood before her. They spoke with the politeness of people who are meeting each other for the first time.

"All in black. . . ?" he whispered dreamily. "Ah! It's hardly snowed on you."

But the magic attraction that each exerted over the other continued to grow. It shortened their breath and made carousels turn round inside their heads. People began to notice them. This society, so often malicious, had kept a special radar for love that other people have lost. An ancient Italy was awakening within them, a certain intensity of passion; an Italy so close in spite of the mountains, and from which a long and stubborn invasion continued to flow.

"Who is that page with the slanted eyes?" asked someone. "Might our cousin have a fondness for. . . ?"

"Singapore!" cut in another.

"I don't think so. But once they reach forty, can you ever be sure? It's a dangerous turning point. They can suddenly become new men."

"Or new women. . . ," assured one of the women. "I've heard talk of a friend who, at that age, discovered she had quite a fondness for her sisters. And I can assure you that, until then, it had been quite the opposite."

"Don't believe it for a minute. There was always a secret inside that eluded her."

"The ambivalence of the human being."

But over there, the wild demoiselle, pointing out three young women to Monsieur A., said to him sadly, "They're superb. How can you still look at me? Go and join them."

The first one had wispy hair, encircled with a cord, like a sheaf of rye. The hair of the second was midnight-blue, with little braids mixed in. The third woman, who was the most aristocratic, had red hair; two English curls hung from her temples to her breasts, so linear that the coil was hardly distinguishable, but shimmered in the twilight.

"The life, the death of trees. . . . I remember," an enraptured old gentleman was telling them, "when all the walnut trees in Valais exploded one spring. It sounded like a cannon firing. They had been completely frozen."

"After this hunting party, we'll leave the tower," Elysée de A. added in a low voice. "I'll hardly have the leisure to live here anymore. But rest assured, I'll keep watch over you."

He took a few steps away from her, then returned. "The jewelry cabinet is locked! My wife distrusts people, even our guests."

He laughed. He must have found that amusing.

Before noon the next day, the hunters headed down from the summits where they had killed five chamois. A thunderstorm was making the tower tremble, and the valley was full of blackish storm clouds rushing constantly northward. Below, the entire forest was swaying its larches and fir trees, overturned like umbrellas. A sharp, whistling sound was heard that had nothing to do with this earth.

"I've never seen such a storm," said Madame de A., astonished.

"But the tower is solid, with walls two meters thick?"

"They are really old stones."

"They alone really last . . . ," the lawyer said emphatically. "I spent an entire winter here once, with Elysée."

In the great hall, the lanterns and candelabra were quickly lit; the fire blazed, and the women's faces turned rosy. The men took apart some long, old Spanish pistols whose springs they made sing with fingers already less skillful than their owners of yore. Card games were organized.

Monsieur de A. woke up the wild demoiselle, who was still sleeping. The festivities had resumed downstairs, but she refused to reappear.

"Your cousins will figure us out," she said.

"It's not difficult to sense two beings in a crowd, who search for each other, pretending to flee. To connect two gazes that turn expressly away from each other. Two voices that stay silent, two smiles given to no one, but secretly meant for him, for me. My love is written on my face . . . and in the end, they'll all see it and tear it apart."

They lay next to each other in the little room for a while. They stayed that way, without moving. From time to time, they looked at each other.

"I wonder why we love each other."

"I know why."

"Why?"

But he didn't respond. She was running her fingers lightly over his head, as if she wanted to retain its shape forever.

"In this face," she observed, "there's all the harmony of an eighteenth-century façade, in the purest style. But it's a funny image, because in fact this face is neither beautiful nor classic—it is fit for a clown."

"Exactly!"

"Now explain to me why we love each other."

"Because you're not you, but another. And me, I'm not me, but another!"

"You find that simple?"

"Yes," he said seriously. "Our love is very simple."

"It couldn't not exist?"

"No, it couldn't not exist. There are a thousand ways of loving, and ours is the simplest. And the devil, I mean God, can't hold it against us."

He held her against him for a moment, in her entirety. Then, the storm having abated, he went down to pack his bags with the guests, leaving her the key to the tower.

VI

He had clearly advised that she stay there. But she had lost confidence and no longer felt safe there. She feared the empty rooms, the large, cold stones. She put a few provisions in a bag and went back down to hide in her cabin.

Underneath the rickety table, she found her little silver man. He was cracked from top to bottom, the foil had come apart. "Oh! What does that mean?" Life as a prisoner was making her superstitious.

She thought back to the night when Elysée de A. had taken her. "One time. . . ," he had murmured. What had he meant? "One single time, one time only, and—never again." That was it.

She slept poorly, ate nothing. But she wasn't short of blankets—even the softest ones—or of sweaters. She was even truly comfortable on her bed of dried grasses, rocking her memories against herself. "One time." The October sun radiated a violent heat. She listened to the sound of the stream. It became the sound of her blood, the absolute draining of her blood. Would she awaken one morning, without a drop left in her and so transparent that daylight would be visible through her body as it is between the veins of a dead leaf? Through the opening in the chalet (it had no door), she looked out at the path of hair-grasses and trampled down Queen Anne's lace. "Elysée walked by here. He saw that tree." She searched for traces of him everywhere.

She would have liked to have lived in another time. But she was ashamed of her dreams and told herself that, in *another time*, nothing could have been any better. We each carry our destiny as a fruit carries its seed.

"I want to erase myself for you, my love. And to me, my existence means little."

"No one will understand. It will be my way of loving you."

"An oblation? No. Not being anything, that's not suffering."

A light humidity rose from the stagnant field where the parnassia shone, white. One night she thought she was seeing the immaculate bird. One day, a helicopter passed over her, headed toward the bottom of the valley, and then returned. Its propeller shone bizarrely in the twilight, like an eye. "The eye of Cain?" But she no longer believed in God.

"It was only our need for love and protection that invented God. Our pride as well. He was an explanation of our suffering. But men have never tried to give a meaning to the suffering of animals and things." The wild demoiselle knew very well that, all around her, animals were moaning, uprooted trees and cut flowers were bleeding. "Human beings have never bothered to invent a future paradise for a weasel, or for a houseleek! But after death, they won't be any better off than either of them. Death is the return to the bosom of the earth, the eternal repose."

Changing color, the larches created a reddish haze over the mountain. She went naked in the warmth of a sun that had lost half of its power. This wasn't the first time she had lived without clothing. She remembered her adolescence, how chaste she had been. In those days, that voluptuousness, hardly conscious, hadn't troubled her. She had learned, too young and too firmly, to push away any so-called impure thoughts. And if nature manifested itself in her then, it was only in her dreams, in a childish way. Something then unknotted itself in her body, plunging her into a state of ineffable well-being. She didn't know its name; she was ignorant of the exact words that would have enlightened her. But, thus liberated, she opened serene eyes onto the dawn, and she offered to the untroubled air of her bedroom and its white lacquered furniture a very beautiful body, untormented by desire.

But now! She loved a man and desired him.

One day, as she stood naked in the solitude of the meadow, she felt a strange, numbing sensation. She thought she was in the middle of a desert, blinded by a brutal electric light. She wasn't dreaming. She truly saw herself lost in the middle of a desert. She was watching her shadow, very black, at her feet. The shadow was the only living presence—she, herself, already felt frozen in death. She remained stationary; the shadow crept and grew longer. Finally, the shadow was so long that it seemed to reach the confines of this mineral world. The wild demoiselle even feared that it would desert her altogether. But a sudden coolness calmed her, and she began to feel reality around her once again.

One night, snow fell. Swirling dry flakes penetrated every crevice in the shack and covered the sleeper on her bed. Around ten o'clock, Monsieur de A. arrived, very worried.

"You can't stay here! I had advised you to stay in the tower. Put on your all your warm clothes and come with me!"

She obeyed. They walked through the stands of hazelnut trees and the alders, which were already white. They clambered up a frosted slope, followed a path underneath fir trees whose tops they could no longer see, and finally reached the naked, narrow plateau.

The curtain of snow, like those curtains of pearls in the doorways of Southern houses, tumbled and tinkled before them. Occasionally, she raised her hand as if to push it away.

"Your fortress?"

"You'll hardly be able to see it today."

They stumbled into the arch of the doorway, which was eaten away by orange lichens. While turning the key, Monsieur de A. pushed on the large lock. He led in the wild demoiselle, who hesitated.

"There's nothing to be afraid of. There's no one here. My wife has gone down for good. So have I; my office is in town now."

"Ah!" she said.

She felt abandoned, and squeezed the little Specter she held in her hand.

"I'll come back up to see you and bring you what you need. They're still looking for you. It's better that you stay in hiding. Your husband's death. . . ."

He stopped, suddenly drawing his breath with difficulty.

"I think everything is resolved as far as people's suspicions of you are concerned, but they could still torment you with interrogations. . . . It's still dangerous. You are ferocious, but fragile. You need a good lawyer."

They lay down together in one of the canopy beds, and he made love to her once again.

"My little virgin!"

Yes. . . ."

"I knew that *they* are often impotent. . . ," he said, absorbed in thought.

He certainly wasn't. But she was amazed that, in spite of the pleasure, love still had for her a flavor of blood and suffering. "Elysée is a real man. I love him, he loves me, and he isn't crazy!"

She told him what her wedding night had been like. She had at first, she admitted, shown a certain fear. Then, while kissing her, her husband, with skill-ful, knowing hands, had tied her up with silk cords. There were four—exactly what was needed—he said. First one ankle, then the other (and hers were ex-tremely thin) was tied to the wrought iron bedposts. He covered her with kisses as he tied them. Starting with her legs and belly, he went up to her breasts, her shoulders, and the length of her arms all the way to her hands. He seized and ca-ressed them while attaching her wrists to the head of the bed. "This is to get you accustomed. . . ," he repeated over and over. Then he slowly opened the little army knife. The second night, they had already crossed two borders, and they were in Spain. Against the whitewashed wall, the gilded bars of the bed's mag-nificent arabesques looked as black as those of a coffin. "Your pink blood and my crimson blood—what a rare mix! What a secret pact!" But he was already be-coming much less delicate in both his words and his bizarre behavior.

By the time the wild demoiselle finished talking, gray daylight was already coming in through the tower window.

Monsieur de A. dressed quickly, covered her with an eiderdown, and placed another three kisses on the delicately paved footpath of the vertebrae along her youthful neck. His was a hard, male mouth, unhesitating, and not very knowledgeable. She received them like a benediction.

VII

He reappeared three days later with an enormous sack on his back, haloed by the scent of the apples and tangerines he poured onto the table. He put the meat in an improvised ice-box. The cartons of rice and pasta, the bread and canned goods, he put away himself in the dining-hall closet. He was one of those men whom love renders paternal. She watched him, a little dazed, sur-prised, and crushed by the joy of this unexpected visit. "I adore you, I adore you, I adore you. . . ."

He must have guessed this. He retorted, "A clown!"

"Yes, and with that . . . such harmony in you, a balance from the heart."
He was smiling inside.

"Are you originally from A.?" she suddenly asked.

"You would have to go back five generations. Our three castles there were also sold, ruined, then restored for those idiotic Sound and Light spectacles. We have nothing left of all our wealth . . . nothing but a row of trees that became regal without us. And now even those chestnut trees will be felled to widen the road!"

"You still have a letter," she said.

"You found it? I didn't know where it was anymore."

Why were they still being so formal with each other?

"In the little room at the top of the tower. Your ancestor didn't seem too happy in the foreign service, or very fulfilled in his home life, either. . . . Was she pretty?"

"Beautiful, yes. And sour."

"There's a great nostalgia in that letter for the canton of Valais, the worries of home life, the peasants."

"It's true."

"And also an emotional subtlety, a suffering, that are tied together, hidden deep within him. . . . It was me he was writing to! I loved this father, this letter to a son."

"Consider it yours, then," he said.

He had left again. Would he return? She ran her fingers over her dry mouth, pressing her nails into the pink flesh.

"Is it possible for me not to exist for him?"

She was speaking alone; she was afraid in the tower. There were too many memories already decaying there. But she didn't want a resurrection, and she was haunted by this certainty: the lover would not return.

Left to herself and her fogs, she penetrated deeper and deeper into the unreal. She performed what she called a "mental suicide," but so naturally that she hardly even realized it. She was lying on one of the sheepskins in front of the fireplace, when the space around her drew itself away. She *saw* herself, standing in the crag of a boulder that hung over an abyss. It was an abyss without a name, a very deep and narrow gorge, with walls the color of slate. She could discern all of its tiniest lines, each twist of the river, the color of the stones, and the outlines of plants on the vertical slopes. She needed no forcing; she threw herself in. But a simple blink of her eyelids was enough to restore to her what remained of her lucidity.

Although November displayed its usual mildness, the sun had nonetheless disappeared. She received only its reflection, sent back by the other face of the mountain. Her side remained plunged in the shadows, except for an hour around noon. She sat at the tower's threshold to welcome it. This all-too-furtive visit reminded her of her lover's last visit. "Come warm me up!" she cried. But she heard only the echo of her plea, a bird rising up over the firs also cried; it was only a jay.

There came a time when even this hour was no more. For her, the sun had stopped living. So she stayed in her cot, huddled up in the covers, in the middle of the knights' hall. She reread the old baron's letter; she even read the housekeeping ledgers; columns of numbers didn't bore her. There she found a father, a mother, brothers and sisters. "I was made for that life, for that time." But she shook her head, with her hair already growing back, all tangled. "That's not true. I'm not from anywhere or any time!"

The forest, so dark at dawn, stayed black all day long and drowned completely in the voiceless abyss of the night. There were no more stars, not a single ray of light, not even the buzzing of an insect.

When the cold became too intense, she tried to light a fire in the fireplace. Her scalp burning, she fell asleep, reawakening when a branch exploded, then falling back into a dreamless sleep, and reopening her eyes in the morning, frozen.

At first, it was her feet she felt were ice. Then her legs, and next her belly became painful. Now, her very soul was cold. She was ashamed of having believed so strongly in that love; she was ashamed of being ashamed. As always when she was distressed, she was flagellating herself instead of trying to take some action. "I loved much more than I was loved. . . ." But hadn't she known that right away? She surprised herself, clutching herself in her arms like a newborn. She even gave up starting fires. Every evening, she heard a muffled sound. A door closing? "The door to paradise!" It was all over; the warmth, the scent of the underbrush, the waves that the wind sketches in the tall grass. The earth breathed no more. Ah! How happy she had been that last month of August, the wild demoiselle!

In a fine powder, the snow began to fall, up higher at first, then down around her, in her, but the day drank the snow, and the rotting stumps all steamed. The pale landscape became so inhuman that she rejoiced. She no longer dwelt in the world of the living. Space pulled itself back once again. She burst out laughing; she was in her desert. A light, no longer yellow, but colorless, metallic, unbearable. She stood in it, rigidly erect, and dead. And her shadow had disappeared. An oversized moon rose in the white sky; it illuminated nothing; it didn't illuminate at all.

Yes, in her dreams and in reality, the wild demoiselle was dying, was no longer eating, was dozing away from weakness. One day, abandoning the little silver Specter in the room at the top of the tower, she decided to flee. . . .

Like all those who are preoccupied by just one or two matters, Monsieur de A., engineer that he was, was absent-minded. He had the sorts of distractions that either soften the heart or irritate. A zero missing from his calculations could entail serious consequences. But forgetting a young woman?

Back in town, he felt some relief. That perpetual tension had worn him out. At the same time, he was dragging along a tender remorse that his new duties made short work of muffling. They even became so demanding that he couldn't go back up to see the wild demoiselle a third time. He had, however, confided the secret and a verbal report of the matter to his cousin and best friend, the lawyer. All in all, he still believed his protégée was safe in his tower.

One morning while working in his office, he was surprised by the hum of voices. The mail was brought in to him. He opened up the newspaper and read this short paragraph:

> *Madame D., who had been missing since August third, has finally been found in the Rhône, not far from the location where her car, a red Austin, had overturned. Her body, which had been caught in the roots of a willow, was miraculously preserved intact.*

"Miraculously . . . !" he cried (or did he laugh?), and a sob folded his giant body in two.

• *11* •

On Misty Ponds

$\mathcal{A}$t first, nothing more than shadows could be seen through the mist, shadows upright on the largest pond. People thought it was a mirage, some kind of reflection, but a breeze swept in, and then you clearly saw young men and young women bathing. They held hands, splashed each other, and dove suddenly. They swam very quickly, and in every direction.

Everyone was quite surprised. But this was only the beginning.

These young people proved devoid of modesty; they were shamelessness itself. They were accused of sodomy, of a thousand strange perversities; exhibitionism was the least of their sins. But the mist returned, and there were your enchanting unfettered shadows, and for a moment it all seemed a dream. But this wasn't a dream at all.

The general amazement kept growing. Where did they come from, these boys and girls who were always naked, with bodies that did not tan but retained instead a pallid, lunar complexion? And their lascivious games were subtle indeed. You could see them all making love as one, glued together more tightly than cantharis beetles, or simply inserting hazelnuts, or red or purple wild cherries, in their ears and nostrils. There was even a serpent seen to penetrate, with the whole length of his body, the intimacy of a woman who seemed to feel nothing but intense pleasure. And the oldest of the town's notables insisted that one of these creatures had given birth, before his very eyes, to a little tree.

The boys had hard muscles and flat hips; the girls carried their breasts high and shaped like hazel grouse eggs, and they had the most beautiful navels in the world. But people began to mutter that their beards and their hair were not real beards and hair, but actually lichens, and mosses, and even leaves that rustled as they walked by.

Especially mystifying, perhaps, were their mother-of-pearl bodies, with transparent skin so white it was silvery; people blamed the mists in which they took their pleasure. A schoolteacher claimed that, on the contrary, nothing made skin tan faster than the sun's rays coming through the fog. . . .

Certainly this combination of light and humidity, these ramparts of reeds, kept a morning mist in place over the ponds; it encouraged this outrageous frolicking, but the stern spring winds would chase it away. And the townspeople waited for spring.

When April arrived, they were dumbfounded. Fires of tree limbs at the four corners of the marshlands provided a fine replacement for the mists. But who was maintaining these aromatic blazes of juniper, dog-rose, and barberry? Even their weightless ashes fluttered as they rose up and yellowed the sky.

People spotted them dancing in rings at night. Yes, these boys and girls paraded around the ponds for hours, ecstatic and untiring. They were sometimes accompanied by goats, does, wild pigs, and strange animals they straddled. It was said that, at their touch, birds and blackberries, flowers and butterflies all grew beyond their natural size. That in their presence, everything revealed secret abilities for excess and ubiquity.

But they were so beautiful, and seemed to pursue earthly happiness with such intense nonchalance that many of the curious observers who went to curse them returned home stupefied. "The wind goes right through their mouths!" they exclaimed. There was a heightened danger of imitation. Some young people from the town joined them. No one recognized their faces. The highest authorities were stirred and decided to bring an end to this new Black Sabbath, one that seemed even more damning than the ancient ones that had come before.

"*Nymphs, tribades, fauns, and satyrs have returned to earth. . . ,*" announced the newspaper headlines. "*Let's stop the shameless youth!*" the local papers screamed.

So it was easy to see them, but they were never heard to speak, or to laugh, or to shout. Not even a sigh. It was, above all, their silence that frightened. There was a stunning gravity in their insolence.

But the oldest of the notables fell madly in love with one of the teenage girls, whose skin was streaked through with dry pine needles. She wasn't the most beautiful, but surely the most capable of unsettling him, and her nearly speechless demeanor only added to her charms. He wrapped her up in a horse-blanket while she was sleeping, and his car took them straight to one of those giant hotels that stand on the mountainsides these days. He carried her upstairs himself, refusing the porters' assistance, and fled into room number 7, which he had just rented for a king's ransom. The bed was huge and covered by a comforter in sea-green silk. He burned incense in perfume-pans to simulate the mist and put on a record, "Frog Songs: A Summer Night."

But although the young captive gave herself willingly (he could not but be impressed by the absolute coldness of her pallid skin), she exhibited neither joy nor sadness. She opened her mouth only for kisses, a sticky mouth that reminded the old gallant of the mud he had tasted in his childhood days. The next day, fearing the touch of her frosty hand, the poor notable was a bit disconcerted. He went out to take the mountain air, after asking the Chinese floor-attendant to bring a frothy hot chocolate, some croissants, and medlar jelly to room number 7. When he returned, the breakfast remained intact on the bedside table. The young nymph had disappeared. But there were long pink worms intertwined on the comforter, the sort of worms found in very rich soil.

Upon returning to town, he alerted the local police (their calves were strong and their fearless members were well seasoned).

But they returned empty-handed, swearing that they hadn't been able to catch a single one of these perverts that slipped through their fingers like little fish[1] that vanished into the reeds and the club mosses, leaving behind a sweetish scent that their German Shepherds refused to follow. They organized more hunts. The people smirked, declaring that these young folks made love in the treetops while the policemen played cards underneath. The tallest and thickest of the pine trees were cut down, but on the ground, their limbs cut off, they proved empty.

The town leaders finally decided to capture them dead or alive, in nets, like birds or fish. Big, sturdy ones were specially prepared. They chose a bright night, expecting one of those processional excursions around the largest of the ponds.

They soon appeared from the darkest part of the forest. Their bodies, steaming and diaphanous, moved forward calmly and noiselessly, with flowers tucked in the most intimate folds of their skin—wild gladioli, anemones, asphodels, male orchids. Stained by crushed strawberries and blackberries, their curls dripped down their legs; they exchanged caresses, casting slow, serene glances over the trees and the surface of the pond. They walked three times around it, evading as if by miracle the bird-catchers' nets. Then they walked into the water.

But there, an even more treacherous net was stretched, controlled by a masterful mechanism. The lovers sank into the waves, which grew ever darker, ever deeper; beneath the weeds, they completed the gestures they had begun. Soon, their heads were all that could be seen, like a hundred cut-off heads on an obsidian platter; then their eyes closed.

---

[1] Bille refers specifically to bleaks, a European freshwater fish known for its silvery scales.

"Get going!" shouted the police, with a devilish violence.

All at once, the circular net emerged.

It was empty. A few water spiders and a couple of dragonflies were the only things tangled in the lines. And a voice was heard, but it was made up of many voices together, a voice that said: "We've been dead for a long time. But your children will eat grapes that aren't yet ripe, and we will come back to life again."

· 12 ·

The Oval Room

About twenty friends had arranged to meet that evening in this castle, which can be reached only by passing through stretches of reeds, then following along a line of ash trees, and next, some very old pear trees, all covered with yellow lichens.

And so, in this castle, I had once again found my great love of old, the love I had forgotten for so many years. I no longer even knew the color of his eyes, or just how that dark lock of hair curled over his forehead. But that day, I saw him unchanged, just as he was before, just as he had inhabited me—yes, inhabited me—for so long. He was pale, with a touch of pink on his cheeks, and he looked so slight in his loose-fitting clothes, so handsome in his oversized eyes, aristocratic as ever, despite his burglar-like demeanor.

I was seduced again, lost in love all over again, but I asked nothing of him.

It was enough for me to be next to him in the darkest room in the castle, breathing in the childhood scent of that love, because that love had been surrounded with toys, with childish rituals, with troubling images. And I saw once again the unicorn, the dollhouse, the willowy puppets whose fingernails were made of feathers, the black Virgin with strings of pearls sewn onto her dress, and the little queen who wore a pink seashell for a crown. Hadn't they been burned or ripped apart by the vengeful lover? No, he who was deserted and dismissed had preserved these treasures of cheap junk, which for us were *treasures*. Perhaps he had also preserved his hatred, but it didn't seem so. He appeared lively and slow, attentive, seductive. And we loved each other—oh! how we loved each other!—with the delicacy and absurdity of first love.

It was autumn, the rustiest of autumns; the vineyards were yellow, eaten away by verdigris; all around us, the earth was soaked with water. The air

105

smelled of rotten leaves and stagnant streams. A marsh nearby was beginning to settle into its winter shape. We had walked all the way around it, our high-heeled boots sinking into the mire and the peat, but we still knew to dash fearlessly onto the wooden footbridges. And I saw what I didn't dare believe; I saw it in the mirror of sleeping water: I was young again, as young as on the very first day.

And when we entered the Oval Room, which was on a level with the park, and we greeted a gathering of people, some known to us, and others unknown; we knew that they had the same desires, the same passions as we did. Life wasn't worth living except on account of one creature and one creation: the first to be loved, and the second to be built.

We weren't thinking of the afterlife, but we were acting as if, after death, something of us should remain, something intangible. Despite the impurities we had accumulated over time, we had all retained a naïveté more shattering than the lamb's because it was conscious and inalterable. Although our egotism was utter madness, each of us daily consecrated a drop of our most precious blood to this ideal.

And we realized—having rediscovered it that very day—that our friends were all in search of an absolute love that tasted of eternity.

The stunning Josyane, who had seen and lived through everything, and whose moonlike breasts swelled under her black bodice, and the dreamy Christina, whose thick, red hair weighed down her shoulders, and the other women: each of them had come to find a lover.

There was also Karik, whom I had trouble recognizing. Her sensible ways were gone, replaced by an Amazon's harsh, proud confidence. She seemed so resolute—with a chain of glass rings around her neck and hips, the nape of her neck uncovered, and the arch of her eyebrows outlined in purple—it frightened me.

Then there was Alberte, the very young adolescent whose skin was so white, tender and cruel as innocence always is.

As for me, I contemplated my beloved, this brother given to me not by nature, but by a fatal destiny. The nervous frailty of our bodies and the strong texture of our souls were identical. We adored the same sun and the same abysses; we could count on our bodies all the same scars. With bleeding fingers, we had wandered through the snows of the desert and the sands of the mountains. We had taken our childhood baths in the same fountain and slept in the same crib. This mysterious fraternity would bind us together until death.

And this castle, rustic again now, with logs piled up in the archways, but where people had once spoken of naming a king—the last descendant of one of Charlemagne's barons—for us, this castle has been freed of its dust. The golden parquets shine; the marble chimneys have been swept out with branches from fir trees; the spider webs have been wiped away, and the nests of the swallows that dirtied the paneled ceilings have been cut down. The vast oval table, made of red oak, has been moved back into the middle of the Oval Room, along with the maple armchairs and the secretaries. But the reaper and the farming tools were still in the courtyard, and, from the terrace, we heard the cowbells from the herds, coming home at dusk. Far off, in the pale fields, two riders in fur jackets trotted by. The boy wore a checkered cap, and the girl, nothing, nothing but her hair that floated freely. The ponies' coats, a dark reddish-brown, vanished in the rising mist.

After dinner, which was served in the dining hall, the guests scattered along the paths through the fields, drifting apart until they were just three or two couples, one couple, sometimes a single man or a single woman.

But instead of disappearing in the groves of the park, as several people did, we preferred to wander through the village, along with the poet Romur and the very young woman. Walking along a grassy path, we nearly bumped into a rabbit hutch. But the girl, who loved domestic animals, had immediately bent her knee with the nimble control of a dancer, and then raised herself back up on the points of her white shoes, under the poet's softened gaze.

We violated the forbidden door of a wooden church, standing alone on the plain. My beloved stepped up on the platform, opened a giant Bible, and delivered a sermon on the spirit and the flesh. It frightened a bird that had nested in the organ, and an orange butterfly, too, but made us laugh out loud.

We responded, "From now on, the spirit and the flesh will never part, not on earth or in heaven."

"What do you know of this, my children?"

"What do you know of this, Father?"

"Poor lost souls! This very night, you will have a few surprises. May the All-Mighty protect you. . . ," he concluded, with an unctuousness that was entirely ecclesiastic.

We went out again and returned through a cornfield where a fox rustled; from a distance, we could see his eyes glowing like the tips of two cigars, but he ran away. Then it was the village and the open windows of a long stable that sent us whiffs of a solid animal heat. We entered, greeting the herdsman, who was milking his ruminants, their pale buttocks rippling under his claps. Quite amused, we read aloud the names that were posted above their stalls: Lucia, Marquise, Mignon, Clorynde, ...

Once again, I looked at my brother *who wasn't my brother*, he was also looking at me in the middle of this stable that was larger than the church. We took turns drinking the warm, foamy milk that the dairyman offered us from a tin cup.

But the poet and the girl wanted to rejoin their lovers, who had gone off in different directions and were perhaps, at this very moment, in the act of betraying them. When we got back to the Oval Room, a hippie couple greeted us. Living together had caused this boy and girl to resemble each other in a striking fashion: their triangular faces were equally pale; their eyes showed the same stately indifference. There was an Indian headband across each of their perfect foreheads, and a braid hung down each back. The others who had taken evening walks had returned to sit and warm up by an intense beechwood fire.

Our host, an old duke with powdered hair, was giving orders to a servant who plunged a ladle into a big bowl that stood on the table. Out of it she drew a ruby-colored liquid made of fine liqueurs and French champagne, in which mysterious spices, strawberries, and cherries had marinated. She carefully poured it into goblets.

"It's the cup of passion!"

Josyane said mockingly, "No, Romur, it's just the goldfish bowl!"

Fortunately, the young lady of the castle was deaf, and the duke, her father, was paying little attention to this gathering.

A concert was to take place, preceded by the reading of a memoir on the customs of the region. But the man who was to read it, the learned ethnologist Lacuse, was absent. What was he doing? His uncouth power, tempered by a hidden gentleness, always aroused a confusion of feelings in those around him. But he liked ambiguity. Instead of forgetting him, everyone thought about him.

"Such an intelligent man!" said someone.

"Not surprising, he's the devil himself!" retorted Romur.

For the first time, I noticed on the poet's forehead two small protuberances that testified, no doubt, to his energy as well as to his imagination. But I saw very subtle pink waves pass under the ivory skin of the adolescent girl, and her gaze began to let out reddish gleams. This creature fascinated me, not only because of her unusual features, but because of her androgynous gracefulness as well.

The chandelier, suspended in the middle of the oval ceiling with stucco moldings, swung imperceptibly, due to the footsteps that could be heard on the next floor.

"Who is walking like that?" asked the duke.

It was soon revealed, as the door opened and Lacuse appeared. He was broad and powerful, and his demeanor was marked by a woolly silence that contrasted with the amplitude of his movements. He didn't speak, and refused to read the memoir out loud.

"It's very boring," he affirmed.

The duke didn't deign to take offense, and simply canceled the promised concert. To the two musicians, a harpist and flutist whom there had hardly been time to notice, he offered a ride in a horse-drawn carriage.

"You still have a carriage and horses!" exclaimed the two women, delighted.

"Have a good trip to the other side!" said Lacuse.

"You exaggerate. . . ." This reproach came from Ramier the explorer, a round, lively young man, behind horn-rimmed glasses he occasionally pushed up to rest on a mass of curls worthy of a herdsman.

Paulette, who was older than we were, but still beautiful in her maturity, contemplated Lacuse admiringly. The duchess stayed. I now noticed that one of her bulging, aged eyelids kept drooping, closing up, while the right one remained open. This made me uncomfortable, so I left all these personages and went to contemplate the family portraits lined up on the wall, which was never flat, but always more or less curved. The ancestors' backs must have gotten chilly when the winter winds came slipping inside.

Suddenly, I heard my cousin Jalvaine, settled next to her lover on a sofa. "Why always bring up Death and survival after death? Let's be satisfied with life."

"Does someone believe in the Hereafter?" asked Lacuse, dropping the memoir. From it rose a cloud of brown dust.

"Not me."

"I do!"

"Don't forget that every affirmation implies a negation."

"We transform ourselves into some *other* thing."

"That's the big question mark," I said, "*the new equation.*"

The servant entered, carrying two platters of little treats, both sweet and salty. Lacuse followed her with his eyes. She walked rather like a barnyard bird and wore a little gold cross on her bare chest. As she passed in front of him, Marietta nearly tripped over a chair. She didn't dare to look at him.

He smiled, and continued: "What does God mean to all of you?"

"An invention that man created because of his anxiety. A natural necessity."

"The Father we all dream of. . . ," sighed a hairy student who hadn't opened his mouth yet.

"A Bogeyman that tyrants have held up in front of the people, since the very beginning of the world!"

There was a silence

"It's the Infinitely good, the Infinitely perfect. . . ," recited my beloved.

His phrase reminded me of my catechism, but I knew he thought like that.

"But why have men felt the need to eat *him?*"

All were speechless at this question from Lacuse.

"Some of you are Catholic. The host is God, you digest it, you. . . ."

"It's love's essential desire!" said Christina.

"Yes, the strongest."

"The eternal. In all primitive tribes, men eat, they suck the flesh and bones of their dead relatives or of their enemies (people also love their enemies) to acquire their merits. It was totally misunderstood by the colonizers and missionaries. They themselves did even better: they swallowed their God."

"In whose name they exterminated all of the so-called savages," said Ramier, bitterly.

"Nowadays, they are killed in the name of Science, in the name of Progress. . . ."

"Who have replaced the gods and who are every bit as malicious."

But Lacuse stuck to his idea. "Why do we eat what we adore, what we love more than anything in the world?" (His tone changed.) "And you know very well that it's possible to love what you scorn! Women, for example, who are only good for one thing."

"What hidden dissatisfaction makes you talk like that?" asked Jalvaine, scandalized.

One of the young women, who had lost her mother the month before, turned quite red.

"I must confess . . . because I myself was completely shocked by it—something beyond explanation happened to me. The day I saw my mother dead, I felt an instinctive need to take a piece of her, of her body, to suck it, to drink her blood even as it chilled, yes . . . even to eat a piece of her poor flesh. To eat it!"

Sobs shook the young woman.

Everyone else was silent.

"It was an irresistible desire to unite myself with her, to incorporate her to myself. Yes, I experienced this hope of a transmission possible through ritual cannibalism."

"Did you do it?" asked some impertinent man.

"No, of course not! I didn't even dare to cut off a lock of her hair. All I could do was kiss her frigid forehead and squeeze those hands, already joined together, that had caressed mine so lovingly when I was a child."

She began to cry harder.

"Stop crying!" ordered Lacuse.

"Now calm down, dear. What you've expressed is normal!" Paulette and her husband Bruno told her.

They were the only married couple among us. They specialized in translations from English. They added, "People speak more spontaneously at a round table than around a square one."

"Really! You think so?"

"Yes, because the absence of angles allows the chain of human sympathy, our electric current, to stay far more continuous."

"Here we are, caught between two ovals!" complained the student.

"The duke isn't coming back."

"He's teaching the harpist to play the flute," said the student.

He pulled a guitar out from behind the sofa and began to play. The pupils dilated in his dark eyes, and I noticed a silver lamé sweater under his half-open canvas jacket.

No one really listened to him. The guests were taking turns getting up to help themselves, dipping the ladle into the huge, glowing red bowl. The two hippies, who stayed out of the conversation, were chewing on slices of bread and butter spread with a thick, green paste made of pistachios or hashish. At the very moment when we heard a galloping horse, a stranger walked into the room and kissed the hand of the duchess, who introduced him: "Mr. Sorday, the engineer."

He was a tall man with white hair. A thin young woman in a beige dress, with a dusky rose feather boa around her neck, accompanied him.

"Good evening! Good evening! We couldn't get here any earlier."

Yet another visitor arrived, wearing a long, crushed velour cape with a little gauze ruff. When she let the cape fall, we saw that she was wearing a very short dress and a leather belt with copper pompons that Lacuse eagerly twisted with his hand. The hand was slender, but the hair on it was as tough as thorns. Suddenly, he let them go. Marietta, the servant, was making another entrance, carrying a tray. Certainly she was beautiful enough to rival any woman in the room, and she even surpassed them in passive gentleness.

I forgot to mention that there was also a proud and wise little clockmaker, a man so small he always went around on tiptoe. Getting old clocks to run again was what made him happy. He was standing on a ladder, trying intently to awaken a seventeenth-century timepiece.

"It's gone to sleep forever!"

"Oh, you're going to bring up death again. . . ," protested Karik.

"Yet every man *eats* what he loves, as everyone should know: some do it with hateful looks, others with words that caress. . . ."

"Stop parodying Wilde!" Josyane shouted at the poet. "You parody everyone." But she looked tenderly at Romur.

Once again, a horse's gallop resounded. It was passionate and wild—and this time, it was loud enough for everyone to hear. Going to the window, I saw a pale shadow pass through the darkness of the park, and I felt the floor tremble beneath my feet. "What is he doing? Why does he keep circling around us like that?" Then I noticed that Lacuse had made the servant sit down on the arm of his chair and was whispering in her ear. She was listening, looking thoughtful. Suddenly, he seized her by the waist, lifted her in the air, and seated her on his shoulders, lithe as any athlete at a country fair. Speechless with surprise and dignity, she forgot to smile at the group's applause.

To tell the truth, everyone had drunk quite a bit from the big bowl, and no one seemed inclined to go upstairs to bed. The old duchess was sleeping, even though her right eye was still open; no one was paying any attention to her. My lover had rested his head on my heart, which didn't surprise anyone, either. He should have weighed heavily on this heart that had betrayed him, but my lover was scarcely heavier than a child. As for the poet, well, he seemed preoccupied with Karik, who paid him little attention.

"But hope haunts men until the very hour of death!" said the clockmaster.

I looked closely at Romur. The shadow of a beard, like a goatee, had appeared on his chin. Maybe it had grown over the course of the evening? And the two little bumps on his forehead were starting to get bigger. He put his arms around Josyane, whose loosely knit black shawl was growing tighter, becoming as thick as fur. They left the Oval Room together. She gave me her hand as they passed by me; it left a scratch on my palm. The adolescent followed them. I noticed that her ears and nose, perfectly pink, were twitching comically.

I looked at Lacuse again, but I hardly recognized him. There was a dark, dreadful force emanating from him, which prevented me from seeing him well. The beautiful servant had disappeared. But for the third time, I heard the frenzied horse make its round, its hooves hammering the ground, shaking the very walls of the castle. It died out, but then returned, even louder, faster, encircling us with its vibration. Did the others hear it? No, they didn't seem to hear it, but how I listened!

Just then, a new light penetrated into the Oval Room, where they had forgotten to draw the curtains over the wide bay windows. The full moon had just risen.

The guests also rose to go out into the park, which was brighter now than it had been at dusk. Dark pools of grass spread at the base of the immense trees, whose dazzling foliage nearly blinded us. I was surprised to hear growls, hisses, and calls. I saw a superb ibex and a panther run by. A white rabbit trotted after them.

I returned to the Room, but a couple of young chamois and an antelope leapt out from the door, nearly knocking me over, and I heard Karik's laugh. The ibex tried to join the antelope, but she disappeared into the thicket. He then turned to the panther, who first eluded his grasp with all her claws out, when a voluptuous "ahhh!" left her panting. They coupled right before our bewildered eyes.

Then a peacock came out of the Oval Room. At first, I thought it was a male, but no! The long feathers with staring golden eyes were merely attached to her own, more modest ones, by means of tiny, adhesive, colorful ribbons. A monkey devotedly carried her train. Where had that one come from? Then a badger and a fat she-fox went by. "That's Christina," I said to myself, "but who's that badger?" A bizarre couple who will perhaps give birth to a new race: little foxes with black and white stripes.

"Come," my lover said to me. "Let's do what all the others are doing."

But I wanted to take a last look at the Oval Room, where the duchess and a few guests still should have been. All we saw was an owl keeping watch, one eye open, and one eye closed. A silver fish was swimming in the ruby bowl; a little guitar sailed among the strawberries.

"But can he live in that liquid?" I asked.

A shrill cock-a-doodle-do startled us. Perched on top of the ladder in front of the old timepiece, an Italian rooster was flapping his green and russet wings.

"Shut up! It's not dawn yet."

And we tiptoed away.

"I'd rather be in a room than out in the evening cool of the meadows and the willow groves," my lover told me.

We were the only ones who hadn't undergone a metamorphosis. And we joyfully went up into the castle, passing through several large, empty rooms, but finally discovering an alcove to our liking. I felt his mouth, so cool on my skin; I loved that kiss, given across so many years! With that gypsy lock of hair falling down over his nose, he was already talking to me in his sleep, for I had always been a living part of his dreams.

"Oh!" he said. "Our ponies have refused to ford the stream; what shall we do?"

"Don't worry, we're sure to find a bridge of branches, further up."

But I could hear him fretting, just like he always did. Soothed by his murmuring, I fell asleep.

Late in the night, we were awakened by shouting. The room above ours was shaking; blows were knocked against the walls; a heavy body fell to the floor. The voice of a man, furious and very hoarse, could be heard heaping insults and words of love on a woman who must have been his companion. She didn't respond.

"They haven't become animals, either. . . ," I said, naïvely.

"It's too horrible; I can't stand it." And my beloved began to tremble.

But we got up and ran to the top floor. The two chamois were frisking about wildly in the granite staircase, their hooves hammering against the steps. A braid slapped against each of their necks.

There was a gray mouse in the flagstone corridor, in front of the door. She moaned, "I've never heard anything like it in my life!"

Forgetting to wonder at a talking mouse, we forced the door with a power I didn't know we had. Paulette and her husband arrived right after us. They were just about to exclaim something, when I saw them suddenly shrink up, turn into cats, and pounce on the mouse.

We stayed on the threshold. It was the maid's quarters, in the attic, illuminated harshly by an electric bulb. There was nothing there but a huge boar, chewing on a last bit of flesh.

But the sound of a beak, tapping at the window, turned our heads. It was a turtledove.

The boar had finished his strange meal. Nothing remained in the room, nothing but a pool of blood on the floor, with a little gold cross gleaming in the middle.

We heard a horse neigh, off in the distance, and the turtledove flew away. We went back down into one of the reception rooms. The duke was there, locking the beige turtledove up in a cage. No doubt he had mistaken it for one of his own. I wanted to ask him what had become of the harpist and the flutist, and as if he had guessed, he said, "They've flown away, too, but they're just parakeets!"

He shook his finger menacingly at a pair of cats, a female and her tom, entwined aggressively inside a basket. The female stretched out on her back and, with a lasciviousness that was completely maternal, she displayed her six little pink breasts. I was hardly surprised to see, swinging from the chandelier, a squirrel who preferred the bronze branches and their opaline flowers to the cedars in the park. He wore a little pair of horn-rimmed glasses, pushed up on the top of his head, and was cracking a hazelnut.

"You're behaving very badly tonight, all of you!" scolded the duke.

"Wait till you see upstairs. . . ," a voice said.

The antelope was standing on the threshold. I had recognized Karik's stubborn forehead and capricious élan: I could sense that she was ready to rip open anyone who disagreed with her.

"You'll see what's left of your Marietta," she said.

A terrible neigh rose up from the park. In the bright moonlight, we saw a white stallion, shaking his long mane and raising his head toward us. He neighed once more and disappeared at a gallop. The duke had come back downstairs, more interested in the stallion than in his servant's disappearance. Struggling in her cage, the turtledove risked hurting her wings on the bars; I opened it and let her fly out the window. She flew in large circles, while down below, the horse, who had returned, was waiting for her.

She set herself down on his rump, and they fled into the forest.

A mirror returned our two faces to us. I saw that I, too, had begun to re-semble my lover. We had the same spearhead-shaped face, sharp and pathetic, with slits for eyes, and the same uncertain mouth.

"Oh!" I said to him. "Since we are now as we were when our love first began, let's lie down on that couch over in the shadow. Caress my breasts, like you did so well back then! Take me!"

But he said nothing. I watched his body dissolve, melt away in a blackish mist. I wanted to touch him, but what was there to touch? All my hand could feel was dark, cold fur. And when I thought I was reaching toward his hair, the length of his elongated face, what I found was the ears of an ass.

I slowly looked down toward my feet. They seemed so far away, so inac-cessible. I was afraid of seeing them either webbed or forked. In terror, I screamed, "Where are my feet?" What was I?

• 13 •

The Girls in the
Forest of a Thousand Mirrors

$\mathcal{A}$ mirror remains invisible in a forest because it reflects the trees. Especially if it is a mirror on both sides: then it reflects them front and back.

At first, in that forest, one noticed only a prodigious number of pines, silver birches, larches, and junipers. Many young girls entered the forest, drawn in by something they could not have named. Perhaps the oval mirrors hanging from the branches possessed a magnetic power. They attracted the girls, who arrived before them, their faces just at the mirror's height. The girls gave a little scream at seeing a head coming toward them, nose to nose, a head with dark eyes or blue ones. Then they recognized themselves and laughed with pleasure. All these cries of surprise, of fear and joy, linked together through the trees and the wind, formed a stream of silvery music.

A young man passing by was attracted in turn by the strangeness of these sounds. He saw all those trees, real or reflected, and those girls with a single body but two heads. The mirrors refused to reflect his, so he felt a violent resentment.

"Why don't I have the right to see myself like them, and to admire myself? I am very handsome?"

The only response was the silence, mixed with the wind's sighs and the young girls' soft cries.

Then he angrily struck a mirror with his sword, since men can hardly live without swords, and the mirror was shattered. But even on the ground, the shards remained invisible. They kept on reflecting branches and little bits of sky; the birds took the pieces for springs and came to peck at them.

The young man tried desperately to see himself in the girls' eyes, but the arrogance in his gaze made them lower their eyelids, and he could see nothing. Enraged, he kept smashing the mirrors with all his might; one after another, they broke and fell. Soon, there remained only one in the forest. The girls, walking barefoot, searched everywhere for that one mirror, tearing the bottoms of their feet on all those bits of glass. There were bloody footprints throughout the forest.

The young man took in the smell of blood, so very sweet, and he heard the music of cries mingled with tears. It brought him a bizarre pleasure, but still he wanted to see his own face, and he began to look for the last mirror.

"Perhaps," he hoped, "this one will reflect me."

In the end, he found it. Many young girls were lined up in front of it and behind, too, since it reflected on both sides, just like at a double ticket window at the theatre.

Indeed, seeing yourself in that mirror was a real piece of theatre. A person was not only shown the freshness of her complexion, the redness of her lips, the brightness of her gaze, the suppleness of her neck, the softness of her hair, but she could also read there her most secret thoughts, those you aren't even conscious of having. And that provided plenty of lessons! One learned the most surprising things from it.

For example, you had always thought you loved your grandmother, but the truth was that you hated her; or that you really wanted to kill your little brother instead of giving him a string puppet for his birthday. You would rather have done this than that, etc., etc.

It was so intriguing, so fascinating, that the girls pushed closer and closer together, forming a barrier that prevented the young man from getting through.

Seized by a terrible impatience, he brandished his sword and cut off all the girls' heads before they could even make a sound!

He stepped over the bodies and walked up to the mirror, which reflected only a pine branch and a fragment of the sky with a bit of cloud trailing across it.

Beside himself, he hung all the heads from the tree branches, using their fine hair, and that reminded him of the days when so many of these heads would hang live from the branches, reflected by the mirrors. Their eyelids had reopened, and in their glassy gaze, finally, he could look at himself.

He found himself truly admirable, and he walked out of the forest whistling the Great March from *Aïda*.

• *14* •

The Red Chair

It was an old Voltaire armchair, with a trace of Louis-Philippe style, found in the barn of an opulent mountain home.

The family's grandson, Archibald, whose grandparents in years gone by had owned proud herds of cows, queens with horns and milk (meaning: best in beauty, best in battle, and best for milk): now Archibald was on a shoestring diet. . . .

He was an artist, a painter, which also means: very sensitive, virile, but narcissistic. And he was in love.

He was in love with a superb, silent young woman. Her hair, eyes, and eyebrows were pitch black, and her body so perfect that each time he saw her, his principal occupation was savoring her from head to toe.

Both were descended from the solid, stocky peasantry, and also shared an inclination to study, not just love but various other sciences. Thus they showed themselves gifted in all things, thanks to the rich, wild soil that had accumulated in them for generations.

She had quickly become an expert in the exercises of love, dressing in a captivating fashion and masterfully applying makeup that turned her face into an ochre-shaded pearl with fluttering mauve eyelids. Occasionally, when overcome by emotion, this face would disappear altogether beneath bangs and long locks of hair that shimmered like seaweed. But her brothers reproached her for these metamorphoses, finding that she had, of late, begun to look like a streetwalker, for brothers are like dragons about their sisters' virtue, when they aren't the ones selling those sisters.

But, with her black boots laced up high, her clattering heels, and her form-fitting skirt, she continued to climb deftly the spiral staircase leading to the top floor of a sordid city house where, in an attic apartment, the painter had set up his glassed-in studio. And always, before and after they made love, she sat in the red chair.

She was his woman, his slave, and his model, and he always painted her half-undressed; that is, wearing purple stockings, breasts exposed, but corseted with unusual whalebone devices that Archibald had also discovered in his grandmother's attic.

Afterward, she curled up again in the red chair, where she often fell asleep.

One day, he noticed that the faded upholstery of the Voltaire-style chair had taken on a brighter new shade; after a few weeks, the studded fabric had turned an extraordinary blood red. At the same time, he noticed that the young woman was growing paler.

"Are you feeling ill?" he asked her.

"Not at all; I'm just a little tired, and I like this chair so much."

"Come now, you don't like it better than you like me?"

"What silly things you say. . . ," she replied, smiling.

At this point, he always painted her sitting or curled up in the armchair. He found that its carmine color showed off the young woman's skin, which grew ever paler, and her hair, black as a truffle.

She added an orange-colored blush to her cheeks and lips, and outlined her eyes in green pencil, but even her eyes, so dark before, were losing their color. He didn't worry much about it; he was like all artists: childish and cruel. He even enjoyed making her jealous by describing the beautiful women he passed in the street: "How she carried her head, and what a rump she had!"

"A pure-bred mare, then," the girl concluded. She was always sweet and conciliatory, but what was she thinking? And what was she feeling?

He'd show off all his muscles and swagger, quite satisfied with himself.

He would tell her his dreams, and she noticed that she was always absent from them. "But," he retorted, "nobody dreams about the people they love!" He deserved to have her repeat to him the burning words that men in the street murmured to her, for she was beyond beautiful: stunning. But she couldn't do it; the words got caught in her throat.

Then her gaze became boundless, taking on the dimmed luster of a black crystal, and she thought, "I don't want to be a suffering machine; no, I don't. . . ." But she stayed with Archibald, and he continued painting her. At exhibitions, people admired his dark compositions, illuminated by a white bosom "lacking only the red stain from a dagger, buried to the hilt. . . ," wrote one critic.

One day, when he thought she was sleeping in the armchair, and he was preparing to paint her again, he noticed with some discomfort that the two front feet of the chair were wearing feminine boots with zigzag laces. He took it as a joke and tried to scold his girlfriend, to shake and wake her up. But his hands felt only the blood-red fabric. The young woman had just disappeared. He looked for her throughout the studio and in the closet that served as their kitchen. He even looked under the bed and in the wardrobe: there was no one.

"She couldn't have left without her boots!" But when he went back to the chair, he saw, with horror this time, that the lightly contoured arms of the Voltaire were clad in black gloves, and he recognized the long suede gloves she wore to the theatre.

"I don't like this joke!" he shouted angrily, and he waited for her to return.

But she didn't come back, that day or the following days, and when he began looking for her in the city, he couldn't find her. Even her brothers had no idea what had become of her.

He had to return home, and he sadly rested his eyes upon the armchair, which he found more and more fascinating.

"My love, my love. Where are you hiding?"

He heard a light sigh, and he noticed that the lemon wood of the chair had developed a surprisingly curvaceous shape. And the arms were inviting him to sit down. He obeyed them. The Voltaire chair became so soft, so pleasing, that he forgot his sorrow and dozed off.

He woke again at the break of day and resumed his search for the girl, all through the city, the country, and the little villages. He came home tired, very late, and his one desire was to fall into the chair, where he began to cry.

But once again, he heard a sigh. As he turned his head on the back of the chair, he noticed that this back, always stiff and straight before, had now grown two breasts. This bosom, so ingenuously offered, comforted him, and he heard a voice like a ventriloquist's coming from the seat itself: "I'm here, my darling!"

Then he put his thumb in his mouth, like when he was a little boy, and fell into a peaceful sleep.

• *15* •

The Villa in the Reeds

*T*he red pheasants were screaming in the reed beds of the Rhône. The peasants from the river's right bank were installing light footbridges of pine across the shallow water. And despite the wind sending sand into their eyes, they keep those eyes wide open to look at the pale house, abandoned forty years ago: *Villa in the Reeds*.

The sun, the moon, and the night dew have proved powerless to erase those few words. I myself read them with amazement from the trains that follow the river.

Not long ago, a man moved into the house. Where did he come from? No one knows. "He sleeps on pillows stuffed with sawgrass," people laughed. "And if he can live on frogs' eggs and duck legs, he's in luck!"

So he knows full well the sickening damp of the marshes, and the dryness of this land where rain is rare. People see him every now and then, seated on a hillock covered with dwarf oaks. Perhaps he is keeping an eye on some secret tracks through the rushes.

He seems sad, bogged down by something, but one day, he comes to life. He has spotted a crimson scarf, flecked with yellow, floating on the greenish water. He climbs down the knoll, skirts around the ponds, running and jumping over the muddy holes. He has just enough time to count the cries of a crow on the shore, and he discovers it.

Her. . . .

Tangled in the reeds, with gray silt eating away at her body. He frees her, cleans off the stiff legs, blows hard at the old topcoat she wears, ties the silk scarf over her tresses of corn, lifts her up. How soft she is in his arms! He walks as if in a procession, but now, it's no cold-fringed holy banner banging against his belly—it's a woman. The *foehn* sings psalms in his ears; in the distance, the snow-capped mountaintops sway against the blue of the sky. For the very first time, he is pressing a body against his own. He can hear the crack of the delicate bones, and he sees, through the holes in the topcoat, the breasts and their little brown points, the mysterious navel, the tuft of coarse moss. He becomes strong, so strong that, with his two hands, he lifts the woman above his head, then kicks open the door, completing its destruction, and entering the *Villa in the Reeds*.

A bed of sedge cradles them. He kneels before his prey, reveres her. He prepares food for her: some wild asparagus dug from the dry sand, a cake of flour and butter mixed with cumin seeds. To drink, he gives her a liqueur in which he has marinated some blackberries. She eats very little, but smiles at him. They fall asleep, their bodies entwined.

The swampy cold invades their bedroom at dawn. He spreads out what remains of the blankets, eaten away by voles. He lights a fire in the middle of the room, among the stones that he has piled there. It is both his hearth and his stove. He brings his beloved a bowl of clear broth. Carefree and playful, she forgets to cover herself. *Confusion has seized hold of the world, and the human heart, too, is becoming ferocious.* But the man at the *Villa in the Reeds* isn't at all aggressive, and his gentleness surrounds him like a cloud of melancholy. He goes out and gathers bunches of marjoram and lush, leafy branches to hide the house's dilapidated state from the young woman. He tells her: "I lost my father and mother, my sisters and brothers, and I was waiting for you. A great tenderness lives within me. Do you love me?"

She keeps smiling, without answering, but her smooth beige body, strangely cool, and strangely fragrant, trembles and presses against his, ceaselessly asking him for love. He lavishes it upon her; he has dreamed only of her since childhood.

There was no rain that winter, only a very fine snow, like frost, that remained. The peasants hardly ventured down to the plains. But from their villages, propped up against the mountainsides, they were astonished to see that light, trembling stubbornly among the reeds in the evening. They believed it must be ghosts, will-o-the-wisps, because they could not believe the man could be so determined about sleeping in that unwholesome ruin. But when they returned to the river to tear down their fragile bridges of bent wood, and they saw the trout reappear from the depths after their stay under the ice, they realized that the man hadn't stopped living there. And to listen to him speak, to listen to him sing—they knew he must have a woman keeping him company! That bit of news did its part to disturb them, to make them jealous. And the man seemed madly in love!

They surprised him bringing a thousand things into the house in cere-monious style. White stones, wild cherry branches in blossom, birds' nests with their minuscule jade green eggs. Springtime *opens the souls even of minerals and plants.*

He climbed back up the hill where the groves of oak trees still hold on to their dead leaves for months, and the pine continues to offer its scent and its chiseled shade. He watched the large green lizards fight and make love, as he sat on the riverbank next to a strange shape that the peasants, from a dis-tance, took for a dosser.[1] But he didn't carry her on his back; he held her on his arm, kissing her often.

He often walked with her all the way to the riverbanks battered by the muddy water from the melting snow. The river, grown wider, let out a muf-fled rumble; there was no way of crossing it now. The ponds swelled, looking for outlets even inside the *Villa in the Reeds.* The man was forced to raise their bed of sedge onto boards that were less rotten, and the fire in his hearth threat-ened to die. But his happiness was undiminished, even if his home became a den for foxes and badgers, even if the April rain fell drop by drop from the beams stripped of their slates. Then, through the holes in the roof, the russet moon shone down on his lovemaking. And when glowworms appeared along the pathway's edges, he collected them to make a crown across the forehead of the silent young woman.

She smiles at him always, and her belly is growing rounder, carrying a child. He caresses her ashy, slightly oily skin. He braids her yellow hair, which makes a dry sound when it breaks. The scarf's carmine fades; it becomes trans-parent, and the silk threads catch in his fingernails.

He scarcely leaves her, except when he goes fishing for tench in the green waters, sliding his hands under the sticky lumps of earth. Or sometimes crayfish in a very dark stream. Or maybe the river-fish, that keep to the sandy hollows.

The peasants took advantage of one of his outings to enter the *Villa in the Reeds.* It wasn't long before they found what they were looking for. They saw *it* lying in the sedge, belly swollen, corn-braids all undone, the scarf tied over the little sheep's skull.

"Oh!" said the oldest. "That's my scarecrow! I recognize it. . . ."

"That's all it is!" said the youngest, very disappointed.

"I had put it in my field, at the edge of the muddy section, I remember—the autumn winds carried it away."

---

[1]From the French *dos* (back): a wicker, cone-shaped, open basket carried on the back for harvesting grapes but also used by the European Santa Claus for toys.

"You topped it off with your daughter Isabelle's scarf—I recognize it, too."

"Two beanpoles for the legs, the old wicker basket for the body, a vine prop for the arms, and the head . . . you see!"

"So that was it, the man's woman?"

"Let's go toss the damn thing in the water."

They threw it into the biggest of the swamps, where the bottom, covered with algae, is malachite green. But the dosser floats, and the water returns the scarf's pink to life, and the wicker belly sticks out. The man spots it on his way back from fishing.

"She's drowned herself! She's dead!"

He threw himself into the water and though he didn't know how to swim, he began to play. Without being in the least surprised, he saw that he was covered with scales; with slow, nimble motions, he flapped his tail and fins. What joy! The water had become a familiar home territory. Through the liquid lace-work, he saw his beloved coming toward him, a queen carp, shining golden-brown, and she was carrying their little one on her back.

· *16* ·

Eight Tiny Love Tales

#5 If I Were A Tree
and You Were A Tree in the Same Forest

My roots would tunnel through the earth and moss, would glide into the crevices of stones, would seek you, would seek you through the darkness, the slow, decomposing night, the scents, the shapeless monsters, until, feeling your roots, they would quiver with joy, with a love so crazed it would arouse the entire forest.

#14 Naïve Prayer to Thank Him for Having
Created the Mountain

Lord, I am walking the Canal Pathway. An easy path: it doesn't go up, it doesn't go down; it ranges along the length of the mountain and it is above the world. The world that You have made. But this place is the fragrance, the incense of the world! It is still pristine, in velvet and dew. Each day at dawn, it emerges from Your hands. The light breeze is Your breath; the sharp, sweet scent is Your scent; the blue shadows, so pure and so dark, are Your Night.

And the upright pines, the tall ones, together, the little ones from after the avalanches, together; they all await You. And me, I remain motionless, my face lifted toward You; I, too, await you.

And all the flowers and all the grasses, and the rustling grasshoppers, and the plant stems and the fragrant pine needles, and the pebbles, and me—we all say THANK YOU.

#36 Gorée Island

Your ship, whiter than the sea-daffodil, passes by this island where, in years gone by, I was the black slave sold with fetters on my feet and hands, like the bronze bracelets you now buy for fun.

In the corridors of death and on the streets of rusty stones, I left behind my blood, my tears; I bit at the forged iron of the skylights; I surrendered my soul in one of those dungeons with three rays of sunlight where prisopes linger.

The following century brought the Chevalier of Boufflers to the island, and I haunted his palace. A nobleman who did a great deal of thinking, but alas, always in haste, as the Prince of Ligne said of him. He could not easily tell me from the shadows, but he did love me. I enjoyed his wit and his spirited way of making love; men are too serious nowadays—I no longer haunt their castles. But perhaps tonight I will enter your cabin through the secret porthole of your ship, whiter than snow-lilies, and in the morning you will tell the captain: "Last night I dreamed of an invisible woman, but she was just perfect for me.

#44 Anguish

Yellow flowers spin through my night. Shadowy suns, why do you torment me? I was hidden in the womb of the mountains, in the childlike freshness of the mountains.

And now, there you are, darting your scorching glances my way. I feel the heat of your ray-tentacles. Why restore to live something that should have died in me? Something I believed was dead.

Love is a cruel beast. Oh! I'm afraid of it now, afraid of this new love. I can already hear the laughter.

So I will have to bury myself to resist you? To resist your strength, the pearls filling your mouth? They will nail me in place, alive.

Your hands *charm*. You have cast a spell on me. You have touched me with your magic wand. Never will I forget that caress. So soft. Ah, yes! I'm afraid.

#66 The Sleeping Woman

For such a long time, I was dormant. A woman nonetheless and calm, nearly happy. I lay in dead leaves; I offered to the sun, to the waves, an invulnerable body. I slid along the mountain grasses, filling my nostrils with vanilla orchids and orange hawkweed. I was the sleepy lover of the moon and the animals, the trees and the monsters. I dreamt of Mongols, pyromaniacs, hideous clowns, and sword-swallowers. The perennial innocent shepherdess, I knew nothing of anguish; but the kite's cry of love, for a thousand years, yes, I hadn't heard it.

But one day you arrived; you took me by the hand. And, to wake me, for I was sleeping still, you said: "My spouse, my sister, I recognized you."

#75 Crazies

I think of the woman who knitted stockings. Endless stockings, long as her nights, long as a day without bread. Always long, lasting days and days.

She wanted to run away; she dreamed of her departure; she slipped her legs endlessly into those endless stockings. That way, she told herself, they will be seven-league stockings, and I will be able to run away.

I think of the man who wrote: "Oh youth, oh happy times—we sang, we danced—the good Lord himself was there in person," on the back of the drawings he completed with the lead of his pencil stuck under his fingernail. (They gave him only one pencil per week.) I think of the little paper cone that helped him sight-read his music. I think of his suspenders, the tanned calves of his legs.

I think of the angel of machines and of blackbirds. Who greased his inventions with excrement. He always wore a hat, the broad wings covered with seeds for the birds.

I think of myself. Who, in a religious boarding school, was considered crazy. Of myself, who darkened each day on the calendar, till my fingertips were black.

I think of you.

#88 Wish

To sleep with the animals, no longer to have any thoughts. In the living scent of wools, of pinewood, of flintstone and hay. No longer to tear this heart on the cutting edges of Love, but to rock it inside the breast like an innocent. No longer to hope, or to regret. To let the hands float in the warm waters and the wind, to walk barefoot on the grass and sand. To breathe deeply, without fear of the future, and to believe that everything is right here, and not on the other side. To know that this very place is the goal. And at last, detached from everything, to indulge in a smile.

#100 Lovers in Stone

She, lying on her heart side, and he, lying on his right side, they face each other.

Cities above him; forests above her; they keep each other.

Lovers for eternity.

Eyes without tears, mouths without kisses, his chest without wheat shafts, her mound without flowers, they find each other at last.

You were my first love; you are my last.

Forever separated; forever more together; they are alive through eternity.

My smile responds to your sweetness. Your desire to my fidelity.

Sleeping spouses who will alone remain awake!

From one edge of the world to the other, they signal to each other.

Lovers alive for eternity.

• 17 •

Emerentia, 1713

I

*T*he girl existed.

She came from *Henry the Green*, a book by Gottfried Keller. As a child, he had heard tell of her; he had seen her portrait in oils darkened by time and found the minister's diary, taken up again here.

II

The plain of the Upper Rhône valley is a vast marshland. A few hills wooded with pines emerge from this expanse of reeds and stiff grasses where only the horse and bull can graze. Dunes—people call them the Islands—dry in the reflected sun; in the wind, they rise up in whitish clouds. The villages keep a distance from them, layered in the foothills below the mountain ranges.

The road was carved out of the rock on the right bank. Sion, the capital, and two other towns built on the most solid hills of this land where, as in Genesis, the mud and the water remain undivided, are the only signs that link it to the world.

III

Emerentia is sitting at the front of the saddle, her little feet against the horse's mane, held tight around the waist. She likes to straddle the horse this way and dominate the world from within the arms of her father, lord of the land.

They are starting to pave some of the town streets with round, white stones from the river, pure as alabaster.

The two riders go down the *Cows' Way* road; they go around the ramparts and dash through the western gate toward the sands and meadows where wild tulips are opening.

One day, they went very far toward the setting sun, out to the swamps of Praz-Pourris.

Madame de M. saw them when they returned. For a long while, she pinched her lips, which turned blue.

"I don't want you to take the little one out like that. It's too dangerous for her. And for you too."

The lord doesn't respond. He admires his second wife and fears her.

Emerentia was five years old when their marriage took place.

The men with fluted ruffs and sugarloaf-shaped hats waited in front of the cathedral; behind them were the lame and the poor. The nave was full, with the notables of the town down on their knees in their emblazoned pews.

A scream.

Two footmen in coal-gray livery with gold buttons break through the crowd. They carry Emerentia, dressed completely in black velvet from which dangle two little violet slippers. A chaperone follows them. They leave the church.

"She couldn't bear the incense," someone says.

"It's more like she can't bear her mother's death. This solemn ceremony must surely have reminded her of another one. . . ."

"The funeral."

"The lord had married beneath himself. Now he's chosen a high-born lady."

One of the women, a commoner, moans, "They say that the little girl scratched at her mother's coffin, that she lay down on top of it, that she was screaming. . . ."

"Dogs that love their master do the same thing."

For a child who doesn't understand it, what is death?

"The good Lord took her from you; she's in heaven. You must pray that her soul rest in peace," the ladies of Sion whisper to her.

Emerentia hates the "good Lord," and heaven, too. Doesn't want to recite the "Hail Mary" or the "Our Father." But they make her go back to the church, into the shadows and the cold of the pillars. The candles burn day and night, but don't warm her. She looks at Christ on his cross, the nude body from which spurt clusters of black blood, the face striped with red under the thick turban of thorns. Here is the Lack, the place of all horrors.

Madame de M., Emerentia's stepmother, is descended from the Great Lombards, those first bankers in Valais, who came from beyond Simplon and grew wealthy in the fourteenth century in this forsaken valley.

The young girl falls ill. Near her bed, her old aunts, her father's gray-haired, mustached sisters, sleepy as marmots in winter, mumble their prayers.

Emerentia howls and buries her head beneath the sheets. A crucifix hangs from the canopy on her bed; she rips it down and throws it out the window. She tears apart her prayer book.

"We'll place her with the holy father in the village of F., as a penitence," says Madame de M.

IV

There are turkeys and black pigs in the village. They don't go as far as the marshes. They stay near the houses that are always sinking a little deeper into the ground because the stones and gravel come down with the avalanches.

But chestnut trees grow along the slopes, and their roots retain as much as they can. Crows caw on their branches in autumn. And down below, where people sink in, only the algae and bright red carnivorous plants move and vibrate like starfish.

The idiots, the goitered, advance through the alleys in a small herd, loving one another, rubbing up against each other. Some of them laugh, showing their black, toothless gums; others snivel and whine. Some have faces that never even quiver, mouths that don't show even the ironic smile of the dead.

At the age of seven, Emerentia is relegated by her noble family to the home of this village curate, well known for the rigor of his faith. Madame Fulkrie, the housekeeper, takes charge of the girl's manners and her clothing. The priest takes charge of her soul.

This man always wore a black tricorn hat with the edges turned up, and a long riding coat. From his sleeves hung lace so stiff that it sounded like castanets when it struck a piece of furniture. The servants starched it on Saturdays, along with his collar bands and the surplices.

What was his relationship with the powerful Bishop? Madame de M. was still stunned that, given his learning and social standing, he had been posted among these ignorant peasants. However, in reality, it was convenient for everyone. She hadn't forgotten that, in the past, she herself had wanted to become a Carmelite. But, forced to follow her family's wishes, she had married the seigneur de M., an inconsolable widower. She couldn't forgive him for it. No more than she could forgive his first wife's young daughter for being so beautiful and so lively.

Emerentia's dark brown locks were strangely intermingled with strands of gold as if, in the darkness of her resemblance to her father, a few rays from her mother had burst through, her mother who was so blond and so sweet.

V

That winter, the Rhône carried along great blocks of ice, the real Rhône; the other rivers, the brooks, ran hidden, noiseless.

The plain became even flatter, smoother and paler, but bluish, like milk with too much of the cream skimmed off. Even the Islands were hardly visible, all covered in frost, transparent, erased from the world. When Emerentia stared at them long enough, they seemed to start moving, to float away.

One day, she spoke of it to the village elders, who said, "The little girl sees what will be."

The vicar questions her: "What is grace?"
No answer.
"Repeat after me: *Grace is a supernatural gift that God gives us freely to bring about our salvation, because of the merits of Jesus Christ.* Did you hear me? Repeat it."
Silence.
"Can we lose grace after having received it?"
Emerentia nods her head.
"I would like you to repeat what you learned from your catechism book. Recite it!"
Off in the distance, the cry of geese. One of them is caught in the ice; it is dying.

On the open panel of his tower-shaped secretary, the saintly reverend writes in his journal:
"Today I received, from the noble and pious Madame de M., the pension due for the first trimester, which I immediately acknowledged, and entered in the register. Afterward, I administered her weekly correction to little Mérette (Emerentia). It was rougher than usual, as I lay her across a bench and whipped her with a fresh-cut rod, not without lamenting and sighing to the Lord that he should bring this sad task to a good end. In truth, the little one cried out in pain, and begged for mercy with humility

and sorrow, but she was no less obstinate in her resistance, and expressed contempt for the missal I had placed under her eyes for her to study. As a result, I allowed her a moment to catch her breath, then locked her in the dark pantry where she moaned and cried, but then she went quiet, until she suddenly began to sing and exult, much like the three saints in the flaming furnace. I listened and recognized that she was singing the same rhymed psalms that she had earlier refused to learn, but singing them in a manner so improper and profane, like the stupid and inept songs of wet nurses and children, that I was forced to see this conduct as a new sort of malice and a trick of the devil."

In her confinement, Emerentia had sung two stanzas from the Feast of the Most Holy Sacrament:

> *Fracto demum Sacramento,*
> *Ne vacilles, sed memento,*
> *Tantum esse sub fragmento,*
> *Quantum toto tegitur.*
>
> *Ecce Panis Angelorum*
> *Factus Cibus viatorum:*
> *Vere Panis filiorum,*
> *Non mittendus canibus.*[1]

To the tune of:

> *Le fils du roi s'en va chassant*
> *Avec son beau fusil d'argent;*
> *Mire le noir et tue le blanc*
> *Par-dessous l'aile il perd son sang,*
>
> *Par les yeux lui sort des diamants,*
> *Et par le bec l'or et l'argent.*
> *O fils du roi, tu es méchant*
> *D'avoir tué mon canard blanc!*

At least, those were the words that Monsieur the Vicar, stiff with anger, thought he heard. It gave him a furious urge to go out and shoot one of those birds, and he left.

---

[1]Bille provided the French translation: "When you see the Host broken, may thy faith not waver; remember that each parcel holds as much as the whole. // This is the Angel's bread, turned Travelers' food; but bread for children only; let it not go to the dogs." Emerentia sings to the tune of an old country song, "*V'la l'bon vent,*" where a girl laments the shooting of her favorite white duck by a cruel prince. The bird is magical and diamonds and gold pour from his eyes and beak while blood flows from under his wing.

VI

After Cardinal Schinner's saber-rattling against the Milanese, the peasant revolts, the murders, and the Reformation (Valais had nearly become Protestant), the country once again fell into the slumber of the first ages.

But it was an uneasy drowsiness that suddenly hardened the wavering ones, made them suspicious and led to a sort of village Inquisition that reeked of the old Jansenism.

When they weren't barefoot, the poor still tied their shoes with bits of marsh-willow. Those who were less poor survived by raising herds of half-wild horses, which they sent out to pasture in the terraqueous plains of the Rhône. The breed, enhanced by a few stallions from the "Bohemians" trapped in Switzerland during the Thirty Years' War, had just been improved again in 1702 when the King of France sent a great number of horses through the valley to provide new mounts for his army in Italy. They left behind young colts among the alders, two thousand pistoles at the tollgate, and many more horse droppings.

The vicarage of F. was not vast and completely lacked seigneurial airs, but it was furnished with heavy tables, bulging trunks, and Renaissance buffets. They had needed to take apart the doorways to get the furniture through.

That earned the vicar a nickname: the Demolisher.

The church, with its wooden ceiling, was of simple design, but it could hold the whole population of the area, which included three hamlets. One of these, invisible from below, was perched high up on the boulders.

In Europe, the admirable mannerism of the sixteenth century was about to transform itself into a more austere baroque. But Valais, closed in by the Alps, didn't easily open to outside influences. Only one ferry and two men provided passage across the river at the Scex gateway. These gaps, and the return of the newly titled mercenaries, were just beginning to endow the townships with graceful buildings and less rigid manners.

This village church where they forcibly bring Emerentia each morning at dawn hardly reminds her of the cathedral in Sion, where, as she used to say, the dark man in the pulpit frightened her. But the smell of incense is the same, as is the guilt-ridden quiet of genuflections and footsteps.

The anxiety returns, submerges her. The little girl drowns in it; she struggles, but can no longer escape from it. She cries, biting her lips, squinting her beautiful eyes to avoid seeing.

At the vicarage, they make her live with the enormous holy books, barricaded with copper fasteners, with covers reeking of sick wild creatures. And when the books gape open before her, Emerentia cannot breathe.

They have confiscated her toys and dolls.

Monsieur the Vicar has taken up his diary again:

"Truly heart-breaking letter arrived today from Madame, who is in all truth an excellent person and a perfect believer. Said missive was moist with her tears, and she made known to me the great affliction of Monsieur her husband, because things show no sign of improving with little Mérette. It is certainly a great calamity that has struck this family, a very respectable and illustrious one, and it surely seems, let it be said with all due respect, that the sins of the lord her grandfather on the paternal side, who was a Godless profligate and a roguish horseman, have reappeared so that they may be expiated in this wretched little creature. Have changed my *tractament* with regard to the little one and now will try a fasting cure. Have also had sewn, by Fulkrie herself, a little dress of sackcloth, and forbidden Mérette to wear any other garment as this penitential garb is most appropriate for her. Her resistance continues unchanged."

After her arrival, Emerentia had gone about dressed in a gown of crimson velvet with gold trim. There was a bounce to her step as she walked. In Russian, *cramoisi*, crimson, means the beautiful ring of a bell; in this case, the color and the child were one. Emerentia wandered along the village street like a dancing, singing bell.

The surprised children snickered at her to cover up their admiration and envy. They threw stones at her. But she turned around and faced them, completely fearless, with an anger that turned her face as red as her dress. They were frightened, stood frozen for a moment, and then fled.

The next time, they let her go by without doing anything at all. She looked at them intently, dared to raise her little fist against them, and then started to laugh.

Their response was respectful—yes, or else they remained openmouthed. And they followed her in silent procession. Before reaching the vicarage stairs, she sized them up one last time. But her expression had such grave intelligence that they were forever subdued by it.

She zigzagged up the stairs, offering them a different half of her face and her smile at each turn.

VII

Above the village, the coppery leaves in a little grove of dwarf oaks make a metallic clatter. Almond trees crown the dry stone walls with rosy clouds. Here, the ground is already warm; down there, the muddy stretches of land breathe out their miasmas.

Emerentia believes the treasures of this world are all around her: the sun, the warm *foehn*, the transparent waters of the river, but she doesn't know that she herself is *the cream and the crown* of this world.

Standing before her, Monsieur the Vicar questions her:

"What is the radiant Trinity?"

There will be no response. The little girl clamps down her deathly pale lips.

"Repeat after me! *It is a God in three persons, the Father, the Son, and the Holy Spirit.*"

She trembles, staring fixedly. It seems that she no longer sees anything; she has the gaze of one blind from birth, but overwhelmingly beautiful, without the whitish glaze. The priest is troubled by this rigidity, this silence.

"I want you to say: *The Father, the Son, and.* . . ."

Emerentia falls to the floor and rolls about, her body writhing while she screams frighteningly.

A maid and Madame Fulkrie come to get her. They tie her up and put her to bed. She must go to sleep without dinner. But can she sleep?

She can, because she dreams. She is seated bareback atop the mane of her father's Arabian horse, but he holds her tightly in his arms.

"You should exorcise her," says Madame Fulkrie to the vicar.

He says nothing.

Perhaps he is afraid? He has never believed in the devil as he does now, in Emerentia's presence.

"We'll see in time," he eventually replies.

For several days, he didn't question her. Then he began again:

"What is sin?"

Silence.

"If you don't answer, you will be beaten with wild rose-bush branches."

Emerentia feared those thorns even more than the leather straps. She replied all at once, without taking a breath:

"There is the sin of life and the sin of death."

The vicar was so surprised—by the fact as well as the substance of her response—that he dropped the catechism. "Why did you say that?" he stammered.

"I answered without thinking about anything, because the catechism is written without thinking. There is *nothing* to be understood in the catechism."

As she spoke, she had bravely looked at him with eyes that were too large, that expressed neither joy nor hate, but a poignant indifference. An adult's child-like sensitivity, petrified, smooth. Her gaze was a black crystal, an unbearable force.

VIII

The next day, Emerentia went out to walk with the village children. She told her new friends that there were mermaids in the Rhône. They don't know what mermaids are; she tries explaining to them, she is familiar with mermaids. There is one in her father's castle, it hangs from the ceiling in the great hall, decorated with antlers and torches.

The children listen to her, credulous and dazzled. From time to time, a pike or an old carp jumps from the center of one of the marshes, and the smaller the marsh, the larger the fish seems. They all shout: "A mermaid!"

"No, a mermaid is half fish, half girl. They even wear lace caps," explains Emerentia.

When she speaks, things become real. Mother silt, animals, trees, plants— all these have flesh and soul related to hers.

The children would say: "Toad's tears, tears of blood."

They point to the red pheasants' eyes, the muskroot whose small flower is blue at first, then green. Emerentia picked the shadow flower, the sword flag, and taught the children their names. The sands were taken over in some spots by a reddish moss.

"Oh!"

In a gray clearing, not completely dried out despite the intense heat, some purple orchids with tiered petals were opening up. The children had never seen so many of them.

Back home, they told their parents that Emerentia, by her mere presence, made flowers rise up out of the mud.

Another day, they went all the way to the Islands. There were pine trees growing on one of them. The children wanted to start a fire, but the little girl forbade them to do so.

"You're afraid of burning like a witch!" mocked the older ones, who knew what was being said about her.

Emerentia remained silent. She couldn't understand—she, who understood so many things—why the flames frightened her so.

They saw red insects with black dots, a butterfly and some loud birds with blue wings that stayed near the children. The large swallowtail lighted on Emerentia's forehead, which glistened with pearls of sweat.

But she arrived late for her catechism lesson and was whipped. Then the vicar wanted to make her recite the *Credo*. She obstinately refused.

"I don't remember the words," she admitted.

He set himself to helping her and recapitulated the first two articles of the *Credo* slowly, while providing patient and obscure explanations:

"And now, what does the third article teach us? *It teaches us that Jesus Christ was conceived by the Holy Spirit, and that his Mother, ever-virgin, is called Mary.* Repeat after me!"

But at the word "Mother," Emerentia is once again taken over by a terrible trembling that will not stop.

The vicar waits, tapping his skeletal fingers against the well-waxed table as if it were a piano. The little girl is distracted by this noise that reminds her of woodpeckers striking the poplar trunks. She calms down.

"Who created you and brought you into the world? *It's God.* Repeat: It's God."

She doesn't answer, because she doesn't understand. In the end, she says: "I wasn't created."

"Scandalous!" shouts the priest. (He had shaken his priestly bands with such agitation that they now hung crooked across his chest.) A seven-year-old child who doesn't know that God created her!"

The vicar breathes with difficulty.

"You will recite the *Credo*."

But Emerentia is silent.

She has returned to the ponds. She is bold enough to go near the great Rhône when she is with the village urchins. The waters are rising, and they had to wade across some streams. Here, the ground becomes hard again; a dwarf lavender creeps all over it. Emerentia walks; she runs; but suddenly, she stops. A small emerald-green creature is frozen in the sand; it has the indifference of death, its eye stone-still. It's a green lizard, the king of catalepsy.

The children gathered around Emerentia don't move either. For a long time, they look at it.

"Is it dead?"

"No."

How does she penetrate this mystery? But she is made of the same invariable and surprising fabric as nature. She felt that she should not disturb this apparent sleep.

They abandoned it. When they had disappeared in the sedge, the lizard rounded its upper spine, stood up on its legs, lowered its head, and pounced on a little coronella snake.

On the plain, over the tops of the rushes, the children could watch the horses and the little black bulls go by. The men drove them off into the distance, and left them there all summer, occasionally coming back for them, in the evening.

Emerentia pulled up some water grasses to make a train for herself, and to hide her legs. She tore the upper part of her coarse cloth tunic, and her white chest appeared, completely flat, with two pink spikes.

"I'm a mermaid!" she said proudly.

Then they all bathed, romping and shouting, also letting their rags go, little by little. The girls dropped their frayed skirts and the boys their poor front-flapped pants (the youngest ones were still in dresses), and they offered their naked bodies to the breeze.

They experienced various pleasant sensations, all new to them. How interesting to see oneself and to see the others, and especially to look at Emerentia's skin, so fine and pale. Their greedy, respectful hands reached out toward it.

The first shock over, they become quite joyful, and let their bodies slide over the dunes. The damp sand sticks to their skin, spangled with shining particles: mica, quartz, tiny specks of garnet.

They get back up and form a large circle. They sing some couplets in an off-key voice, couplets which must also be acted out:

Plantons la jolie vigne
La voilà la jolie vigne
Vigni, vignons, vignons le vin!

De rivière en pisse,
La voilà la jolie pisse,
Pissi, pissons. . . .[2]

Some landowners bringing their bulls back from the pasture saw them and reported everything to the vicar.

He passed judgment on the entire horde of children. They were smart about defending themselves and pretended they had been playing "Stripped King," also called "Fooleries King." (This royalty obliges the person on whom it is inflicted to be undressed by degrees: head dress, one sleeve, two sleeves, one button, and so on. Barring a vigorous resistance on the part of His or Her Majesty.)

"Naturally, your queen was Emerentia."

IX

"What on earth is she always telling the children?" the fathers and mothers wonder. Is she telling them evil stories? Maybe she is trying to make contact with the devil.

---

[2] A traditional wine-drinking song: "We'll plant in the vines/ Here's the pretty vine/ Vine in, wine in // From brook to piss/ There's a jolly piss/ Pissy piss-in. . . ."

Nothing surprising about that, thought the priest. Her grandfather was interested in the *Great* and the *Small Albert*.[3] He himself, while visiting the lord, had spirited them from him and brought them back to the vicarage, where he occasionally read them. He had also read with great interest the trial of Michée Chauderon (fateful name!), a witch burned at the stake on April 6, 1652. First, she had been stoned by the women and the children. Then, the doctors had searched for the spot that could feel no pain, sticking long pins into her body. . . . That lack of sensitivity is a sign that someone belongs to the devil. She had confessed to having seen the Evil One at Eaux-Vives in the form of a big red hare.

The vicar sighs. Or rather, he whistles: his chronic bronchitis makes muted sputtering sounds in his chest. He has taken up his diary again.

"Today, found myself constrained to break off all contact and communication between the girl and the village children, as she has run wild through the woods with them, then bathed in the pond, hanging on a tree branch the little penitent's tunic that I had *ordered* for her, sang and danced before them, completely naked, and incited her companions to participate in mockeries and naughty games. Severe punishment administered."

But she escapes once again toward the Rhône, whose gray waters roll ever higher. Slowly, they invade, separate the grasses, cover most of the Islands.

This causes no harm to the willows and sallow-thorn but the pines are shaken and lose the last bits of earth from their roots.

Alone, now, Emerentia leans over the spotted salamander. And she throws crumbs from her bread into a stream for the trout. She feels good; there is extraordinary jubilation at the center of her body.

A few children have seen her and they join her. One of the old willows no longer has any branches, but some strange bulges on its trunk. It is hollow, and the children hide inside it.

They pushed each other to follow Emerentia into the hole. They so filled it that the tree broke open with a crashing sound, and left them, still squeezed together, screaming in terror. The little girl jumped first; the willow, splitting in two, collapsed without doing them any harm.

When they returned to the village, they said, "The grandpa willow exploded, and it shouted, too."

"Emerentia was with you?"

"Yes."

"So now she gives orders to the trees, and they obey her."

"She knows how to cast spells on people, too," grumbled an old woman who feared dying like the willow tree.

---

[3]Books of magic by Saint Albert the Great (c. 1193–1280), a Dominican philosopher and alchemist.

Emerentia gave no orders to the trees, but it is true that she saw them as living people. Their limbs, for her, were arms; the holes dug out by the birds, their eyes and mouths, and the wind blowing through their branches, their voices. And when she passed by them, sauntered between them, she felt irresistibly drawn, held back by these beings that she guessed were harmless and loved her. One day, a larch caressed her cheek with a branch. She was shaken by sobs; that hand recalled to her a distant and forgotten sweetness. A gesture her wet-nurse might have made? No; despite her good heart, she had only displayed a kind of brusque tenderness. No; this must have been how, at the dawn of her life, her mother caressed her.

X

Now it is dangerous to venture into the reed-beds. The water has invaded everywhere.

The herds of horses and the red bulls still take their chances and go there. Choosing the most stable ground, they wade through the troughs with mud up to their chests.

One day, Jean-du-Moulin, the best horseman in the village, takes little Emerentia to ride behind him. She grabs on, her two fists tightly grasping his leather belt.

Jean-du-Moulin's hair is very dark and curly; he is just barely nineteen years old. Early on, he had been an imp running through grass as tall as himself; then he grew up, grew tall and strong, but his mop of hair kept its outrageous black morel gleam. His life out in the open air, in a land where too many people lived in confinement, turned his skin dark and his eyes bright. The girls liked his gaze, the color of the river when the snow is just beginning to melt, a very beautiful gray, but already a bit cloudy.

His friend—and occasional enemy—was Clair-du-Vannier: a stocky redhead, muscular and nimble. He could ride young bulls, and he could fall, when needed, from atop absolutely anything by rolling himself up into a ball.

So those were the two boys, who, although they hadn't yet turned twenty, were men already. They managed to understand Emerentia. In their own mysteriously rough way, without ever cajoling her, smiling at her with their ogre-like teeth. They carried her off on their horses as soon as she could escape from the vicarage, raising her up higher than their own heads, but with the respect the priest shows for the host.

And what dancers, those two! Superb, and slender at the hips, with large but beautiful hands. It wasn't until much later that those of their race grew heavy, no longer singing and dancing, but thinking only of work and getting rich.

Jean-du-Moulin was the first who dared stand up to the vicar. He was supported by Clair-du-Vannier and also by the village schoolteacher, who admired Emerentia's grace and surprising knowledge.

In the village, people said she that the three men were crazy for her: "She bewitches them with a single smile. That surely proves she has a power that isn't Catholic."

"Even Monsieur the Vicar is taken in. . . ."

On the desk, the feather pen scratches and the tiny cup of gold powder waits to be shaken over the purple ink. The repetition of adjectives is surely due to the anger that moves the writing hand.

"Today, great uproar and annoyance. A tall, solid, good-for-nothing, the young Jean-du-Moulin, came and argued with me about little Mérette, claiming that he hears her screaming and crying every day. I was in the midst of disputing with him when the young schoolmaster also arrived, the fool, who threatened to file a complaint against me, then threw himself at the wretched creature, embracing her with all his heart, etc., etc. I immediately had the schoolmaster arrested and brought before the bailiff. Now I must be sure to get Jean-du-Moulin, too, although he's rich and rough mannered. As for myself, I would be inclined to believe what the peasants are saying, that the child is a witch, if such a notion weren't contrary to reason. In any case, the devil is in her, and with her I have undertaken a very troublesome task."

The vicar even went so far as to talk about a female *succubus*, to which the teacher had replied: "Today, such creatures exist only in brains rotted by too much carnal abstinence. And you, Monsieur the Vicar, are more at risk on this point than the men of the village, who are healthy, if not holy."

He went on to say that Protestant ministers were perfectly right to marry. And that. . . . But he couldn't continue: guards had come to take him away. The children no longer went to school, and surrounded the vicarage in the hope of seeing Emerentia again at one of the windows, or at least hearing her pretty voice, that sweet chiming sound, directed to them again. But they heard nothing.

XI

"That's her?"

The painter bows down. He is quite surprised. The little girl curtseys quickly and looks at him.

He finds her beautiful and, at the same time, dreadful. He wonders why the asymmetry of Emerentia's features, hardly noticeable as yet, makes such an impression on him. "How can I translate this contradiction?"

She spreads open her arms, standing up very straight, visibly happy to be in her brocade dress with the goffered ruff around the neck and the *garde-infante* that swells the skirt above her waist.

"You cropped her hair?"

The artist had been told of his future model's splendid hair.

"It was necessary for physical and mental hygiene," the vicar replies.

He doesn't admit that, in the village, the louse is king. The pink or white louse, or brown or gray, depending on the age and the color of the scalp.

The painter can't refrain from saying, "What a shame!"

And when they bring him some skulls for his painting, he remarks ironically, "You collect them?"

But he quickly adds, "The little one is lighter. That will be less tiresome for her, and, in the left hand, she will be able to hold a flower."

"A flower?" The vicar is stunned.

"Every lady whose portrait I have the honor of painting holds a flower. Each flower is a symbol."

"As you wish."

The vicarage is dark, with shutters closed, but outside is the summer in all its violence. Out there, the floating flowers that people call roses of the Rhône are opening up. It's also the flower of the dead, as those who cut them die by drowning.

In Upper Valais, a whole mountainside has collapsed, undermined for too long by subterranean waters. The springs had multiplied inside it like veins, forming pockets, dark lakes. But in the end, these voiceless streams found ways out, began to roar, bringing forth yellow sand where vast pine forests would spring up.

The silt, the trees have invaded the plain. They pushed the river toward the right, just below the rocks supporting small towns, shaking the dungeons, the watchtowers, and the churches, painted with frescoes of the Last Judgment. A cardinal burns among the damned.

Closer by, the Black Wood has just been set ablaze by the shepherds' Saint John's Day bonfires—there's no shortage of wood, but rather of bread—and it crackles. The sweet scent of the flowing resin can be smelled all the way into the village. The peasants breathe it in, and it makes them tipsy: their sense of doom is lifted.

The wind carries this reddish smoke, still alive with sparks, all the way to the vicarage, but birds can be seen dropping from the sky on the damp steppe.

"All week long, I've hosted a painter that Madame sent to me so that he could do a portrait of the young lady. The grieving family no longer wants to keep the girl, but only a portrait, as a sad reminder to use for contemplation or in penance, and also because of her great beauty. The lord, in particular, does not want to renounce this plan."

Blackened tree trunks appeared in the Rhône like snakes that sank, suddenly rising when caught by the stones, and then off again, pulled in by the swirling eddies.

Along the banks of the river, at the risk of being trapped in silt, peasants pulled in these floating wrecks using poles fitted with hooks. The river grew even wider; the swamps doubled in size. From these swamps rose up mists that traveled as fast as the wind. A rumbling of clouds above the rumbling of the waters: it created an uproar like that of a military invasion.

Off in the distance, the geese cry—spiteful cries, torn like the rushes.

"Every day, Fulkrie serves the painter two jugs of wine which apparently do not satisfy him, as he goes to the Red Lion every evening, where he plays with the *chirurgo*. He's a rather haughty type, so fairly often, I serve him a woodcock or a young pike that go on Madame's trimester bill. In the beginning, he tried inventing schemes and offering favors to the little one, who took to him immediately. I made it clear to him that he was not to interfere in my procedure. When someone went to get Emerentia's coat and her Sunday clothes from storage, and she was dressed once again with her headpiece and her little belt, she showed great pleasure and began to dance. But that joy soon turned bitter when, following the instructions from Madame de M., I sent for the skull and gave it to her to hold. She didn't want to take it, and then, for the painting, cried and trembled while she held it, as if it were red-hot iron. Actually, the artist claimed he could paint the skull without a model for it, but I did not agree to that, because of what Madame had written: 'What the child suffers, we suffer also, and in her very suffering we are given an opportunity for penance, as much as we can do for her. Thus, let Your Reverence falter not in your devoted care and education. If, one day, as I pray to almighty and merciful God, the little one should come to receive, somewhere, light and salvation, she will no doubt rejoice heartily at having already atoned to some extent for the obduracy which our unfathomable Lord has seen fit to inflict upon her.' With these courageous words before my eyes, I judged it an opportune occasion to make the child undergo a serious penance with the skull. In fact, we used a child's skull, small and light, as the painter complained that the shape of a large man's skull clashed with the small hands, according to his art's *regula*, and she also held this one more willingly. In addition, the artist also gave her a little white rose to hold, which I was willing to tolerate, because it can be seen as a good *symbolum*."

XII

Emerentia was no longer sleeping at night. She would slowly glide out of her high-legged cot and draw close to the window, tilting her shaven head forward and listening to the sound of the river. She was afraid. But she experienced a temporary freedom while the others slept. No eyes were upon her. Neither the shadows nor Satan worried her. The presence of the living people surrounding her was more fearsome.

Were those piglike snores really coming from Madame Fulkrie? During the day, the woman was dignified to the point of aggressiveness. Sometimes, while dreaming, the vicar would cry out, and the distant sound would reverberate through the long corridors.

Emerentia would shiver; she would feel the wind turn icy cold, and would climb back up into bed.

The Rhône kept growing wider. The meadows of the plain were completely flooded; some wooden bridges were torn away. They had to bring in flat-bottom boats to get from one side of the river to the other.

Swollen cattle could be seen floating through the eddies, their feet in the air; and good luck to any horse that lost its way.

Because of all this, Jean-du-Moulin and Clair-du-Vannier forgot about the little girl. But *they* had known how to love her; for they knew fondness from fondling. She looked too much like the little Madonna in Majesty that the girls took out of the sacristy at the feast of Corpus Christi to parade on a platform through the village.

When the waters receded, they decided to take her out again on their horses, each in turn. They snatched her away twice under the very nose of the vicar. The laughing amazon was clinging to Clair-du-Vannier's short coat. The horse stopped short, sank its head up to the eyes in a pond to eat a plant, and the poor jacket, worn out as it was by sun and rain, dirt and smoke, split apart. A piece of the frayed cloth remained in the hands of Emerentia, who fell into some clumps of reeds without much harm.

But he noticed nothing, and continued on.

When Jean-du-Moulin came back for her, she was gathering up black shells, singing to herself. He was bold enough to bring her back to the vicarage, and his eyes (blue with a bit of gray) didn't even blink when they encountered the vicar's. He, however, did blink. "I'm not going to be frightened by this would-be bandit from the Islands. . . ," he muttered through clenched teeth.

"Suddenly received today a counter-order with respect to the painting, and must not send it to town, but rather keep it here. It's a shame, given the good work done by the painter, who was completely charmed by the child's gracefulness. Had I known this earlier, the man could have done my own portrait on that canvas to justify the expense, since all that splendid food is entered in the account book on top of his salary."

"He sure likes his food, the holy priest does," said the villagers. "But it's not a sin, except during Lent and on Fridays."

But when the peasants saw a flock of woodpigeons drop suddenly onto the vicarage roof, the old folks became jealous, and the old wives were sure that the little one was using some magic to bring them in.

"They fall right onto his table! And the vicar reaps the benefits!"

Yes, he very much appreciated dining on the chestnut-stuffed birds. But Emerentia cried, pushing her plate away.

From the wainscoting hang a rifle, a saber with a steel hilt, and a flintlock pistol made entirely of chiseled ivory. He takes up his diary once again.

"In addition, I have received an order to terminate all worldly instruction, most notably the Latin, which is no longer considered to be of use. Fulkrie must also stop her spinet lessons, which seems to make the girl unhappy. Rather, from now on, I must treat her like a foundling and simply ensure that she create no public scandal."

All that remained for Emerentia were the religious services. She wasn't to miss any of them, neither matins nor vespers. Certainly the church in F. was less tomblike than the one in the capital, and the incense wasn't as rich. But she remained voiceless there, consistently refusing to sing the psalms. Only one thing pleased her: the ballet of the choirboys who came and went in bright red robes and lace skirts, swinging to the rhythm of the bells and the genuflections.

One day, she opened her mouth and said: "I'd like to be in the choir."

This desire was met with much laughter: "That's only for boys!"

Girls haven't the right to do this, to do that, Madame Fulkrie was always repeating: it's not appropriate. A young girl must stay modestly in her place and never draw attention to herself. Hadn't the vicar himself pronounced from the pulpit: "'All women should die of shame at the mere thought of having been born female,' said Saint Clement of Alexandria."

XIII

A servant led the Grand Vicar into the parlor. "Donatille!" The priest called her back. "Bring us Mérette."

"She doesn't want to come."

"Make her come." (He thought better of it.) "No." Then, turning toward the envoy sent by Monseigneur the Archbishop: "She has a nasty disposition. I didn't understand why the family wanted her portrait. It would only worsen this vain child's pride."

"Pride and vanity are two different things," the curate permitted himself to remark.

"She is possessed by pride and also by vanity." The vicar had seized the large skull that sat atop his secretary. "This is what I should have made her hold. Only this could have given her cause for reflection. She has none."

"Surely you will be kind enough to show me this portrait."

"We have hidden it away in the attic."

Then the priest crossed himself, mechanically, but backwards and completely involuntarily, which upset him a great deal. The Grand Vicar was watching him pensively.

"Monseigneur sends you his greetings. . . ."

"François-Joseph Supersaxo, direct descendant of the celebrated George?"

Whenever he received visitors from the capital, the priest, knowing he was under suspicion—God only knew of what!—always faced them with an icy demeanor, looking askance at the intruders.

He suddenly remembered that the fencing around the house was decorated with little wrought-iron monsters, and he was unable to hold back a smile, which helped him recover his poise. But the vicar insisted that the painting be brought to him.

"Is that really her?"

Donatille picked off a few spider webs; a spider scampered across the floor.

"When I knew her, she was very beautiful and so bright. Nothing escaped that child's fine understanding. I heard her one day. She knew more Latin than some students do."

"She refuses all religion!" the vicar cut in.

The envoy leaned over the unfinished painting, done in oils on the back of a chessboard. The artist had time enough only to trace the outlines of her dress. It is dissolving; only the artfully pleated ruff holds up the strange head like an iron collar, and the silk pinafore, the wrists edged with golden lace are also faithfully reproduced. But where is the diadem-shaped headpiece that sparkled with sequins and pearl arabesques?

In this painting, Emerentia has only a black bonnet, like a priest's cap, and in her hands, a faded flower that looks more like an arnica than a rose. And, on her face, all the helplessness of a little girl who has been brutalized.

"Such chaotic features. . . ," murmured the vicar. He added: "It's dark in here."

He turned toward the windows, divided into small leaded panes, and veiled with curtains, and he noticed how the furniture exhaled a rancid odor. The servants rubbed it with a mixture of old walnut oil and salt.

"Mérette has an aversion to God and perverse leanings that remove her from the circle of humanity."

"You don't really think. . . ?"

"She has no sense of sin, no respect for holy things! She is an offspring of the Lord of Disorder."

"Nothing escaped her extreme sensitivity," repeated the envoy. Nature itself is pagan, and childhood is so close to nature. . . . Let us not cast away the flowers when we try to separate the wheat from the chaff."

"You have no idea!" The priest grew angry. "It is frightening."

"I heard that she had the gift of second sight. Those mysteries are not without explanation. The Counter-Reformation already set fire to enough stakes—let's not add a little girl to the flames!"

"Her mother came from a lowly background. Monsieur de M.'s first marriage was a scandal."

"I knew her. She was a wholesome person, simple and good," the envoy replied.

He was silent.

"Emerentia is ill. . . ," he finally said.

"These maladies are more pretended than real. And therein lies the bizarre."

"And here it lies," echoed the Grand Vicar in a voice no less bizarre. "Her whole family is waiting for her death. Wishing for it. . . ." (Suddenly he felt filled with revulsion.) "The girl is only seven years old!"

"She is all too precocious," the vicar sighed. "If you only knew. . . . The devil can take on the sweetest forms. He can show pearly white teeth, and his smile can be charming."

The envoy felt uncomfortable, despite all his worldly experience. He remained troubled by the painful question the portrait asked: those two painted eyes, one larger than the other, the uneven eyebrows, an ear poking out slightly, and a mouth closed tightly on a scream. Perhaps the artist had been clumsy?

"Remember her grandfather! His forefathers had embraced Calvinism. At Sion, they spoke of nothing but driving out the clergy. The bailiff had it posted on the cathedral walls: 'Hildebrand de Riedmatten, last bishop!' Without the Capuchin armies. . . ."

"I think about it constantly. That was a sign. A lesson for us. . . ," the envoy responded. "We must acknowledge it with complete humility."

"You dare to speak of humility with regard to such heresy, the devil's own invention!"

And the priest spit on the ground. The Grand Vicar turned away in disgust. "That man has no manners whatsoever."

"Protestants pray alone, but they do pray. As for us, we are lucky to be surrounded by a legion of angels. Do not frighten them off, Monsieur le Curé! Beware of your Jansenism."

"Is that a warning?"

"There is within you more violence than you think."

"It is given to me to defend Our Lord Jesus Christ of the Holy Roman and Apostolic Church!" shot back the priest.

"Children are fragile; that little girl. . . ."

"She has a terrible power!"

XIV

Every evening, Donatille pushes Emerentia's head so that it leans over a porcelain basin filled with a mixture of schnapps and water from the fountain. Into it, she dips a small comb with long, fine teeth, with which she scrapes the young lodger's shaved head. Bothered by the alcohol, one, two, three lice fall.

"My dear little lice!" says Emerentia.

But her hair is growing back. The housekeeper turns it into thin braids, pulling forcefully on them. The girl cries. Then Dame Fulkrie ties them with a little leather string.

Each morning, she dresses her in the sackcloth tunic.

They have forbidden her the company of other children, but they allow her to go into the garden, where the pear and peach trees, shaped into distaffs and fans, are starting to lose their leaves. There is thyme, sage, and tarragon.

Out on the plain, the waters have receded, and the banks have turned white again. Emerentia escaped through a door left ajar, and she runs all the way down to the nearby river. In the liquid transparency, the trout seem to swim in pure air, their shadows accompanying them. They draw near the riverbank and recognize Emerentia.

Jean-du-Moulin has also seen her. He draws near. She didn't hear him arrive.

"I've come to say goodbye," the man says.

The wild geese are still crying out in the marshlands. This is the land of malaria, of growths that hang like pinkish ornaments from the necks of poor people. They can't make money on these vast expanses of communal land. No compensation is granted to those who have no livestock. And the peasants waste away in idleness, sitting by their front doors, shaking with fevers that come and go like the horses in the distance.

But there are the others, the clever ones, the rich ones, who always have a whip or a pair of shears in their pockets. They go down to the stable at dawn, and they chase cows, goats, pigs (their wild boar friends, joke the nobles), beyond the village gardens; they close the gate and let the animals wallow about.

They plant grapes in bowers on the sunny slopes, tear out the stones and pile them up into labyrinthine walls. They drink their little wine that turns fine and clear, if they know how to wait. As for the old folks, well, they're more likely to drink their coffee water.[4] "It takes away the pain."

Jean-du-Moulin and Clair-du-Vannier have had to leave for the war. Dark hair and redhead, brown eyes and teal eyes, both at war in a far-off land, to save the Toggenbourg.

From his pulpit, the vicar had accused them of debauchery. He singled them out for recruitment to the couriers from Lucerne.

He continues with his writing, which he considers a duty. But he suddenly stops, resting his worn out, barbless quill pen. He listens. He is transfixed by what he hears.

This time, it's not a psalm that Emerentia is singing in the next room, but rather, in a Gregorian style, and with infinite sadness, the words of "La Porcheronne":

> *Quand Guilhem de Beauvoir*
> *eut les talons tournés,*
> *Dut s'habiller de serge*
> *et les pourceaux garder.*

A moment of silence, and then the voice resumes:

> *A gardé sept années*
> *sans rire ni chanter;*
> *Au bout de la septième*
> *elle s'est mise à chanter.*[5]

---

[4]Bille uses the popular expression "sock-juice" for bad coffee, from the socklike coffee filter invented in 1710.

[5]"The Pig-keeper" (title indicates a girl): "When Guilhem de Beauvoir/ Had walked away/ She had to wear serge/ And watch pigs all day.// She tended to pigs for seven years/ Without a laugh or song/ But at the end of the seventh year/ She turned her voice to song."

"Yes," he muttered in a low voice, "it's one of those shameful songs the French peddlers carry with them."

And, keeping time with his finger, he began to hum along, but then checked himself, as if caught in a sacrilegious act, and got to his feet. "Must I exorcise that child?"

In truth, when it came to Emerentia, an inexplicable emotion made him fear these practices, though he knew them quite well.

"Let us pray to the Lord," he said more loudly.

XV

In the church square, the bear shook himself and began to dance. Quite a few people had already gathered there to watch it. The showman had it on a chain, and carried on his shoulder a little animal wearing a tricorn hat like the vicar's, and a red jacket with long tails.

The peasants were familiar with bears. They had encountered them in the mountain forests, and, when they killed one, they cut off the front paws (the hands), and nailed them above their front doors. The paws dried out and turned a brownish color, like the mushrooms that grow on tree-trunks.

"But the little animal? What's that?"

"A wizard, a miniature wizard!" someone shouted.

"It's a monkey," said Mérette, looking out the kitchen window.

The vicar was meditating in the drawing room and Madame Fulkrie was out on a visit; the little girl took advantage of the moment to go out on the front terrace of the vicarage. On seeing her, the monkey began turning the crank on a gaudily painted box. She clapped her hands and dashed up next to the bear. She lifted her arms up into the air, bounding on the tips of her toes, so beautifully alive and joyful that the spectators applauded. The monkey stood straight up, and took off his hat in a grand wave to the crowd. Everyone thought that he had waved to Emerentia.

"She knows the animals' language, and they respond to her."

Indeed, the bear was looking at her, turning toward her his round, melancholy eyes, sniffing her with his snout, caught in a muzzle made of two iron and leather circles from which dangled a cord. The man, who was smaller than the bear, wielded a stick that was taller than both of them. In the end, the women became frightened, and barricaded themselves in their shabby homes. Their husbands, knowing the collection was about to begin, disappeared. Only the children remained.

But Dame Fulkrie, warned in time, came to get Emerentia. She shut the girl in her room, and double-locked the door.

The children learned to station themselves at a corner of the vicarage yard so they could have one of the servants bring their friend gifts: bitter almonds, hazelnuts, wild figs with tough, purplish skin, but a nice flavor. Donatille always gave them to her; the other maids were not inclined to do so, fearing the housekeeper's wrath.

Jean-du-Moulin was gone. Perhaps at this very moment he was dying on a battlefield, or in some mutiny, his head tilted back, his beautiful gray eyes filling with mud. And the inconsolable Clair-du-Vannier? What was the drinking binge, what sort of forced inaction was he using to drown the last scraps of his spirit?

They must have remembered the sky over their mountains, a darker blue than anywhere else, and that nice glacier wine[6] to slake their thirst. But they must also have thought of the little princess imprisoned in the vicarage at F., even more lonely and miserable than they were.

And the school teacher? No one had heard a word about him.

One last time, she managed to evade the vigilance of her wardens. Instead of heading down toward the Islands, she began to clamber up the rocky trail that went above the village leading to a chestnut grove. She took off her shoes and walked barefoot through the rough caresses of the lichens and the dry leaves, where chestnut-husks with harmless points rolled. The air was so warm that she took off her ugly sackcloth dress, and her little body blossomed in the autumn sun that shone right on her face.

Such a marvel, to have a body, hands, feet, a soft belly, and that mystery one must always keep hidden. Why? The *shameful parts*, say the servants and Madame Fulkrie.

This is a birth; it is as if she had been dead, and now, she is alive again. She admires her round arms, despite their thinness, her knees, her little toes, and the force that moves them, the lightness and harmony of her limbs. Her ears, too, she touches them—what a joy to hear! Her eyes, she fingers their eyelashes— what a joy to see! She closes them; she can still see through her eyelids, but everything is red.

Nonetheless, her back hurts, spotted with bluish bruises. But she hears them calling her, looking for her.

She tears up some grass and makes a bed for herself, burrowing into the thicket. The rocks have retained the warmth of the sun. She covers herself completely with leaves and falls asleep.

The "holy man" has pulled down the front of his secretary. It sounds like a guillotine. One day, a servant broke her fingers in it.

---

[6]Glacier wine is a Valais rèze wine, stored at higher altitudes in barrels that are never emptied but added on to when wine is drawn for special occasions. Some barrels can be over a century old.

"The vicar knows how to write!" people say admiringly.

Writing is still a magical power in this illiterate country.

"Emerentia also knows how to write," say the children.

But they have stopped teaching her anything at all, and soon she will no longer remember how to read, or even how to trace a letter.

"The day before yesterday, little Mérette left the house and we felt a great anguish until we tracked her down today, around noontime, all the way at the top of the chestnut grove, where she was sitting in the sun, unclothed, on her penitent's habit, warming herself to her heart's content. She had undone her braids and placed a little crown of beech leaves on her head; she had also hung a sash of these same leaves around her body, and had spread out before her a *quantum* of beautiful strawberries like those with which she had filled her belly. When she saw us, she tried to scamper off once again, but, ashamed of her nakedness, she tried to put her little tunic back on, which fortunately allowed us to catch her. Now she is ill and appears to be confused, because she speaks without making sense."

XVI

"Emerentia doesn't come down into the courtyard anymore to draw triangles and make circles with her little stones," people noticed.

"That's why the pigeons don't come to the vicarage roof so much anymore. . . ."

Emerentia could no longer throw them bits of her bread, or tell them the pretty names that she had invented for them in the past: "My silky, my opaline, my wholly white Holy Spirit." Those words that she had known, that she had sung, were beginning to recede from her memory. She was slowly slipping into a lightless swamp where the algae smothered her, waving covetously around her.

She felt a need to hide. They found her sprawled underneath her bed. One day, she fell asleep clutching in her fist a pearl that had fallen from her headpiece, back in the days of the portrait. She had found it in a groove in the wood floor.

Through the small glass panes of her window, she still watched the plain and especially an island of alders where no one had ever walked, because the water around it was too swift and too deep. One evening she saw flames scurrying about the islet.

The villagers, too, had seen the flames: "It's the witches sabbath. There are women out there."

The girl knew a little about the sabbath and the ogress-eels that the servants spoke of so often, but she asked: "How did they get there?"

"The devil gives them black wings to fly," said Madame Fulkrie, fixing a suspicious eye on her.

"Witches fly naked on brooms. . . ," Donatille whispered.

Emerentia envied the witches.

But she had stopped frolicking. She didn't play hopscotch anymore, and she let her bony arms hang down along her sides. She was no longer that bit of quicksilver, of mercury that rolls along, taking on a thousand forms: that malicious girl who mocked the perukes of the prominent citizens who came to visit, calling them "Parakeet! Parakeet!" That naughty girl who had once stuck some dried burdock flowers to the frills of the housekeeper's dress; who broke her mother-of-pearl rosaries; who, one day, had thrown holy water in the vicar's face. (He had threatened to plunge her into the font.)

One night, she dreamt of her dead mother.

The girl was walking along the bleached-out dunes and could see her, calling in the distance. She tried running toward her, but kept sinking into the unsteady ground. And her mother, in the distance, was telling her a word that she could not hear because the wind was blowing too hard. She felt the underground water rise up around her legs, her thighs, her belly, and that terrible force sucked her in.

Bathed in sweat, she opened her eyes, but she didn't dare to wake Madame Fulkrie.

The hamlets comprised some thirty hearths. Now, the villagers stayed in their hovels made of daub, stones, and tree trunks, badly squared off. In the same room, men, women, children, sometimes even hens and pigs, sought among one another the warmth they needed. The "slow indolent ones" who had spent months sitting in doorways, dreamily contemplating the plain, were now relegated to the recesses in the stables. People brought them food in little troughs. They were useless, dead weight, but they were not mistreated.

"It's a good thing that, in 1644, the State took pity on us poor folk. It freed us from mortmain and the variable tallage," the old ones said.[7]

The young ones, the wealthier among them, went to the fairs in the cities, all the way to the big lake, to sell their horses. On returning, they often get married, as young as seventeen, to girls only fourteen or fifteen years old.

---

[7]Mortmain: a lord's right to his vassals' properties at death, which makes inheritance impossible for the vassals' relatives—used ironically here, since they own nothing.

Snug in their hoods, the women servants miss the two handsome boys in exile: "Jean-du-Moulin isn't here to protect Emerentia anymore."

"Nor Clair-du-Vannier to put her on his stallion's crupper and lose her in the rushes."

"It's the vicar who made them leave for the army."

"He was jealous!"

And they furiously throw heavy logs into the stoves. Outside the house, they tell people that Emerentia has lost her mind.

"The madman doesn't weigh much on a scale, a pebble from the Rhône weighs more than he does!" declares an old man.

"You yourself don't weigh much, either," Donatille retorts. "The vicar thinks the little one is possessed; I heard it from Dame Fulkrie."

They're grinding the ears of corn that have dried all autumn long, hanging from the beams on the front walls of the house, but at the vicarage, the priest prefers corn from Naples, and he feeds the other to his animals.

The little girl has stopped eating. She sleeps, or pretends to sleep. She is wasting away so markedly that the housekeeper is frightened: "She caught malaria at the Islands. Or maybe it's the Maltese fever?"

But no one calls for the doctor.

They have taken from her all that most suited her, those things that lived within her: kindness, the tenderness of natural beings and animals, the grace of growing things, the mother forest.

The village children still think about her. At evening gatherings, they tell extraordinary stories about Emerentia: "Artus, the Emperor of the Marshes, the big red and black bull, walked up to her. He pawed at the dust, he gave a nasty bellow, but Emerentia, she raised her hand to pet him between his two horns. He turned meek like a lamb."

"And," the captivated children added, "she spoke to him."

XVII

"Little Mérette is back on her feet, but she is continually more altered, and is becoming completely simple-minded and mute. According to the consultation with the *medicus* that we called in, her reason is either wandering or is clouded, and she now requires medicinal treatment. Not surprisingly, he offered his own services for that task, and promised to restore the child's equilibrium, if only we would place her with him. But I can see that, for M. Chirurgus, this is all about the good boarding fee he would receive, not to mention the gifts from Madame, and I informed him of what I thought was appropriate on this subject: to wit, the Lord Himself appears to be bringing his own plan for his creature to a conclusion, and human hands would neither know how to, nor be able to change anything about the present situation."

Emerentia dreams in her bed with its turned columns. She is in a huge forest, where the trees are so tall that she can't see their tops, but their white trunks come together like the *pillars of the cathedral*; they begin to squeeze her so tightly that she suffocates. She screams.

"Why do you twist about as if you were on the grill?" grumbles Madame Fulkrie, who hates being woken up during the night.

At the first light of day, a silent Emerentia is led directly from the vicarage doorway, kept both locked and bolted, to the church. For these few steps, the housekeeper holds the child's fingers in her own and one of the gruffest of the women servants crushes the other little hand in her palm. They have sewn her a hooded dress made from the local brown cloth. She looks like a dwarf monk.

One day, a horse that doubtless remembered her got into the church, walked up to the choir, stopped, and hearing her arrive, returned to post himself under the porch. How superb he was then, emerging from the shadows, the dawn lighting up the strands of his mane down his forehead!

The little girl smiled, called him, and tried to run toward him. But Madame Fulkrie's stiff arm snapped like the string on a bow and forced her back into the vicarage. A servant with a stick had to chase away the sacrilegious horse who was determined to stay.

The following day, after Mass, she was locked up in the church for having once again torn and stomped on her prayer book. But she felt better there, freer, surrounded by a peaceful darkness, illuminated by the little eternal lamp. Her enemies had vanished and God seemed less frightening. She observed the statues of saints in their golden niches, and remembered her dolls.

What had happened to them? Her two favorite ones? The one in a mouse-gray muslin gown, trimmed with violet braid; the other, dressed in a long riding skirt of crimson velvet and a feathered hat. They were grand young ladies, these wooden dolls whose faces were covered with slightly scaly plaster, but their eyes, painted in black, with eyelashes in dotted lines, and their very red mouths and cheeks, were intensely alive.

Were they dead? Thrown on the fire? The little girl wondered. Her trunk, with its wrought-iron fixtures and all its contents: her dresses, waistcoats, undergarments embroidered with openwork, games, cup-and-ball toys, teetotums, everything had been sent back to her parents. Neither the priest nor the housekeeper liked the thought of that trunk in the vicarage, not even under lock and key. It represented temptation for their boarder and perhaps, for them, remorse. But in truth, they had no sense of remorse, convinced that they were working for Good and never flagging in their battle against Evil.

Emerentia shook the bells used at the elevation of the host. Their silvery sound was hardly reassuring to her. She climbed up on an altar and tried grasping a statue of the Virgin that entranced her, but it was in a glass cage and the panes wounded the girl's fists. She remembered a faraway day, during her mother's illness, when her nanny had taken her on a pilgrimage to Notre-Dame-de-la-Garde. They had left in a carriage drawn by two horses, then they had walked through the forest, where the nanny had carried her in her arms, as the Mother carries her Child. Above their heads, the pine branches slid by, and Emerentia breathed those sylvan scents for the first time. The chapel, with its cone-shaped roof, was white like the Lady who inhabited it. A sign between the two porch pillars read:

ADRIAN DE RIEDMATTEN
BISHOP OF SION
PRINCE OF THE HOLY EMPIRE
COUNT AND PREFECT OF VALAIS
GRANTS AN INDULGENCE OF FORTY DAYS
TO ALL WHO SAY HERE
FIVE OUR FATHERS AND HAIL MARYS
1695

But today, Emerentia is alone. She doesn't want to stay in the church any longer. How can she escape? She grabs a candle from an iron stand bristling with nails, and walks along the walls, looking for a way out. She comes upon a door and opens it. This is the sacristy, where she sees the tall cross carried in processions, and the bell that the bell-ringer and the priest used to plunge into the lake, way up on the mountain, *to plead for rain*, when drought destroyed the village vineyards. But the effort was overwhelming, and one day, one of the penitents abandoned the procession, crying, "The swamps that cover my land, down on the plain, have no need for your litanies!"

She also sees the basket for the consecrated bread, the ivy-garlanded candles for protection from storms, but what most astonishes her is: the yellowish beeswax figurines, the ex-votos. They are in all different shapes: arms, legs, eyes, and heads, but the prettiest ones are the statuettes of men and women, little girls and boys. She picks up a family: mother, father, and child. She caresses them.

"Mérette, you can come now!" calls Madame Fulkrie.

To find her, she had to go all the way in to the sacristy, where the candle was guttering out. Emerentia quickly hid the treasure she had just stolen under her tunic, tied at the waist with a belt made of rope.

And so she had her dolls. She hid them behind her bed, where the broom hardly ever reached, as even the servants no longer took much care of the girl. She dressed up the effigies in remnants from chasubles that still had a bit of silver or gold thread.

But they were discovered. They, too, were taken from her.

XVIII

Emerentia lived—but was she really living?—cloistered between chests shaped like tombstones, sideboards with pewter pitchers flanked by heavy chains. Such furnishings didn't surprise the little girl; they resembled those in her father's castle. Nonetheless, she missed her little armchair; it was just her size. Here, everything was too high, too big for her, especially as she so often felt tired. And at the vicarage, there were none of those lovely cushions of damask, no tapestries with people on them. During her illness, they had also taken away her little cat. The girl asked how it was doing. They told her it was dead.

In November, there had still been some golden-blue days with mauve sunsets, but Emerentia, too feverish, had been unable to see them. At present, she saw other things, things that existed for her alone. She heard sounds that she was the only one to hear and sometimes, responding to those sounds, she would call out inarticulate words. Her movements, once so harmonious, became jerky and brusque.

On a strangely voluptuous piece of furniture for a vicarage, an ebony settee inlaid with mother-of-pearl and covered with purple padding, Emerentia lay down one day.

Giant dragonflies flew around Emerentia; she sensed the rustling of their wings. Images buried deep inside her now rose to the surface, from that ancient compost that survives within each one of us. Reptiles that had vanished millions of years ago reappeared. She recognized them: lizard, serpent, triton, tortoise, but these were frighteningly large, and they threatened her with their elongated necks, their fangs, beaks, and claws, and their pulsating breasts. They had reddish overtones, with scales that clattered like armor. She didn't like them; she was afraid of them.

Then she saw a Three-Faced Christ. One, a frontal image, was flanked by two identical profiles. Two eyes sufficed for the ensemble, but there were three noses and three mouths. And these three mouths, at the same time, said: "I am the supreme Trinity."

And everything went black again.

"The weather is getting milder," the peasants said. "We're going to have snow."

It already shrouds the mountaintops. Everyone can feel it coming; the smell of snow glides over the plain. In the villages, all motion has stopped. They are waiting.

Neiges blanches et rouge sang
Sang de vierges et neiges d'anges,[8]

the servants sing.

And the spiky flakes, whiter than white—nothing is whiter than snow—rustle, hesitate among a thousand currents of air, then huddle up together, multiply, collide with each other. In long strands and webs that mingle and struggle with one another and then unravel, they weave the cloak with no beginning and no end, the seamless cloak that covers the earth.

The bedroom window at the vicarage is left ajar during the night; Madame Fulkrie sleeps, and the woodstove creates a wall of warmth between her and the countryside. The snow is for Emerentia alone. She inhales its scent and climbs up on the stone bench; she leans forward from the deep recess of the window; her hands reach out. They become flecked with snowflakes; the snowflakes burn. She turns, then leans back and, offering them her body and her face, she calls to them:

"Snowflakes, little snowflakes!"

They cover her. She opens her mouth, leaves it wide open and doesn't mind that the cold hurts her teeth. With her blue lips she snatches the snow, rolls it on her tongue and swallows it.

Numbness settles into her body. She closes her eyes, soothed, and gets back up into her bed.

The second night, the housekeeper caught her, tore her away from this delight. Punished her. Closed the window. Forbade her to open it again. Stoked the stove till it was red hot.

But they didn't beat her anymore; they fed her once a day, as they did with the "indolents." She ate, or didn't eat.

In the middle of one night, she began screaming so loudly that Madame Fulkrie woke up filled with terror, lit her candle, and got up to go look.

"I'm bleeding!" the child cried.

---

[8]"White snow and red blood// Virgins' blood and angels' snows."

"But where . . . where are you bleeding?" questioned the housekeeper, troubled about the real age of the onset of puberty. She had started menstruating at the age of fifteen; Emerentia was seven.

"Everywhere."

The little girl was holding her arms out from under the quilt, and she could see clusters of coral-colored grapes on them. "I'm bleeding! I'm bleeding!" Horrified, she opened her chemise and saw the same coral clusters of blood.

Madame Fulkrie abruptly tucked the sheet back down. "There's nothing wrong with you. Nothing at all. You dreamed."

The villages have capsized in the snow. All that remains are their black doors, open for the scream, like those caves in the cliff-sides where dwarfish folk live in the Mountains of F. But black lines also take shape in the white expanse, gouged out by passing carts.

And time passes before the fixed retinas of Emerentia's eyes.

Emerentia, Emerentia!

She studies Madame Fulkrie, who is sleeping. The housekeeper has enormous teeth, which her dry lips don't quite cover. Is she laughing? No, she doesn't laugh. But now the little girl knows that Madame Fulkrie's teeth *are watching her.*

XIX

The blocks of ice were melting over the ashy water of the Rhône. You could hear the wooden bridges cracking. The whole earth drank up the snow; the sun became fierce, and all at once, the plain turned green.

The yellowish mounds in the swamps became covered with tender sedge, and catnip grew between the alders. The horses, free again, grazed on the bulrushes' new shoots. Birds returned from Africa: hoopoes, curlews, bitterns, and wild ducks.

Up from the bottom rose the water-fern that looks like a long four-leaf clover, and the silvery chubs with their shiny scales. From the muddy throats of geese came shrill, monotonous sounds.

But the stony vineyards were still desert lands. A pinkish dust rose up from them, stirred by the *foehn*. This sand penetrated into the houses, filling mouths and making them thirsty. Drinkable water was rare; the water from the limestone beds brought on goiters.

The children are back in the Islands. They go through swarms of mosquitoes and come across the little brown scorpion and the white ants that leave tracks alongside their footsteps on the soil. The boys throw themselves into the mud, slide flat on their bellies, with their fingers spread apart and their legs in the air. The girls imitate them awkwardly; they aren't familiar with such games.

Emerentia is no longer there to teach them the pavane, to show them how do kipps and arabesques. The pearliness of her fingernails used to amaze them.

They fill their lungs with the sour smell of dead water teeming with life. The great crested grebe and the harrier flutter about once again in the osier beds. Burbots reappear at the surface of the ponds. Here, toads are coupling, the bowels of the earth are opened, and bubbles rise up like incense.

Emerentia's orphic power endures. Her invisible presence leads the children onward. The horses whinny as if to call her; she alone, with Jean-du-Moulin and Claire-du-Vannier, could approach them. She even curtsied to them, and they admired her with their wide, oily eyes. Today, they scamper off, crushing the boisterous vegetation. Jackdaws land on their backs, pulling out hairs for their nests. But sometimes a foal drowns in the unstable footing under these waters, or is injured by broken reeds, dangerous as knives.

They spent the night outside, hardly sleeping, grazing until late, then they would close up into little herds, and sleep for two or three hours. They got back up at dawn.

"But mules sleep standing up," a shepherd said. "And they snore loud."

He mimicked the sound and the peasants laughed. The mule, still very rare, was scorned. Horses and bulls, they had lived there since the beginning of time.

Still sequestered, Emerentia has stopped moving, has stopped speaking. Does she still hear anything? At night, perhaps. She sees the horses galloping toward her as one. She falls and they jump over her like a wild storm, like trees that pull up their own roots and bound into the sky. She sees her father again, mounted atop one of the horses. She holds her arms out to him, so that he can take her with him, but he turns away and leaves her.

Emerentia thinks about her father.

"Where is the skull?" thunders the vicar.

The little child's skull that the painter had included in the portrait of Emerentia. Madame Fulkrie and the maids were scurrying through the vicarage, but couldn't find it.

"It must be returned to the churchwarden for the ossuary."

"But, Monsieur le Vicar, I can't bring you what is no longer here."

"Where did it go? So skulls have wings like bats!"

"Don't mention those disgusting animals to me!" the housekeeper says. "Yesterday evening, one of them brushed up against me, and I heard a definite laugh as it went by. It sounded like Romain's wife, who just died in childbirth."

"The idiots! They all choose that time to die. . . ," the priest said, in a strange voice. "I never knew my own mother."

"Why, I knew mine all too well!" she retorted.

"We are all of us orphans, all the favorite children of Our Lord Jesus. And the Virgin Mary is our only mother."

Annoyed, Madame Fulkrie dared to reply: "No one can say that those parents are taking much care of your orphan girl! She is wasting away, and she will end up dying. That, after all, is not something to be wished for. Think of your reputation! I suggest that you let her get some fresh air. In the garden, under lock and key."

Monsieur le Vicar doesn't fail to note this new occurrence in his diary: "The child, in her stupor, seems to enjoy excellent health; her cheeks are bright and rosy. She now spends the entire day in the bean patch, where she stays out of sight and needs no care, provided she causes no further scandal."

XX

Yes, Emerentia basks in the sun, just like lizards and village idiots.

In the vicarage garden, there are breaths perceptible only to her ears: the eagerness of the bees around the greengage tree, the tunneling of the roots, the stubborn growth of the evening glories.

The children have not forgotten her. They know of a gap in the high wall that surrounds her, and through it, they pass presents: a little jade-green egg, the round fruits of dwarf oak trees—just like marbles—a jay feather, some nuts. She digs holes in the ground to hide these treasures, then she covers them up. On top, she arranges little pebbles, lining them up and laughing to herself.

"Witchcraft!" the frightened servants say, and they run away without even speaking to her. But each morning they bring her a bowl of milk, a winter pear, and a piece of rye bread tinged with saffron. They look upward, keeping an eye out for birds; a crow slashes the sky, wings outstretched, as if crucified:

"He's from Sion," Emerentia murmurs.

One day, a snub-nosed sand viper came into the garden. The little girl wasn't afraid; she caressed his cold back. On the other side of the wall, the vine growers are burning the hedges; fire has always made her uneasy. She moans when she sees their glow lingering through the shadows: nests explode; snail-shells turn black. She knows this.

The bean flowers start to open and garlands overtake their wooden stakes, forming an ever more leafy tent where Emerentia takes refuge. The tendrils crackle around her. She no longer thinks of fleeing. Does she still remember the world?

In the sermon for his Sunday Mass, which Emerentia no longer attends, the vicar likes to repeat these words from the Gospel: "In truth, I say this unto you, unless you become as little children, you shall not enter into the kingdom of heaven."

But when the children meet him in the street, they no longer greet him with the politeness they have been taught. From behind, they toss a bit of mud on his cassock. They even dared to climb over the wall and bring their friend a little metal daisy found on a grave, and dolls made of cornhusks, with moist, greenish-blond, grassy hair that Emerentia braids and ties with ribbons she has artfully taken from Madame Fulkrie's petticoats. At night, someone would come out to take her to bed.

"In the middle of the bean patch, we have discovered that Mérette had arranged a little parlor for herself, where she received visits from the peasant children; they brought her fruits and other *victualia* that she properly buried to keep as provisions. We also found there, buried in the ground, the little child's skull that had disappeared long ago, and that, for that reason, we had been unable to return to the churchwarden. She also attracted and tamed sparrows and other birds, which caused substantial damage to the beans, but I was unable to shoot into the clumps, because the little girl was there. *Item*: she amused herself with a poisonous snake that had gotten through the wall and nested near her. *In summa*: we have been forced to bring her back into the house and keep her indoors."

In the vicarage, Emerentia once again finds that smell of incense that she can't tolerate, the stale smell of paving stones scoured with black soap and of bodies badly washed. The smell of prayer. She no longer dares to enter that drawing room, that quartering-room where the vicar usually stays.

"She's a daughter of the lord Disorder," he repeats to anyone who will listen, in a desperate voice.

He is alluding to her grandfather, the Lord of M., that libertine and perverted horseman, but he's on the brink of believing that Emerentia was born of the devil, just like Luther.

In the kitchen, the maids chatter, Madame Fulkrie being out for the day. One of them says: "This morning, when I swept the dining room, I found half a watermelon that had rolled under the table. I picked it up and I saw. . . ." She stops; she can't say another word.

"You saw?"

"I saw *her* face. I recognized the little one's face, quite pale, pretty, with her eyes closed."

The others kept silent.

"And then I thought: 'My, this watermelon looks like Emerentia. . . .'"

The women laugh.

"Don't laugh! It was her! Shaped just like her: the nose, the eyes, the chin, but even paler than she is now."

The laughter has stopped.

"I threw it to the dogs."

The "holy man" keeps his journal scrupulously: "Her rosy cheeks have once again disappeared and the *chirurgus* claims that she won't last much longer. I have already written to the parents."

XXI

Lying in her four-poster bed, Emerentia dreams.

She leaves the vicarage, and in the street she sees a shepherdess leading three animals. These animals, a calf, a goat, and a pig, walk and are alive, but completely undressed. That is to say, all of their skin has been taken off. Their flesh appears just as it does displayed in the butcher's stall. This "operation" has left them vicious; they try to bite the little girl, and she is so afraid that she quickly goes back up the stairs to the house.

She wakes up, her heart pounding as if it might break. She gets up and softly, in the moonlight, goes down to the garden. Using her shovel, eaten away by rust, and all her remaining strength, she digs herself a hole and slips into it. The larvae and earthworms are her silent companions; she avoids doing them harm. Joyfully, she breathes in the cool and putrid smell of silt; she swallows a fistful of it.

Emerentia has buried herself in the motherly entrails. They tuck her in, slipping around her neck, between her hands, her feet. She listens to the pale flower with the little black stain growing above her. Is she born? Perhaps she never came into this world. Emerentia sinks into an insurmountable languor.

"Today, poor Mérette must have left her bed before dawn, slipped in among the bean plants, and died there, for we found her, dead, in a little ditch that she had dug in the earth, as if she had wanted to nestle within it. Her whole body was rigid and her hair, like her nightgown, was damp and heavy with the dew that had landed in limpid drops on her pale pink cheeks, as it would on an apple blossom. We were tremendously awed by this and I found myself today in great embarrassment and confusion, as our Lord and Lady arrived from the city just after my housekeeper had left for S. to buy some preserves and other provisions so that we might honorably entertain Their Highnesses. Thus I didn't know what to do first, and there was much coming and going, and the servants had to wash and dress the little corpse and at the same time prepare satisfactory refreshments. In the end, I had them roast the fresh ham that Madame Fulkrie had put in vinegar eight days ago, and Jacques, the valet, caught three of those tame trout that still come close to the garden here and there, although we stopped the fortunate(!) Mérette from going down to the water. I was lucky to get through it honorably enough with these dishes that Madame greatly enjoyed."

Yes, the servants had washed the frigid little body and dressed it once again in the beautiful brocade dress from the portrait, which was still big enough, as Emerentia had stretched out like a plant deprived of the sun, but had also become terribly thin. They smoothed the folds of the skirt around her legs—they had removed the pad from the garde-infante—and her feet were showing, with their fragile ankles. They found a pair of fine Cordovan flat-heeled shoes that the housekeeper had hidden, and put those on her.

It had been a long time, a whole year and more, since Mérette had been tended to with such care, such love.

She was displayed according to custom, in front of the vicarage, laid out in her child-sized coffin. She lay so lightly on the white silk cushion that her body didn't even make a crease in it. Four glowing tapers flickered in the bright daylight. The entire village filed by, sprinkling the young deceased with a box-wood branch dipped in holy water, making the sign of the cross. Then she was carried into the vicarage drawing room, more candles were lit, and the funereal wake began:

Some old women dressed in black were on their knees: "*Lord, give her eternal rest, and let the light that never fades shine upon her!*"

"*To you is due all praise, oh Lord, in Zion. . . .*"

"The poor, dear little girl no longer knew what she was doing," said the vicar. "Her mind had grown confused."

"We are not responsible," sighed Madame de M.

The Lord her father could be heard crying and wiping his nose.

And on with the "Ave Marias," the "Our Fathers," and the "Apostle's Creed."

The parents, accompanied by Monsieur the Vicar, retired to their chambers. Donatille brought a cup of coffee to each of the old women in black:

"Emerentia use to sit for hours on the riverbank watching the fish. She must have put a spell on them, because they all came right up to her, wagging their tails, rising halfway out of the water. You could have caught them with your bare hands."

"She didn't go without. They had nice fried fish on Fridays at the vic-arage. You could smell it all the way at the other end of the village."

"That Madame de M. was a stepmother. And stepmothers. . . ."

"They want to kill the first wife's daughter."

"Emerentia's mother, the real one, what was she like?"

"Who knows!"

"She was a commoner."

"And the lord?"

"He was a lord."

"Really? A spineless lord he was."

"The little one was disowned."

"Abandoned."

Writing below the thirty closed drawers of his secretary, Monsieur the Vicar enters in his journal:

"There was great sadness and we spent over two hours praying and medi-tating on death, and equally as much in melancholy remarks on the unfortunate sickly condition of the dead little girl, as we are now brought to admit, to our great consolation, that the origins of this condition were found in a fatal disposi-tion of her blood and her brain. Moreover, we also spoke of the great gifts she had, on the other hand, of her frequent, charming, and wise flashes of inspiration, and her impromptu observations. The whole of our brief earthly intelligence will not be enough for us to make sense of all these diverse things. Tomorrow morn-ing, the child will be given a Christian burial, and the presence of her well-born parents is most fortunate; otherwise, there might be resistance from the peasants."

The old women in black have started praying again: ". . . *at the sound of the last trumpet, for the trumpet WILL RING OUT, and the dead, incorruptible, will come back to life. . . .*"

"A child-witch!" whispers one.

"Shut up."

"*Place me among your sheep, and separate me from the goats; seat me at your right hand. . . .*"

The more the night advances, the more the old women in black, amid the tinkling of the medals and the rosaries, experience a holy terror. Their lance-like faces, narrowed by their knotted scarves, fatigue, and despair have grown harder:

"They dare to put her in sacred ground?"

"She's rich people's daughter."

"But the first wife, she was poor, a peasant-woman like us!"

"There are even those who say: one from the street, right from the gutter."

"The lords and ladies have only contempt for us. Without us, what would they eat?"

"Nothing but the lemons and pomegranates that they ripen behind glass walls, in their sunburnt gardens on the terraces of Sion."

"That they ripen? That they kill."

"They killed her."

In the most beautiful bedroom of the vicarage, on canopy beds, the lord and lady of M. are not asleep. Madame turns toward her husband: "I always told you. You spoiled that little girl too much. I saw right away that Evil had entered into her. Do you recall the first time she and I met face to face?"

The lord of M. winced without responding. He remembers the look that his wife had given the *other's* child.

"She looked like your father, and, without a doubt, too much like her own mother."

But, in the end, they both doze off, relieved by this rapid end for their wild child. She was blessed and given the Last Rites; she will be buried within the Church.

XXII

The geese are calling around the ponds. It is dawn, now. The old women with the black scarves that hang down their backs like broken wings drink fresh cups of coffee. The maids form a circle in the drawing room and their voices grow louder than the geese.

"The poor little one couldn't stand it."

"No one can stand it."

"Oh, that racket, the call of the geese!"

"She buried herself, all alone."

"No one has ever seen that before."

"One day," says Donatille, "I went up to the attic, and Jean-du-Moulin's dog followed me, and when he saw the portrait, he started to moan."

"That's not natural."

"She liked rats too much. Even toads and spiders. . . ."

"If she hadn't been a nobleman's daughter, she would have found her final rest at the stake."

In the schoolhouse, the children cannot believe that Emerentia has died. And yet they saw her yesterday, in her coffin, and they went to the Islands to gather marsh orchids for her, but they found none. "That's because she's no longer with us."

They have been forbidden to go though the cemetery gate, as have been the peasants who are furious that this child of the Devil should be buried in holy ground. But the new schoolmaster cannot prevent the children from watching the funeral procession go by.

Four men in leather jerkins carry the little coffin on a cloaked platform. The father and mother follow. The arrogant ruffle swells up under Lord M.'s gray beard; his velvet doublet is black; the chains on his ceremonial sword gird his waist. Madame's triple collar rises, pushed by the wind. She must use both hands to make sure that her dark taffeta dress wrought with jet beads doesn't fly up. The uncles and cousins, the magistrates carry gold-knobbed canes and at every moment, their feathered hats are at risk of turning back into birds.

One of the little urchins spits at them and says: "My lords, know that soon, only your wigs won't be rotting in your graves. It's the only thing the worms won't eat."

These personages, whose solemn demeanor was disturbed by the spring *foehn*, didn't hear him.

On the white silk cushion that smells bitterly of boxwood, the little girl slowly emerges from her sleep. In her absolute darkness, she knocks into the hard wood. She tries to push back the low ceiling that is suffocating her, but her fingers have no strength and the points of the nails make her fingers bleed. Her mouth has no voice.

It feels like a summer day, very warm already despite the cold night. The plain and its foulness are veiled in a fog that creeps along. Around the villages, the fields of saffron shine brightly.

In her night, Emerentia's lips tear apart. From between them comes a long scream. The scream. The gravedigger, the peasants flee. The schoolmaster raises his stick to hold back the troop of children.

She runs; Emerentia is running, and her little tiara has fallen off in the cemetery. She loses a shoe; her feet are so thin that they no longer fill the shoes. She is limping, but she is still running; she goes through the village and climbs up toward the chestnut grove. Her heart hurts too much; she tries to walk; she falls.

And when the men, slower than the children in their pursuit, found her, they realized that she had died a second time.

"This day has been the most marvelous and the most terrifying of all," the vicar writes, "not only since we have been involved with this catastrophic creature, but also in all the days of my peaceful existence. Indeed, when the time had come—on the stroke of ten—we formed the procession behind the little corpse and went to the cemetery while the sexton tolled the bell without much zeal; the sounds were practically pitiful, nearly muffled by the violent, gusting wind. And the sky was also dark and heavy; there was not a soul at the cemetery, aside from our small company. However, outside the walls, all the peasants had assembled, stretching up their necks out of curiosity. But, at the very moment when we were about to lower the little coffin into the grave, we heard an extraordinary scream come out of the coffin and we were filled with extreme fear, such that the gravedigger leaped out in a single bound and ran off. But the *chirurgus* had run over and promptly detached and removed the cover; the little dead girl stood up as if she were alive, pulled herself out of the grave, and looked at us. As the rays of Phoebus pierced the clouds at that very moment with a strange and burning brilliance, she appeared, in her yellowed brocade and with her shining little crown, like a young fairy or an imp. Madame her mother immediately fell into a deep swoon and the Lord de M. collapsed crying on the ground. I myself remained frozen in place with wonder and fear and, at that moment, I was firmly convinced this was a sorcerer's trick. But the little girl came to herself and scurried off like a cat through the cemetery, toward the village. Everyone ran home filled with fear and locked their doors. School had just let out and the band of children was in the street; when that gang saw what was happening, they couldn't be held back; a great horde of them started running behind the little cadaver and chasing her, the schoolmaster following behind, armed with his stick. But she had a head-start of about twenty steps on them, and didn't stop until she reached the chestnut grove where she dropped down, lifeless, upon which the children, swarming around her, cajoled and caressed her, all in vain. We learned all this after the fact, because, in great confusion, we had taken refuge in the vicarage, plunged in deep desolation, until the little cadaver was brought back. She was laid out upon a mattress, and Their Lordships departed immediately after, leaving a little stone plaque with only the family coat of arms and the date, 1713, engraved thereupon. At present, the child is once again laid out for dead, and we haven't the courage to go to bed, so afraid are we. But the *medicus* is at her side and he is now of the opinion that she is finally at rest."

XXIII

M. the Vicar shakes his long goose-feather pen pearled with black blood, and with his left hand, meticulously rolls the ruffles on his cuff back above his wrist:

"Today the *medicus* declared, after several experiments, that the child is really dead, and the burial discreetly took place and nothing more happened."

He heaves a strange sigh. Nothing more.

Lord de M.'s castle can be seen from a great distance. But the ivy that will bury it completely has only just unfurled three little leaves at the foot of the great tower.

Nothing more.

• 18 •

The Halloween Fiancés

Her eyes were purple, the light purple of autumn crocuses in the sparse meadows of the late season.

He was a soldier. A short soldier and thin too. Halloween day, he went down to the train station of the town, to meet his fiancée.

He is happy to see her, and sad. He is always sad. He says it's because he is poor, and town life is difficult. She is just the reverse, happy, full of laughter. To look prettier, she trimmed her coat collar with a piece of rabbit fur bought on sale, made herself a hat; its lustrous fur now gleams around her young face. She is holding a bouquet of mums.

"It's for my aunt's grave, she's buried here."

The graveyard is full of people and the last bees are here, too. He looks so sad that people turn around to look at him. Not at her, she is smiling.

"Now," he whispers, "I suppose you want to visit the living, your uncle, your cousins."

"No, today I want to be with you, just with you alone."

Happiness, love's expectations make her feel light, a little nervous, but they weigh down her companion's slender shoulders.

"And you wrote that you were bringing me a little present: what is it?"

"Oh, he says, it's my mother's idea."

"I'm so excited! Show it to me." He looked melancholic.

"I'll show it to you when we reach the village up there."

She looked up. Her fiancé loved trekking outdoors because he came from the city, and she loved him, she did.

"Way up there? That's a long way."

"No more than an hour, and the path is very beautiful."

"All right, so in one hour I can see your present?"

173

She pretended to frisk him but he backed off a bit, startled.
"You are funny, are you afraid?"
He gave no answer.

The autumn day was mild. It wrapped the graves with tenderness, pouring down upon their tiny flowered gardens a strange light that is more delicate than the summer light.

The young man and the girl climb slowly above the plain with the Rhône waters, a pale flow below the rocks. A bluish mist is curling around the town's bell towers. On the path, leaves flutter about like butterflies. The fiancés are walking hand in hand.

They talk about the future and the children they will have. "But we'll have to know how to live without much money. . . ." They also talk about working in an office, a tedious occupation. At times they hug each other and kiss on the mouth. And a shower of leaves falls on their heads.

But the young man is already tired. Military service is exhausting. He drops down on a slope, she sits by his side. There a good grassy hollow, right there, and some shrubs too, and nobody in sight. He lies back, his face to the sky, closing his eyes. She is not one bit sleepy, such life energy fills her! She fondles a tuft of wild thyme full of gray grasshoppers that bounce out of it and turn blue or red as they spread their wings. She takes a deep breath and looks at her fiancé.

He's fallen asleep.

She does not budge, does not want to wake him. He looks dead. They sleep so poorly in those barracks. But she is disappointed. She had looked forward to it so much, hoped for something else. She could have given herself to him that day. But he does not even seem to feel like it.

His eyes open. "Did I sleep?"

"Yes, you slept."

"It means trust, I feel very trusting toward you. If only I could earn a little more money."

"Yes, of course," she replies, "but you should not think of it all the time."

They get back on their feet and start climbing again. Over there, by the side of the trail, a cross is standing. They pause in front of it. The medieval sculptor gave Christ very long, very straight toes.

"They call him *The Dancing Christ*," explains the fiancé. "It's a famous statue."

They stop talking as they enter the village, also reputed for its bone repository. The young man suggests they visit it. But then his fiancée exclaims:

"Before seeing all those reminders of death, I want to see my present."

"Of course, I forgot."

"I'm dying to find out. . . ."

He pulls a tiny square box from his pocket and opens it.

"Since we are . . . engaged, my mother thought it was a good idea for me to give you a ring."

The purple eyes grow deep purple with pleasure. "Oh! I really didn't dare hope for. . . ."

It is a silver ring, but instead of a pearl or a gem, she is looking at a small piece of yellow bone inserted in the setting.

"What is this," she asks, almost annoyed.

"My first tooth. My mother kept it. It's a family tradition. She had it set on a ring. She thought you would be pleased to have it."

"A tooth!"

She is frustrated, disgusted. "Just because I love this man doesn't mean I should melt over an ugly bit of yellow bone! Ah! I wish they had never thought this up." It was worse than no present. She could certainly do without jewelry or expensive dresses. But that tooth!

"So, so this is my engagement present," she mumbled: a tooth, a little tooth! She did not say another word and stuffed the case into her purse.

He was ill at ease, too. Uneasy and unhappy. To find a little comfort he invited her to snack on a little cheese, fresh bread, and a glass of yellow wine.

When they came back down into the valley, night had already fallen. Candles were shining on every grave, planted directly in the sand. This strange vegetation would burn until daybreak.

They walked by the children's square. Tiny porcelain angels were frozen in their flight, inside their white glass-bead haloes. The fiancée thought of the dead children's little teeth. Their mothers would never have dreamed of making them into rings: they were patiently resting in their earthen cases awaiting the great Resurrection Day.

The Glass Violin

$\mathcal{E}$ach house in this little town was just like all the others: made of plain gray stone, with green shutters. Everyone looked just like his neighbor, had the same habits his neighbor had, ate like his neighbor, spoke like his neighbor, and dressed like his neighbor. Not a single one was a poet, a painter, a musician, an evil person, or a good person. They didn't know what those words meant. There were no people in love, either. Everyone thought only of himself. They had never heard laughing, or singing, or crying.

A stranger would have found all this uniformity quite boring . . . but none had ever come. And he would never have been able to explain to the people what the word "boring" meant. It would have been impossible, because these people had never known any other way of being.

And that's how things would still be now, if a strange little man hadn't arrived in town early one morning. Where was he from? How had he discovered the road that led here? They never did find out.

He walked slowly because he was old and very tired. Everyone was quite astonished at his long, thick hair, because everyone here kept his hair clipped short. His clothes were shocking as well: dirty and ragged, while theirs always looked brand new. The wrinkles in his face surprised them, too; they had never seen a face that looked worn, like something that has been used for too long. Their faces were always smooth and pink.

They didn't laugh because they didn't know how to laugh, but they watched him with their dull, steady eyes. That seemed to annoy the little old man. He made a face at them, but they didn't even flinch, and their faces displayed no sign of anger. He yelled insults, but no one showed anger or shame. He sat down in the middle of the street and thought. Suddenly, he struck his hand to his forehead: he had just had an idea, a marvelous idea. His eyes lit up and the corners of his mouth curled into a knowing smile.

He took off the leather bag he had been carrying on his back, unfastened the straps, and delicately took out a longish bundle, wrapped up like an infant in swaddling clothes. The people attentively followed his slightest movements; those at the far ends of the street had moved in closer. He unrolled the layers of cloth, one after another, and finally took out a strange and complicated object that drew the sun's rays and compelled them to dance: it was a violin made of glass.

The villagers had never seen anything like it; the old man noticed—not without pleasure—a certain interest among the people. He gave a little laugh, stood back up, grasped the object by the neck, rested the other end on his left shoulder, and tenderly placed his chin upon it. In his right hand he held a transparent bow that he made glide gently over the violin's strings. The sounds that came out were so crystalline and so pretty, the villagers felt that, for them, life had just been transfigured.

The music gamboled, sobbed, stretched, forming spirals and angles in the blue sky, falling back down over the town in an enchanted rain. With a touch of gentle madness, it insinuated itself into each person's soul. Little by little, their bodies felt ruled by it as well. An irresistible force shook them, and their torsos swayed. Their feet, so stupid until then, came to life and began tapping the ground, their legs keeping time. Their arms spread out like wings, and they felt light, so light . . .

Everyone was dancing in the street around the little musician. The children held each other's hands and formed circles. The gentlemen and the ladies, the young men and the young women, all looked at each other in mutual admiration. "They are graceful and their eyes shine like stars," thought the men. "They are handsome and strong enough to lift us in their arms as if we were flowers," thought the women. And they were all happy. The sounds came more rapidly; they were dizzying, and the children were jumping, and the grown-ups were turning faster and faster . . .

Then, all of a sudden, there was a sound different from the others, the last sound: the musician stopped playing; the glass violin had just crashed on the ground. The little old man was lying next to it, exhausted from having played so long and so passionately. Stunned, the villagers stopped; they still didn't understand what had happened to them. The parents were breathing hard, the young people kissed each other, and the children began to cry because it was over.

They gathered around the musician and begged him to keep playing, but the little old man could no longer hear them, because he was dead.

This made the people very sad, and for the first time, they knew what tears were. But they also had happiness enough to console them. Life had become precious to them. Each day brought them new sensations; their eyes and ears were open. First, they noticed that it was springtime, and that the town was surrounded by meadows that stretched out all around it; these had turned a joyful green, and the trees were covered in flowers and bees. For the first time, they heard the blackbird whistle, and they were delighted. To express their happiness, the girls sang, and the children told stories. The men felt a need to invent things. They now loved what had, in the past, been a mere mechanical occupation, and they started making all kinds of things.

And soon there were artists and poets, because the music of life had awakened within them both joy and suffering.

• 20 •

The Messenger

$\mathcal{I}$ was walking through the forest with a little boy one bitter fall evening. The forest was already completely dark, when a very long and luxurious car, richly upholstered, as black and shiny as a hearse, stopped. A young man with dark hair and eyes, whose beauty and gentleness were nearly heavenly, looked towards us and, with utmost graciousness, invited us to get in.

At first, I declined, claiming that my house was nearby, but he insisted. . . . We got in the back seat; he turned on the crystal fixture, and we completed our journey through the forest in a style princely enough for a drawing room.

As he let me out in front of the hunting lodge where my husband was waiting for us, he realized who we were. He expressed a desire to meet my husband, because he so admired his music, he said, with all the fire of an impassioned adolescent.

I found his beauty troubling, and I envied my husband for inspiring such enthusiasm.

We went into the lodge. I was quite fond of that little wooden house, surrounded by wild animals that no one ever bothered. My husband was too involved in his music, and my sons in their trips around the world, to give a thought to hunting. For a long time, the Aesculapian snake was the familiar serpent on the north side of the house; the south side hummed with bees that had swarmed inside the double wall of fir and pine. They lulled our sleep as our heads rested there. The wall on the east side was broken up by oblong windows, each one fitted with a bar that the birds used as perches. They especially liked those windows because the pines with their branches (and they with their beaks) tapped right at the glass: just the day before, I had seen the prettiest wren there. To the west, the wide bay windows opened over a wheat field, some clumps of trees, and a meadow where sheep lived. And in the attic, where no one ever went because there was no stairway or ladder, a squirrel sometimes rolled his hazelnuts and shadbush seeds up there.

Then the vast forest that surrounded us on all sides took over again, held back, in the old days, by the bend of the Rhône that could be heard in the distance, and today by fires that were more and more frequent.

"My name is Isidore," said the young man.

We started at the name, as if it were an enigma.

"You've built your house over the dead from the great battle...."

"Oh! The forest is big," said my husband.

"It's true," I added. "I always wondered about those marks in the ground, like trenches, at the edge of the forest...."

"It's not here that you'll find a skull on a bronze sword, like the one they just discovered at the gates of Sion," said Isidore. "But you are surrounded by the dead!"

We were somewhat unsettled. What could he mean?

"There are perhaps fewer dead here than in any city neighborhood."

"And the trees, what do you do with them?"

"In any case, we don't cut them down," my husband replied.

"In many of these trees, there suffers a man's soul." He put his hand over his heart.

"Those souls smell sweet, and I love to hear their moaning," I murmured, with a smile.

But I saw that he wasn't listening to me.

He was looking ecstatically at my husband. Alas, I wouldn't be the one to win over this magnificent youth. All I had was the music of a voice vibrating endlessly, like the halo of a red moon around his body.

[He leaves, becomes lost in the forest and the fog. The car is still there.
They open it; there is a coffin inside.
The young man still doesn't return. They call the authorities.
The coffin is opened. Inside it lies the young man.][1]

I looked at my husband, who looked at me. Our hands joined together, and, gently, we began to shake.

---

[1]The segment in brackets is only Bille's outline for the rest of the story, but she did have the all-important closing line written out.

About the Translators

Monika Giacoppe is Associate Professor of Comparative/World Literature at Ramapo College of New Jersey. She first discovered Corinna Bille while studying French at the University of Lausanne's Ecole de Français Moderne, and has remained fascinated by the author ever since. She has published on writers including Corinna Bille, Anne Hébert, and Nicole Brossard, and maintains an interest in translation theory and practice, as well.

Christiane P. Makward (D. Lit. Sorbonne) has been Professor of French and Francophone Studies at The Pennsylvania State University for nearly thirty years. Besides Corinna Bille, her interests in contemporary literatures in French include Caribbean women's theatre and novel, and contemporary women writers generally. She has published several books, translations, and many articles in the field of feminist literary criticism.